Help us Rate this book...
Put your initials on the
left side and your rating
on the right side.
  1 = Didn't care for
  2 = It was O.K.
  3 = It was great

_LR_	1 2 ③	
_ec_	1 2 ③	
_HK_	1 2 ③	
	1 2 3	
	1 2 3	
	1 2 3	
	1 2 3	
	1 2 3	
	1 2 3	
	1 2 3	
	1 2 3	
	1 2 3	
	1 2 3	
	1 2 3	
	1 2 3	

DATE DUE

JUN - 7 2012		
JUN 2 0 2012		
JUL 0 7 2012		
JUL 2 8 2012		
AUG 1 7 2012		
SEP - 4 2012		
NOV 1 3 2012		
MAY 1 6 2014		

DISCARDED

DEMCO 38-296

CALICO BRIDE

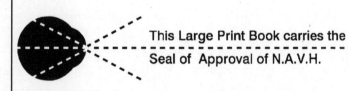

This Large Print Book carries the
Seal of Approval of N.A.V.H.

CALICO BRIDE

JILLIAN HART

THORNDIKE PRESS

A part of Gale, Cengage Learning

GALE
CENGAGE Learning·

Detroit • New York • San Francisco • New Haven, Conn • Waterville, Maine • London

GALE
CENGAGE Learning®

Copyright © 2011 by Jill Strickler.
Buttons & Bobbins Series #3.
Thorndike Press, a part of Gale, Cengage Learning.

LIBRARY OF CONGRESS CATALOGING-IN-PUBLICATION DATA

Hart, Jillian.
    Calico bride / by Jillian Hart. — Large print ed.
        p. cm. — (Thorndike Press large print Christian historical fiction)
    "Buttons & Bobbins Series; #3."
    ISBN-13: 978-1-4104-4485-1 (hardcover)
    ISBN-10: 1-4104-4485-6 (hardcover)
    1. Montana—Fiction. 2. Large type books. I. Title.
PS3608.A7857C35 2012
813'.6—dc23   2011049581

Published in 2012 by arrangement with Harlequin Books S.A.

Printed in the United States of America
1 2 3 4 5 6 7 16 15 14 13 12

For the Lord does not see as man sees;
for man looks at the outward appearance,
but the Lord looks at the heart.

— *Samuel* 16:7

CHAPTER ONE

Angel Falls, Montana Territory
July 1884

"Thank you, Mrs. Olaff." Lila Lawson closed the cash drawer. "Please come again."

"Of course I will. How can I resist? You have such a pretty display of summer fabrics." The kindly elderly woman hugged her brown-paper-wrapped package. "Once I sew this up, I am coming back for that beautiful lawn. You promise not to sell it all until then?"

"My word of honor." She intended to snip fifteen yards of the delicate fawn-colored material off its bolt and hold it beneath the counter. It was her prerogative as the shopkeeper's daughter and it was the least she could do for Mrs. Olaff, who was a loyal, longtime customer.

The front door swung shut with a jingle of the bell hanging over the doorway and she was alone in the mercantile full of pleasantly displayed merchandise. Again. She glanced out at the street. Why couldn't life be more like a dime novel? On the other side of the perfectly spotless windows — she had cleaned them to a shine this morning — a parade of people, horses and wagons, fancy buggies and humble, handmade carts hurried by. Everyone was going somewhere, doing something and it seemed as if the merry sunshine called her name. The whole world was out there and excitement could be waiting around every corner.

She retraced her steps to the fabric counter at the far end of the store, the tap of her shoes echoing against the high ceiling. The sharp briny scent of the pickle barrel seemed to follow her as she circled around the edge of the counter. Her skirts swished and rustled in the silence.

How about a little excitement, Lord, please? Just a little diversion, something to break the monotony.

She picked up her pen, dunked the tip into the ink bottle and resumed her letter to one of her best friends, Meredith, now a teacher at a small summer school north of town.

Dear Meredith,
Dull. That's my life in a single word.

8

Ever since we graduated not a single exciting thing has happened. Lorenzo Davis hasn't stepped foot inside the store. I would even welcome a visit from Luken Pawel to break the monotony. But everyone from school is busy with new jobs like you, or on their family farms like Earlee and Ruby. I miss you all. Not only that, I'm bored. Did I mention it?

Lila chuckled to herself, imagining Meredith would do the same when she read the letter — if she wasn't completely bored by its dull contents. Not that Lila didn't appreciate her blessings, because she thanked the Lord every day for them.

She had a comfortable life, a wonderful father, a sister she loved and friends she cherished. Plus, all the fabric she could want to sew. The bolts surrounded her in dignified rows of blacks, browns and grays, cheerful calicos and lively ginghams. Being around the fabrics perked her up, the bright spot in a long day's shift of standing on her feet.

"Lila!" a discontented woman's voice called from the door behind the long front counter.

That would be her stepmother.

"Don't tell me you are standing around

again?" Eunice Lawson pounded into the doorway, her round face pursed with annoyance. "Can't I take one afternoon off to have tea with my friends without the store falling apart?"

"No."

"No, what?" Eunice waited, sour disapproval wafting through the air to compete with the pickle brine.

"No, *Ma.*" The single word was like an arrow to her heart. Her mother had died when she was fourteen and having to call the woman her pa had remarried by the same designation hurt in more ways than one.

"Be a good girl and be helpful. I left a list to keep you busy all afternoon." Eunice tossed what she probably thought was an encouraging smile before storming out of sight.

Oh, joy. Why couldn't she be allowed to sit quietly and sew during the quiet moments in the store, as Eunice did or the hired lady who came on Saturdays? Lila blew out a sigh, listened to her stepmother's footsteps knell up into the second story and went in search of the list. She found it tacked on the wall behind the cash drawer and frowned at the first item.

Move pickled herring barrel and scrub floor beneath.

At least that would break the monotony. She tapped over to the little supply closet and gathered the essentials she would need.

This wasn't the excitement I was hoping for, Lord. How did the saying go? Be careful what you pray for. Amused, she dumped water from the pitcher into the bottom of a pail. It wasn't as if she had been terribly careful or specific in her prayer, had she? So she didn't intend to complain about the outcome. She grabbed a bar of soap from the closet shelf and made a beeline for the fish barrels.

Try to love your work, Lila, she told herself. Some days she did. Other days, not as much. She set down the bucket and put her shoulder into the first barrel, took a deep breath, tried not to breathe in the fishy smell and gave it a shove. Why couldn't her life be more like a book? She feared her life might always be placid and humdrum, the way it was today. Since she had already read every volume in last month's shipment of dime novels she was out of reading material and her thirst for adventure went unsatisfied.

As she grabbed the mop, a loud, shocking series of rapid pops erupted from the street, noisy enough to echo in the store. The smooth wooden handle tumbled from her hands and the mop hit the floor with a *whack.*

Was that gunfire? She whirled toward the window where the orderly pace of the afternoon had turned into a frantic blur. Horses reared, women ran into the nearest shops and buggies sped by, all heading away from the center of town. Cries rang out as another series of bullets fired.

What was going on? She found herself being drawn toward the door. Angel Falls was a quiet town full of honest and hardworking folk and very little trouble, until recently. Last summer, a train had been robbed just east of town and only one of the men responsible, Finn McKaslin, had been caught. Crime had grown since. She had heard of a few reticule snatchings, several horse thefts and two shops had been broken into. But gunfire had never rang on the streets before.

Was it coming from the bank? She opened the door and poked her head out just enough to see down the empty boardwalk. Many blocks away saddled horses ringed the front door of the bank while two men stood guard with Winchesters at the ready.

A bank robbery! Panic licked through her, shaking her from head to toe. Shots fired again from the bank. Were the people inside afraid? Hurt? She thought of Meredith's father who owned the bank and she gripped the edge of the door for support. *Watch over them, Father. Please keep everyone safe.*

The institution's ornate front doors swung open and a handful of men dashed out, their faces covered with bandanas, rifles clutched in hand. There was something menacing, defiant and cruel about them as they mounted up and gazed around the empty streets. She gulped hard, watching a very tall, very thin man hop onto his jet-black horse.

A sensible young lady would look away. A smart young lady would duck for cover, but this was better than any dime novel. Riveted, she watched as the bank door burst open and a man dashed out, rifle raised. He got one shot off before fire erupted. He fell on the steps and didn't move.

Her jaw dropped. Her heart stopped beating. Was he dead? Her knees gave out and she clung harder to the door, rattling the overhead bell. *Lord, let him be all right.* The outlaws didn't care. They beat their horses with the ends of their reins, shouting harshly. The animals bolted, galloping full-out down the street. They were coming her way!

Danger. She slammed the door shut. Her

limbs felt like pulled taffy as she clamored behind the solid wood counter. She gripped the wooden edge with clammy fingers, her knees buckling. Horse hooves drummed closer, the beat of steeled shoes against the ground rattled the windowsills. Men shouted, guns fired, glass tinkled and something zinged to a stop in the counter in front of her.

A bullet? As her knees gave out completely and she sank down onto her heels safely behind the counter, she caught one last glimpse of the robbers speeding past, spurs glinting in the sunshine. A bank robbery wasn't the kind of excitement she had wanted. She swiped at her damp bangs with one shaky hand. Somehow she was sitting on the floor. It was not exactly the way a heroine in a dime novel would handle danger.

The door rattled open and a bell chimed. No other sound blew in on the still air. Not a single clomp of a horse's hoof, not a drum of shoes on the boardwalk. It was as if the entire town was holding its breath, afraid the outlaws would return, afraid it was not safe. Her pulse hammered like war drums. Was anyone there? Or had she not shut the door properly and it blew open?

She took in a deep breath, willed the

trembling from her knees and pushed upright. Still a little wobbly, but she was not afraid. This was her first taste of adventure. Surely if there was ever a next time she would do better. She had grown up protected and sheltered and for that she was grateful, but she liked to think she had a courageous spirit. She smoothed her skirts and studied the store. The door stood open. No one was there. Right away she noticed the odd distortion in one of the glass panes. There was a little round hole just like a bullet would make.

A bullet. Her heartbeat skipped again. She skirted the counter to take a better look and she saw a man sprawled on his back on the floor in front of the open door with a blood stain blossoming on his white muslin shirt.

"M-miss?" he croaked in a baritone that sounded as if he were out of breath, as if he were a heavy smoker. The tin badge on his chest glinted as it caught a ray of sunshine. "You wouldn't happen to carry bandages, would you? I would like to buy a few."

"A few?" He was joking, right? What he needed was medical attention. She lifted the hem of her skirts and dashed to his side, heart pounding, knees shaking, her breath rattling between her ribs. Blood spread across his snowy shirt like a bottle of ink spilling. She knelt down and she reached to help him, but what did she do? She'd never seen an injury like this before. "You are going to need a great deal more than a couple bandages."

"I'm being optimistic," he panted between winces of pain.

Optimistic? He looked as though he was he going to die. The hard planked floor bit into her knees as she bounded into action. His rugged face turned ashen. He looked familiar. "You're the new deputy."

"Guilty." He wheezed in another sputtering bite of air. Muscles worked in his impressively square jaw, the sort of jaw a hero in a book might have. Dark brown, almost unruly hair framed a face so rugged and handsome it could have been carved out of stone. "Burke Hannigan. You're Lawson's oldest daughter."

"Yes, I'm Lila. You look a bit worse for the wear, Deputy Hannigan." From a shelf she snatched a stack of soft flannel squares, cut for baby diapers, and retraced her steps. "It looks as if you ran into a bullet out on the street."

"I've done worse and lived."

"You shouldn't be so cavalier. Look how fast you're bleeding." The crimson stain had grown larger and brighter, taking over his entire shirtfront. Her hands trembled as she plucked a piece of material from the stack and folded it into fourths. "It was brave of you to try and stop the bank robbers."

"But I didn't succeed. I couldn't run fast enough." He gritted his teeth, obviously as pained by that as by his wound.

His chest wound, she realized as she laid the cloth directly above the obvious bullet hole in his shirt. "Better luck next time."

"I didn't know a woman like you believed in luck." He winced when she applied pressure.

"It's just an expression, as I'm not sure you are the kind of man God would help." Maybe this wasn't the time for humor, but the wounded deputy laughed, sputtering with each deep rumble and, horribly, she felt the warm surge of blood against her palm intensify. "Perhaps you should lie back and stay quiet."

"If I wanted a woman to tell me what to do, I would have married one." He reached for a second piece of cloth and folded it, his bloodied fingers leaving marks on the flannel. Sweat broke out on his forehead at the effort. His chiseled mouth tugged down in the corners, making his hard face appear almost harsh, but his deep blue eyes radiated thankfulness and a depth of feeling that only a man with real heart could give. "I just need to catch my breath, and then I can go."

"You aren't going anywhere, Deputy." He definitely could have stepped off the pages of one of her beloved novels. The alpha hero, rugged and brave, tough enough to take a bullet to the chest and still want to right wrongs and capture villains. Very hard not to like that. "I'm going to fetch the doctor."

"I don't need a doctor." He clenched his teeth. A tendon jumped along his jawline. He was hard muscle and solid bone beneath the flat of her hand. His heart beat oddly fast and heavily, as if something were indeed wrong. He gasped in a breath, stuck the cloth on his other side and applied pressure.

He'd been hit by two bullets? Maybe she was a little in shock, too, since she hadn't noticed. When she plucked another cloth off the stack and added it to the one beneath her palm, her hand was coated red.

"You must have real bandages in this store —" He stopped to pant and wheeze. More blood oozed between her fingers. He wrestled with each breath. "Fetch them. I can patch. Myself. Up."

"Even most men would have enough common sense to lie in the street where they fell." She added another cloth to the pile. Light chestnut wisps fell down from her braided cornet to frame her face. "You are going nowhere, Deputy."

"We shall. See about that." He gasped. If his head would stop spinning, he would be all right. It was probably from the blood loss. That was easy to fix with a bandage. "I just need to catch. My. Breath."

"That looks like it might take you a while." She pressed him down by the shoulder until he was flat on the floor again. "To do so would be at your great peril, and I am not going to let anything happen to you. You collapsed on my shift and that makes me responsible for you."

"I had to get a bossy store clerk." He considered it a good sign that he could quip. "I can't lay here."

"You already are." Her soft alto brooked no argument. She was a willowy, petite young lady with big sea-green eyes and a perfectly dainty oval face. She had delicately carved features, high striking cheekbones, a softly chiseled jaw and a nose gently sloping and cute as a button. Lila Lawson's rosebud mouth pursed. "Don't sit up until this bleeding stops. No, don't even think about it."

"It's a. Free country. I can. Think what. I want." He figured as long as he had some sass, he wasn't knocking on death's door. Yet. It would take more than a few bullets to stop his mission, but in truth he was feeling a little woozy.

A little help here, Lord. Just a tad. He sent the prayer up, hoping the Good Lord would see fit to hear him.

"It's a free country, yes, but you are in my family's store, which means it's my store." She added another diaper to the pile on his chest, her hands wet with his life's blood. Compassion lurked in the depths of her eyes, green threaded with sky-blue. The most beautiful eyes he'd ever seen. "Can I trust you to lay here? I want to shout up the stairs. Someone has to fetch the doctor and I know if I leave you alone in this store to do it, you will drag yourself out the door on your hands and knees."

"Not sure. About. The. Hands." Being as he couldn't much feel them. He felt as if he were drowning, like the time he was held under the surface of the Yellowstone River when Kid Billings had taken objection to being arrested. He'd come near to dying that day. It felt a lot like he was feeling now. Boy, the pain was sure getting worse. "Maybe. I'll. Rest. A. Spell."

"Good decision." Her smile softly curved the innocent corners of her sweet mouth, a mouth obviously made for smiling. She leaped to her feet. "Don't you die on me."

That was starting to be his worry, too. His throat tightened. He hated to have it end like this. He hadn't done nearly enough with his life. There were promises to keep and a mission to finish. He watched Lila's pink calico skirts swirl out of sight and listened to the light *tap, tap* of her shoes on the boards. His vision began to darken at the edges. Regrets hit him. If he died right now, would he have done enough to earn his salvation?

He didn't know. He listened to the faint murmur of Lila's voice, the dim patter of shoes growing close. A shiver shook him so hard his teeth rattled. Iciness gripped him although it was the middle of July, the day hotter than a roaring stove top. He hadn't shaken this hard since he'd been caught in the teeth of a North Dakota blizzard chasing Wildcat Willy all the way to the Canadian border.

"My sister is running to fetch Dr. Frost." Lila returned, her lovely face a perfect picture of concern. She really was very comely. His chest tightened gazing up at her, feeling cold sweat bead on his forehead and roll off his neck. Her soft hand lighted against his cheekbone. "You are making me worry, Deputy, and I want you to stop it."

"Sorry." He gritted his teeth together so they wouldn't chatter. He looked like a weakling in front of her, shaking and trembling and sweating. Not to mention the bleeding. If he could will himself well, he would. She leaned away from him for a moment, leaving his sight only to bob back in again. Something warm and scratchy covered him. A wool blanket.

"That should help." Serene in the midst of crisis, she added another diaper to the pile on his chest and pressed painfully down. "You, sir, are the most troublesome customer I've had yet today."

"I try to stand out." He gasped, hating the weakness and that he was showing pain. "Don't like being. Second fiddle."

"You're one of *those* men." She rolled her eyes for emphasis, lightening the mood, trying to distract him from the blood staining the blanket. So much blood. "First you're too tough to let a bullet wound stop you, and now you need to be the center of attention."

"Trouble." He sputtered out the word.

"You very much are. My stepmother is going to insist we bill you for this." She hoped he didn't notice she was shaking as hard as he was.

"Put it. On my. Account."

"You don't have an account." He was knocking on death's door and he hadn't lost his sense of humor. Tenderness gripped her. She liked this man, and he was dying right before her eyes. She could do nothing but watch. "If you want to start one, we will need a letter of recommendation from another merchant where you have an account and a letter from your employer to verify your job."

"Will do. Right away."

Lord, let him be all right. Don't let him die.

Footsteps pounded on the boardwalk outside, distinctive taps and the faint jangle that made Burke Hannigan's eyes turn dark, his every muscle grew taut and he launched a few inches off the floor, only to cough, sputter blood and collapse back onto the wood planks. It didn't sound like the doctor. Dr. Samuel Frost didn't wear spurs.

"You have to lie still." She grabbed another fold of fabric to hold over the wound. "I've decided not to let you die, so you will simply have to comply."

Sadness darkened his blue eyes. He shifted slightly beneath the blanket, breathing faster as the footsteps pounded closer. Someone hollered a door or two down the boardwalk, the sound carried clearly through the open door.

"Hannigan? Where are you?" His boots struck like hammers, his spurs rang with menace. "Don't tell me you're dead because that would make my day."

What a horrible man. It could only be the town's sheriff. How he was voted into office remained a mystery for more than half the good citizens of Angel Falls. A shiver trickled down her spine and spilled ice into her veins. He was coming their way.

"Take this." Deputy Burke Hannigan's whisper vibrated with pain. His compelling gaze latched onto hers, his plea going soul deep. "Hide it. Promise?"

Something pressed into the palm of her hand and she didn't look at it. With a nod of agreement, she automatically slipped it into her skirt pocket as boot heels and spurs struck the boards outside the threshold. A shadow fell across her, and when she looked up Sheriff Dobbs swaggered through the doorway as if he owned the place. She felt Burke stiffen beneath her fingertips as his every muscle tensed.

"So, you're not dead after all, Hannigan." The sheriff scowled. "But the day ain't over yet."

CHAPTER TWO

Dobbs. Burke's mouth soured at the sight of the snake. No, thinking of the sheriff as a snake did a disservice to reptiles everywhere. He blinked hard against the fiery pain scorching him, rasped in a breath and locked gazes with the villain. He did not blink. He'd learned long ago to never show weakness to a bad man.

"It takes more — than an outlaw — to stop me." He bit out the words as if the double bullet holes weren't affecting him one bit. "Don't give away — my job — just yet."

"I'll put up a post. I was plannin' on it anyway." Footsteps struck the floor with a bully's force, the only power left a man with no heart and a black soul. "You're a lightweight. Never should have given you the job."

Lightweight? Burke didn't let the insult bother him. He was a good half foot taller than Dobbs. He knew what Dobbs was. He had gotten a good eyeful working for him the past few months. "I'll prove myself."

"I doubt it, boy." Dobbs lifted his upper lip in a sneer.

Burke's vision blurred. That couldn't be a good sign. Reality wavered around him like a mirage. From the blood loss no doubt. His teeth clacked together like a train's iron wheels on a track. Pain consumed him like flame. He was fading fast. Lila's pretty face hovered over him but her image blurred, too. He caught a pinch of concern, a fluff of cinnamon-brown curls and sweetness. So much sweetness. The pressure of her hands felt distant on his wounds. The world slowly began to melt away.

Keep the badge hidden, he wanted to tell her. *Keep your promise to me.* But the words would not come and he couldn't say them in front of Dobbs anyway.

"Looks like I ought to put you out of your misery like a downed horse." Dobbs bit out with a hint of laughter.

"What a horrible thing to joke about." Lila's gentle alto held a note of dismay. "Step away from him. I don't need your brand of help."

"Just tellin' the truth, gal. Life is hard. You ought to toughen up and accept it."

Easy to feel Lila's outrage and distress. Her emotions seemed to vibrate through her gentle touch. She was all he could see — every other bit of his surroundings had gone. She was a smudge of creamy skin, rich brown curls and pink calico, and he clung to her image, remembering her sweet beauty and rosebud smile.

"Ignore. Him." He coughed out the words.

"I intend to. Hold on, Deputy." She ignored everything but him. Voices murmuring at the doorway, the strike of her step-mother's shoes on the stairs and the scary amount of blood soaking her hands and her dress. "Don't you leave."

"Won't." The one word cost him. His eyes drifted shut but the hint of a smile touched the pale corners of his lips.

"Deputy?" Her heart crashed to a stop. "Burke?"

"That's life, missy." The sheriff scoffed. "No sense tearin' up about it. First you live, then you die."

Her faith taught to turn the other cheek, so she ignored him. She collapsed back on her heels, shaking. Tears scalded the backs of her eyes. Was Burke dead? She couldn't tell if he was breathing. She laid two trembling fingers against the side of his throat. Nothing. Nothing at all.

Wait. The tiniest flutter pulsed against her fingertip. He lived. Relief rocketed through her. Now that she was a little more calm, she could see the barely noticeable rise and fall of his chest. He was holding on, just as she'd begged him to.

"Stand aside, Dobbs." Dr. Sam Frost's terse demand betrayed his tension. Were the wounds mortal? Worry crept around her heart and cinched tight.

Please, let the deputy be all right. She rolled back the crimson hem of the blanket for the doctor, who was already kneeling and reaching into his medical bag. He worked quickly, pulling out his stethoscope and leaning in to listen. Two deputies pushed into the room. There was no disguising the doctor's concern as he straightened.

"Lila, you need to leave the room now." The doctor tore apart the deputy's shirt. Buttons flew and hit the floor with ping sounds.

"No, I'm staying." She braced herself but nothing could prepare her for the sight of Burke's chest. Two seeping wounds tore into his flesh, marring his perfect physique.

"Lila! Get away from that man." Eunice tromped around the corner of the counter. "He has no shirt."

"But the doctor might need help." She

swallowed hard, feeling woozy at the sight of ruined flesh and bone. Sympathy pains cut deep into her. She hated feeling so helpless. "I have to do something."

"You will avert your eyes and come with me, young lady." Eunice grabbed an elbow and Lila was wrenched to her feet. All around her movement and flurry and voices drummed dimly in her head.

"On three," the doctor ordered and along with other men lifted the unconscious deputy onto the front counter.

"What do you think you are doing?" Eunice demanded. "We conduct business in this establishment. How will we serve our customers?"

"Mrs. Lawson, human life takes a higher priority." Dr. Frost appeared pained, hardly paying her any attention as he poured a solution from a brown bottle onto the separate wounds. "I need better light. Lila, find me some lanterns. I need to operate."

"Someone had better reimburse us for our lost profits," Eunice announced, although it didn't appear as if anyone were listening.

Lanterns. They had a whole shelf of lighting needs. Lila twisted away from her stepmother's grip and dashed down the aisle. Her fingers felt wooden as she opened a can of kerosene and poured it into the first lamp she grabbed.

"He's not gonna make it, Doc," Dobbs commented. "Don't think the sheriff's office is gonna pick up your bill when he dies."

"I'm not worried about the money." Dr. Frost sounded busy and annoyed, although she couldn't see him because of the shelving and the way her stepmother stood like a barricade between her and Burke Hannigan's bare chest.

"I'll take that." Tight-lipped, Eunice twisted the lantern from Lila's grip. "Fill another, but that is all. We can't spare anymore expense than two lanterns."

"Does the deputy have family in the area?" the doctor asked, strained as he lighted a match to his scalpel to sterilize it. "No? Any next of kin?"

"He didn't list a soul on his application." Dobbs's spurs clanked against the planks as he headed toward the door. "No one cares if he dies. I'm leaving. Good luck, Doc. You'll need it."

Lila wondered if Burke could hear what was going on around him, if he was touched by the sheriff's callous disregard for human life. She felt dirtied by the words, as if they had somehow brushed against her soul and she was glad when the door slammed shut. She set the can on the shelf; the lamp's reservoir was full. She ran with it toward the deputy. Blood streamed out of wounds the doctor investigated.

"One didn't go too deep. Hit a rib." As if that was good fortune, Dr. Frost dropped a bullet into a pan with a *clink.*

"Go upstairs, Lila." The hard set of Eunice's round face held a warning. She took the lamp. "Go. No argument."

"But —" She had a thousand arguments but she bit her tongue. Disobeying her stepmother would only upset Pa. That was the last thing she wanted. As hard as it was, she forced her feet to carry her across the room and toward the door to upstairs. When she looked back, she couldn't see anything of Burke but his thick dark hair, tousled as if he'd just run his fingers through it. What happened next was God's will and so it was to God she prayed as she took the stairs one at a time with Eunice on her heels.

"Nothing so terrible has ever happened here before." Lark huddled in the corner at the kitchen table with fearful eyes. "All those gunshots. Do you think they will come back? Oh, do you think we are in danger?"

"Not likely." Lila used her most confident voice to reassure her little sister. She shut the kitchen door behind her, making sure to listen for Eunice's footsteps, which were heading into the parlor. "If you're worried, I can stay with you for a bit."

"Yes, I would like that." The girl tossed a cinnamon-brown braid over her shoulder — a shade matching Lila's — and sighed with great relief. She was a sweetheart, the identical copy of their mother. "You know Eunice. She told me not to be silly."

"She means well." She went straight to the washbasin.

"But she isn't Ma." Lark nibbled on the edge of a sugar cookie. "Do you reckon she's right? That this town will become lawless and we will have to sell the store and move? I don't want to leave the store."

"I can't see our settled town going to rack and ruin easily, not if Eunice has anything to do with it." She rinsed the blood off her hands. Burke's blood. "Everything will be fine, just you wait and see."

"What about the deputy? Is he really going to die like Eunice said?"

"No." Her stomach twisted up tight as she remembered the flash of his deeply blue eyes. Sadness gripped her as she grabbed the bar of soap and lathered her hands. "We're going to take good care of him so that he lives." ·

"Isn't his family going to take care of

him?" Lark put down her cookie, no longer hungry.

"The sheriff said he doesn't have any family." That was even sadder. If Burke passed away, no one would care and no one would mourn him. She set down the soap and rinsed in the basin.

"He has to have someone somewhere." Lark wrinkled her freckled nose. "Everybody has family."

"I don't know. Who knows if Dobbs is right?" She grabbed a towel and dried her hands. Lark was right. How did someone get to be all alone? Everyone came from somewhere, even a handsome deputy with a killer smile.

"Oh, I know!" Lark bounded off her cushioned chair and dropped to her knees next to the paper box by the stove. She rattled through the folded newspapers. "You are talking about the new deputy, right? That's what Eunice said when she told you to stay up here away from him."

"Yes." Lila swallowed her resentment, remembering Eunice's parting admonishment. "Why?"

"I remember reading something. Let me see." She plucked out a paper and leafed through it. "Here it is. Burke Hannigan."

"That's him." A spark of interest thrilled

through her like joy on a sunny day. She gripped the back of the chair, stopping herself from thundering around the table and snatching the newsprint from her sister. She was merely curious, that was all, wondering about the injured stranger. "What does it say?"

" 'The town of Angel Falls welcomes new deputy Burke Hannigan. He hails from Miota Hollow near Miles City, where he worked as a deputy before the town burned to the ground in a grass fire.' " Lark paused to comment. "Oh, that's too bad. I read about that early this spring. It doesn't say he has family."

"Then the sheriff was right." Did she sound casual? She sure hoped so. As she hung up the towel, her pulse drummed in her ears, making it hard to hear as Lark bowed her head and continued to read.

" 'He's a bachelor and this reporter has surmised he is not willing to settle down, so be that a warning to you ladies who might be interested in catching our new deputy's eye.' " Lark stopped again. "There is no mention of any relatives, so he really must be alone. How sad."

"Yes." She thought of him in the room below, stretched out on the front counter. Her palms went clammy and her knees weak. He didn't look strong enough to survive surgery. He'd lost so much blood already.

" 'He is, however, skilled with a six-shooter,' " Lark read on. " 'According to Sheriff Dobbs, he received a perfect score on the marksman part of his interview.' That's all it says about him." Lark folded the newsprint with a rattle and tossed it back into the box. "I wonder what happened to him? Why is he all alone?"

"We may never know." She remembered the deputy's sense of humor as he stubbornly denied the seriousness of his wounds. A ribbon of tenderness wrapped around her. He may have no one to care, but he had her. No one should be alone.

"Girls?" Eunice poked her head around the door. "Bring out more cookies. My friends will be staying longer than usual. No sense going out on those streets until we are certain all is safe."

"We're not safe?" Lark's eyes widened.

"The robbers rode away," Lila pointed out, wanting to reassure her little sister. "Nothing is going to happen. We'll bring the cookies."

"That's my good girls." Eunice let the door swing shut. Her steps tapped away and the faint murmur of lady's voices rose and fell like music.

"I've said a prayer for the deputy." Lark neatly scooped cookies off the rack and onto the platter. The tangy scent of molasses filled the air.

"I have, too." Lila leaned close to help and something in her pocket made a muted thunk against the counter. The badge. She'd completely forgotten about it. Why had he given it to her? She remembered the glinting tin star, which had been pinned to his shirt. She didn't remember watching him remove it. How odd.

"I'll take these in," Lark volunteered, seizing the platter and whisking away from the counter. "If Eunice sees you, she will find some other chore to keep you busy."

"Thank you." She had the best sister. She waited until the door had swung shut before she plucked the badge out of her pocket. It wasn't in the shape of a star. It wasn't made out of tin. It was a heavier metal in the shape of a shield.

This wasn't what he'd been wearing pinned to his chest. She squinted at it, her heart hammering. Streaks of blood coated the emblem and obscured the raised words ringing the symbol. A few steps took her to the washbasin. She dropped the badge in and reached for the soap. Two rubs and the badge shone in the sunlight slanting through the kitchen window.

Montana Territorial Range Rider, she read. The words made a banner above the rifle and horse symbol. Lila's knees went out and she collapsed into a nearby chair.

Burke was a Range Rider, a territorial lawman who answered directly to the governor. The organization was the highest arm of the law in the land. What was he doing in Angel Falls? Why was he wearing a deputy's badge on his shirt? She dried the shield with the hem of her skirt, remembering the plea in his eyes when he had pressed it into her hand. *Hide it. Promise?* he'd asked.

The door swung open. "Lila, it's the doctor."

Her stomach fell to her knees. She slipped the badge into her other skirt pocket and pushed shakily to her feet. What if it was bad news? What if Burke hadn't made it? Icy trembles spilled into her veins as she padded on wooden feet. She stumbled to the door, where the doctor spoke to Eunice.

"Deputy Hannigan is stable for now." Dr. Frost's quiet announcement made the air whoosh from Lila's lungs. Burke was alive. She gripped the edge of the door frame. Relief tripped through her.

"Although he is gravely weak." He spoke

37

in low tones, so his words wouldn't carry to the trio of matrons seated in the parlor. That didn't stop the ladies from leaning on the edges of their seats, keen to listen in. "He is far too injured to move right now."

"What are you saying, Doctor?" Dismay wrinkled Eunice's nose. "Are you saying he has to stay here?"

"Yes. Until I'm sure his bleeding has fully stopped it is too risky to move him. He could die."

"His life is important," Lila spoke up, her voice scratchy. She was aware of the weight of the badge in her pocket as she stepped forward. "He must stay."

"Not here, he can't." The woman drew herself up to full height and set her jaw. "What would people say?"

Lila grimaced. She knew how Eunice could be. Eunice always got her way. Now what did she do to help? What should she say? She could not reveal Burke's secret, but neither could she fail to protect him.

"That hardly matters, ma'am." The doctor frowned. Genuine concern drew lines into his face. He had married recently, and love had polished away the distance and stoicism that always used to define him. "The deputy's life comes first."

"I am a practical woman, Doctor." Eunice

planted her hands on her plump hips and leveled the medicine man with a look that would have undoubtedly stymied the bank robbers into retreat if she had been standing in line at the bank. "There is my husband's business to consider. Can you imagine anyone wanting to shop here with a dying man on display? They would all run down the street to our competition."

A touch of inspiration struck her. Lila straightened her spine and squared her shoulders. "He stays here. He's a servant of our town and he was injured in the line of duty. If you make the doctor move him and he dies, word will get out and it could hurt Pa's business. It could put a stain on our family reputation."

"I had not considered that." Eunice's indignation faltered. Her forehead crinkled as she pondered this new angle.

"I'll fetch some men to move him," the doctor said with quiet authority. "You will need to ready a bed for him. And, Lila? You likely saved his life."

"I did?" She shrugged, aware that Burke was still critically wounded. "I didn't do much."

"You kept a cool head in a crisis and you applied pressure to the wounds. You did a good job. I'm sure the deputy will be grateful."

"I just want him to recover." She swallowed, pleased to know she had made some small difference to the man with the bluest eyes she'd ever seen. "I read what to do in a novel."

"Then you had better just keep on reading." The doctor winked as he backtracked to the stairs. "Never know what useful things you will learn next."

"That's all you need, a reason to keep reading." Eunice shook her head as she returned to her friends. "Go fix up a pallet for that deputy in the storeroom. He's not staying upstairs in our home. When you are done there, you can clean up after him. I fear the floor will never be the same."

Nor will I, Lila thought. She grabbed Lark by the hand and ran to the linen cabinet. She intended to make Burke as comfortable as possible.

CHAPTER THREE

The store was silent. Only one man stood vigil next to the front counter, where Burke lay as if already in death's clutches, his face white as the muslin sheet covering him. A terrible aching seized Lila as she drew nearer. He was a substantial man, dwarfing the entire counter, and yet he appeared vulnerable. Close to death. She braced her fingertips against the counter, her throat dry.

"It's good of your family to take him in." A junior deputy, Jed Black, cleared emotion from his throat and nodded toward the stairs. "Do you have a bed ready for him?"

"No. My stepmother thinks it best he stay down here." She knew how uncharitable it sounded. She crept closer, careful not to step on a squeaky floorboard although she suspected a loud sudden noise would not wake him.

The man was a powerful force, even in

sleep. When she brushed her fingertips on top of his hand, his skin felt cool. Shadows bruised the angles of his face, the rest remained bloodless. His chest rose slightly, still breathing.

Lord, let it stay that way.

"You will feel better in no time," she assured him in a whisper. If only she could will strength and life into him like the heat from her touch.

"Lila!" Lark's voice echoed faintly in the stairwell. "Help!"

She tried to turn away, but it was as if a magnetic force held her in place. Tears seared her eyes when she remembered his striking blue eyes and the depth of feeling she'd seen in them, the unyielding determination not to give in to the weakness of his injuries and the strength of his character she'd sensed in their conversation. A strange honeyed sweetness swirled through her, feeling strangely like respect. It was not fair so strong a man could be this fragile. She walked backward, unable to take her gaze from him.

"Lila!" Her sister's call was muffled by the feather topper she clutched. The thick bundle of encased feather down blocked most of the girl from sight. "I found it. But I'm stuck."

"You're stepping on a corner of it. Don't move." She rushed up to scoop the half tumbling bundle and together they carried it down the last of the steps. "Thanks for finding this. I know it couldn't have been easy."

"Eunice doesn't know. I waited until she was in the kitchen getting more tea for her friends." Lark paused to glance over her shoulder. Her eyes widened with sadness. "He doesn't look as if he will be all right."

"Come." She tugged on the topper, knowing what her sister saw. Sadness gripped her. This wasn't the kind of excitement she had in mind when she'd prayed for a break in the monotony, either.

If only she could rewind time, so the deputy with the soulful blue eyes and wry smile could be whole again. But not even God would turn back time, for it marched forward, each moment giving way to the next without mercy. She shuffled into the storeroom and together they dropped the topper on the wooden pallet. A light dusting of white flour puffed upward, residue from the heavy bags she had just finished moving.

"This doesn't look too comfortable." Lark swiped brown curls from her face. "If I were hurt, I wouldn't want to lie down there."

"Don't worry, I will make it nice for him. The topper will help." She grabbed a corner and shook. The scent of mothballs wafted upward along with another puff of flour dust. When she folded it in half, the thick down made a fairly comfortable mattress. "See how I moved the pickle barrel over for a little nightstand?"

"The lamp looks homey." Lark bobbed to fetch the folded sheets from the top of the stack of fifty-pound flour sacks. "I'm going to run up and get some pillows. I'll be right back!"

She darted out of sight, hurrying earnestly, only wanting to help. Lila shook out the bottom sheet, and warm feelings of the best kind filled her up. She loved her sister.

In the store, the front door opened with a jangle of the overhead bell and heavy boots clamored across the plank boards. She tucked in a corner before whirling to peer around the doorway. The doctor had returned. The tension dug into his face and she spun away so she couldn't hear his words. She knew what the medical man was going to say. Burke was worsening.

Cast Your care upon him, Father. She shook out a top sheet, dread quaking through her.

"On three, boys." The doctor counted down, with a heave she could hear them lift the unconscious man from the front counter. Hesitant footsteps told her they carried him gingerly, careful not to jostle him.

She worked quickly to tuck in the last corner just as the men huffed and puffed in her direction. She flattened against the wall so they could squeeze by and deposit him on the makeshift bed. She'd never seen anyone so pale and still alive. Burke lay on his back, his dark hair tousled, his powerful physique motionless. She remembered his laughter — how promising and rich the sound — and his insistence that he was fine even as his life's blood streamed out of him. He was a good man, she was sure, and a good man should not die.

"What chance does he got, Doc?" Jed Black hitched up his gun belt.

"He's strong and he's young. He has that going for him." Dr. Frost appeared grim, as if he were digging for hope. "I will do my best."

"Appreciate that." Jed tipped his hat. "He hired on a bit ago, but he has helped me out of a jam a few times. He doesn't deserve two bullets to the chest."

"No one does," the doctor agreed. "Thanks for helping."

The men shuffled out mumbling their

goodbyes, and the sunshine tumbling through the small window felt like shadow. An unbearable sorrow claimed her for this man she did not know.

She wanted to know him. In her favorite novels, the hero always lived. He fought bad guys, faced perils, doled out justice and lived to fight another day. Maybe a quiet, boring existence wasn't so bad after all. She was safe, she was happy, healthy and whole. Not everyone could say the same.

"Lila, if you could fetch me a chair, I would appreciate it." The doctor knelt to lay his fingertips against Burke's wrist, feeling for his pulse. "It's going to be a long day. My guess, an even longer night."

"Of course." She tore herself away, hurrying to fetch what the doctor needed, but the responsibility she carried for Burke remained, a link to him she could not explain.

Burke was hot — sweating hot. His skin burned. Droplets beaded on his forehead. A rivulet trickled down the back of his neck, under his collar and down his spine. His mouth felt like a desert floor, the air too sweltering to breathe. His nightclothes stuck to his damp skin, smoking in places where the fabric burned through. The pain was nothing as he felt his older sister's arms clamp around him, holding him captive and keeping him from racing into the burning shanty. Tears mingled with sweat and grit from the smoke.

"Lemme go!" he yelled, frantic, watching the orange tongues of flame rise from the kitchen window and gobble up the roofline. "Mama! Papa!"

"We can't help 'em." Ginna's tears dripped on the top of his head. Her sobs shook him, but she didn't let go. "We'll get all burned up more."

His throat was too dry to speak. The fierce heat from the fire seemed to evaporate his tears. He watched the window just like Papa said, but no one came.

"I'll get your mama and be right out," their father had promised, handing Burke through the open window and into his sister's arms. He could still hear his pa's voice in his head. "Ginna, take him into the fields and keep him there. Don't come near this house no matter what happens. You do what I tell you. Do you understand?"

"Yes, Papa." Six-year-old Ginna had sounded so brave and her bravery remained as she sat down in the soft carpet of growing wheat, taking him with her. Her iron hold did not relent. "We have to do what

Papa said. We have to stay away from the fire."

"But it's burnin' 'em up!" He choked out sob after sob watching the fire shoot up into the sky. Terror and grief tore through him, trapped in his soul. The heat became unbearable and the fire consumed him. It melted the ground at his feet and burned away the memory like the dream it was, leaving him in bed gasping for the surface of consciousness like a drowning man.

"It's all right." A cold cloth covered his forehead. A woman's gentle touch brushed the side of his face. He was still drowning, but at least he could draw in air. Lila's next words came from farther away and were not directed to him. "Does he have a fever?"

"Yes, and it's getting worse," a man's voice answered, one he dimly recognized. Not the sheriff. At least he could be relieved at that. "Ice is on its way. Fetch me some tarps. I'll need to ice him down."

"I'll hurry." Her soothing touch vanished, her sweet presence faded. The pad of her shoes and the rustle of her skirts became silence and he was drowning again, pulled back into nightmares that were not dreams at all.

"Let go, Ginna!" The fire had grown like a monster in the night. "Lemme go!"

"No. I c-can't." Sobs choked her and rocked the both of them. Overhead thunder rumbled. The hot wind gusted and stirred a whirl of red-hot ashes into the air. The roof collapsed with a mighty crack. Flames and burning debris shot up into the blackness.

"Mama." He whispered the word, knowing his mother would not be coming for him. His father would not be following her or sweeping him into his big strong arms ever again. "Papa."

Ginna finally let him go, her raw hands sliding away from his middle as she slumped sideways into the bed of wheat, overcome by tears. He stumbled onto his knees as rain began to fall in hard drops that hit the ground like hail.

Nobody came. The night ticked away, the dawn drew color on the eastern horizon and the sun rose. Finally Ginna took his hand and said kindly, the good big sister that she was, "We must go find the neighbors."

His feet felt heavy. The heat of the fire stayed with him both on his skin and in his heart. The midsummer morning was soon scorching and sweat dripped off his forehead. The sun blazed like a white-hot fire in the sky. Such a long, sad walk. Two miles away, the Dunlaps' shanty came into sight. Mrs. Dunlap glanced up from watering her garden, dropped her bucket and came running. Ginna's hand slid out of his and that was the last time he saw his sister. In this dream that was his past, he searched for her long and hard. But she was gone and he was alone.

Until a faint cold penetrated the nightmare. He heard a woman's gentle alto reading to him, her words so faint he could not distinguish them but he clung to the sound. He no longer felt lost and forgotten. For as long he could hear her voice, he was not alone.

"Lila, it is past your bedtime."

She stopped reading, marked the place on the page with her thumb and squinted through the half dark with tired eyes at her father standing in the doorway. "Can I stay up late, just this once?"

"It's not good for your health, child." Pa padded into the fall of the lamplight. He was a robust man, although some vital part of him had never recovered after her mother's death. "No, you must come to bed."

"But, Pa, I want to stay and help."

"The doctor is here." He pinched the bridge of his nose. "The deputy will be in good hands. If anything changes, I'm sure Doc Frost will let us know. Come, now. Your stepmother is very concerned about your reputation."

"As you said, the doctor is here, as well." She was loath to put down her book. She glanced at the man on the pallet and felt tethered to him in a way she didn't understand. She needed to help him. "I'm in the middle of a scene. At least let me finish the part where the Range Rider is backed into a canyon and out of bullets. Please?"

"You'll have to dangle for a bit, I'm afraid." Pa held out one hand. "Perhaps you can sneak in here when no one is looking tomorrow and read the rest of the scene for the deputy. Not that he can probably hear you."

"He can." Reluctantly, she shut the book's cover. The lamplight caressed the man on the pallet, who was fighting a fever, sweat sluicing down his face and dampening his dark hair. Earlier, when she had rejoined the doctor after the supper dishes were done, Burke had been restless, tossing and turning. After two hours of reading, her throat may be scratchy but he was resting calmly.

"I promise not to leave his side." Dr. Frost withdrew his stethoscope from his medical bag, which sat at his feet. "His fever is the main concern. If it hasn't broken by morning . . ."

A lump formed in her throat, making it impossible to answer. Sadly, she pushed off the stool and backed away from the foot of the pallet. Would he die in the night? She resisted the urge to smooth his tangled hair and dry the sweat beading on his granite face.

"Lila, you're dawdling." Pa stood in the hallway, waiting to close the door. "The deputy is not your responsibility."

"It feels as if he is." It took effort to force her shoes to carry her across the threshold. She took one last glance over her shoulder, surely not the last time she would see him. He lay motionless as if only a shell, but she remembered his smile and his humor. She reluctantly placed one shoe on the bottom stair. She could not explain why with each step she took up the staircase, she left a piece of herself behind.

"Pray for him," Pa advised as he closed the door tight behind her. "It's all any of us can do for him now. He's in God's hands."

"Will you pray for him, too?"

"I already have many times. I hate seeing this happen to anyone so young."

"How do you know anything about him?" She clutched her book. He was just like the hero in her favorite series of novels. Maybe that explained the quick, innocent spark of her interest in him. "He hasn't been in the store, has he?"

"Not that I remember. A while back he stopped to help me when a spoke broke on the delivery wagon." Pa ambled into the fall of light from the upstairs lamps. "At least a few of the town's other deputies would have kept on going, but he dismounted, moseyed up and took over the repair. Expert at it, too. Had the spoke jury-rigged together and back in place in half the time I had been wrestling with it."

Not only an expert marksman but he excelled at wagon repair. Burke was definitely an interesting man. Lila crept down the hallway, where light spilled from the room she shared with Lark. "He struck me as the type of man who would stop and help someone in need."

"He never wanted so much as a thanks in return. I tried buying him lunch, inviting him to a home-cooked meal, but he wouldn't have it. He keeps to himself, that one." Pa lightly tweaked Lila's nose. "You get some rest, my dear. You worked hard to help the doctor today. You showed compassion your mother would be proud of."

"Thanks, Pa." She didn't know how to explain that she'd felt drawn, as if she had no other choice. That wasn't the same as compassion, more like duty and responsibility. She felt inadequate as her father padded toward the parlor where Eunice awaited him. Eunice put down her needlework to speak to him in low tones. Lila turned away, dragging her feet down the hall. Heaviness weighed on her, exhaustion that turned her bones to lead.

"Is he any better?" Lark popped into her doorway.

"No. His fever is severe." She bit her tongue to keep from telling how concerned the doctor had been. The shadows deepened in the hallway like living things seizing her. She could not give in to hopelessness. "I was going to pray for him again. Will you join me?"

"Yes." Lark locked her arm in Lila's and they ambled into the bedroom together.

"We surrender their spirits to the Lord." The minister's words lifted on the hot summer wind that stirred the grasses next to the open three graves.

Burke clasped his hands behind his back, bowed his head forward and squeezed his eyes shut. The images of those coffins sitting in the graves remained etched on the back of his lids. He was so sad no tears

54

would come.

"They are in a much better place, little boy." Mrs. Dunlap rested a heavy hand on his shoulder. "Do not be sad. Think how happy they are in Heaven."

Her words did not comfort him. The sun blazed as if it were the house fire burning him up, too. He wished for Ginna's arms holding him tight around his middle. He wished for Pa's rumbling voice when he told a bedtime story and the comfort of Ma's gentle fingertips as she would clean away a swipe of dirt from his face. He wanted them back. More than anything, he wanted them back.

"Ashes to ashes, dust to dust," the minister went on, talking about things Burke did not understand.

He did not want to understand. He wiped sweat from his forehead with his sleeve. He'd never been so hot. Feelings bunched in his throat, as sharp as knives. The grief burned him up from the inside, the way the fire had burned the house. He wanted to be in Heaven, too. That's where Pa was and Ginna. He wanted his Ma. But dirt shoveled down on the coffins and he was alone.

"You are a good boy. Not a single tear." Mrs. Dunlap patted him on the top of his head. "Good, she's here. Do you see that nice lady?"

He didn't want to look, but he did. He tugged at his buttoned collar because the air was suffocating him. A lady in a black dress climbed down from a buckboard. Her hair was pulled back so tight it stretched her face. Not a speck of dust rising up from her footsteps on the street dared to settle on her skirt. She walked like a soldier, like someone who did not like little boys.

"Is this him?" She had a rough voice, like the wood Pa had split to make the kitchen table before he sanded it. "Is this the orphan?"

He did not know what an orphan was.

"Yes, poor thing." Mrs. Dunlap gave him a little push between the shoulder blades. "We would offer to keep him but we've raised our own. At our age, it would be too much."

"I understand. He's not your obligation." Stern lines kept the black dressed lady's mouth from hardly moving when she talked. "He looks small for his age."

"He took a bad case of diphtheria last year. I remember his mother feared losing him."

"The scrawny ones have a hard time being adopted." The frown lines dug deeper on either side of her mouth. "Come along, boy. I don't want any nonsense from you."

"No, ma'am." He glanced over his shoulder but Mrs. Dunlap simply nodded as if he were to go with this stranger. The minister clapped him on the shoulder and walked away. Everyone left except for the man with the shovel tossing dirt into Ma's grave.

Blistering heat scalded his eyes and felt likely to peel away his flesh. He took one step with the black dressed lady and all light faded from the sky, all color from the earth. There was only darkness as he died inside. No longer his ma's little boy, his pa's only son, his sister's baby brother, he was nothing at all.

CHAPTER FOUR

The morning felt unnaturally quiet as Lila splashed in the washbasin in the corner of the bedroom. Maybe it was the early hour, that's what she tried to tell herself as foreboding trembled through her. Outside the curtained window, no birds sang, no shadows moved, even the wind held its breath as if waiting. She knew, because she'd peeked between the closed curtains. Clouds stood ominous in the sky, heavy like black wool and pressing on the air.

"Lila!" Lark punched her pillow and groggily yawned. "What time is it?"

"It's daylight." She dropped her toothbrush into the holder, gave a final glance in the mirror, fluffed her bangs with her fingers and spun on her heels. "Don't worry, I'm done. Just be glad you're not old enough to work in the store yet."

"I wish, but Eunice doesn't trust me to." Lark yawned again, hauled the covers over her head and muttered incomprehensibly. She didn't move, drifting back to her dreams.

Lila quietly closed the door, her skirts rustling as she tiptoed down the hallway. The house was silent, the kitchen dark, the cookstove unlit. Looked like the coast was clear. Eunice wasn't up yet to thwart her morning mission. She intended to check on Burke and nothing would stop her. Not even the terrible tight sick feeling digging deep into her stomach.

She was afraid for him. She had lain awake half the night listening for any sound that might hint to her how the deputy was doing. The doctor did not leave, no one came to assist him and the downstairs remained silent as she descended the stairs. She avoided the squeaky spots and pushed through the door into the store.

Dr. Frost stood at the front counter, rolling down his shirtsleeves, his medical bag on the floor beside him. Exhaustion lined his grim face and his shoulders slumped as if with defeat. Had Burke died? Her knees gave out and she clutched the door. Cold horror breezed though her, leaving her unable to speak.

"Lila. Good." The doctor reached for his bag. "I've got another patient to check on.

Will you stay with the deputy?"

"You mean he's alive?" The words rasped out of her tight throat and her dry mouth.

"His fever broke an hour ago. The worst is over."

Thank You, Lord. Her knees felt firmer. "He lost so much blood. He will recover, won't he?"

"He's otherwise healthy and in his prime. I don't see why not." The doctor managed a small smile. "I have other patients to tend to. I won't be long. Keep watch over him, Lila, will you?"

"With my life." Her attention rolled back to Burke. She couldn't help it. Her fingers tingled as if unable to forget the memory of touching him. It was an odd sensation that was part lovely and part sweet.

The front door opened with the chime of the bell, but her attention was on the storeroom. Faint light filtered into the small hallway from the single window. A thin muslin curtain did its best to hold back the sun, but large streaks spilled onto the floor and the pickle barrels and onto the pallet. The deputy lay on his back, the sheet to his chin, breathing normally in sleep. She'd never seen a more welcome sight.

"Lila, what are you doing down here on your own with a man?" Eunice's scolding echoed in the store. Her skirts snapped as she stalked closer. "Do you have no common sense?"

"The doctor asked me to keep an eye on him." She hurried into the hall, praying her stepmother would not wake him. "He's improved. Isn't that a blessing?"

"The blessing would be having him out of this building. That is what I'm praying for." Eunice tapped her foot impatiently. "There is no chaperone here. No one to safeguard you."

"I don't need a chaperone. I don't need safeguarding." It wasn't easy keeping her frustration out of her tone. Eunice was a practical woman, something her father appreciated very much. She loved Pa and arguing with his wife would only upset him. Lila sighed. "I have work to do down here before I can open the store."

"I suppose Lark can help me in the kitchen." Eunice's gaze narrowed as if she were trying to ferret out the truth. "You will stay an appropriate distance from him, and I will come down to check on you. Don't think I won't. I won't have anyone in this town saying I didn't handle this situation properly."

"Yes'm." She thought of Pa and how it would hurt him if she was anything less than respectful to her stepmother. She bit her lip to keep silent. She thought of all the good Eunice did — kept the house, fussed over Lark, made sure the business ran smoothly. She was a great comfort to Pa's life.

"I don't want you going into the room. Do you hear me? Don't you step foot beyond the threshold as long as you are alone with him. I need your word, Lila."

"You have it." She pushed aside the misery threatening to take over.

"This is for your own good, you'll see." Pleased, Eunice smiled and patted Lila's cheek. "I'll have Lark bring down your breakfast. Don't forget about the herring barrel. I want this floor spotless before a single customer arrives."

There was no way to avoid the fish barrel. Lila sighed and went in search of the mop. She found it on the floor right where she'd left it yesterday afternoon. The sudsy water had to be changed and that would lead her to the back door. Eunice said she couldn't go inside the room so she kept her toes on this side of the threshold.

Shadows hid him. The lamp's wick was out and the muted light from the window fell across his chest but couldn't reach his face. She bit back her frustration. She needed to see him. Maybe it was her sense of responsibility returning. Yes, that had to be it. She was a very responsible sort. She had also given her word to the doctor she would watch over him. His breathing remained regular and his slumber deep. If she had the wish to lay her hand across his forehead to make sure the fever was truly gone for good, she did not take a step forward. She'd made a promise to her stepmother.

It took all her strength to tear away from the doorway. She had a floor to scrub clean, barrels to move and the front section of boardwalk to sweep. That would keep her busy and perhaps take her mind off the man.

It did not.

Burke came to consciousness slowly. First there was only shadow and a distant pain that constricted his breathing. As he surfaced, he was aware of a muslin sheet beneath him and over him, the softness of a feather pillow, the scent of pickles, herring and something he couldn't quite recognize. Cinnamon, maybe? His mind remained foggy and it took effort to try to open his eyes.

Where was he? He struggled to force his eyelids apart. Sunlight spilled through a nearby window and exploded like dynamite in his skull. He ignored the discomfort but he couldn't see much through the glare. Shelves full of canned goods, cartons and stacks of bulky sacks. He heard the scrape of a chair nearby and in the distance the muffled rattle of a wagon passing by on a street, no, a narrow alley, judging by the echoing clip-clop of a horse's hooves. He was somewhere in town. Pain radiated through him. He was hurt. His mind remained foggy. What had happened?

It was the dreams he remembered. The red ashes raining down from the sky, the flash of lightning in the storm, the dirt tumbling into his mother's grave. He could still feel Ginna's arms around him, although he hadn't been that boy in twenty years. He tried to lift his head and a sharp-edged blade of pain sliced through the dullness in his foggy brain. He exhaled sharply. Laudanum. He'd been under its effects before. This wasn't the first time he'd been shot in the line of duty.

"Burke?" He recognized the voice, soft like a melody, as gentle as a hymn, as arresting as a sonnet. Skirts rustled and a chair scraped closer this time. "Good morning, Deputy. Can you hear me?"

Lila. He remembered her. She hovered over him, burnished with the blazing light.

Her green-blue eyes studied him and he could read the concern. For him. His heart thumped. It had been a long time since anyone had bothered with concern for him. He licked his lips and found them cracked. His tongue felt like sand. He tried to speak but no sound came. Just pain.

"You must be thirsty." She slipped from his view. All light bled from the room. The tap of her shoes, the rustle of her petticoats and the drip of water told him she was not far away, but he could not summon the strength to turn his head so much as an inch to find her.

Vulnerable. Defenseless. He didn't like being either. He was alone in the world, he had to keep his guards up. His pulse kicked, galloping frantically. It all came back to him. The assignment, arriving in town, holding back when he saw Cheever riding shotgun with Slim's gang. That didn't stop Cheever from shooting him. The outlaw must be still mad over his pa's death.

"Here you are." She returned, coming between him and the blinding sunshine and touched a tin cup to his lips. "Drink slowly. You can have only a few sips at a time."

The cold water wet his lips and rolled across his tongue. He swallowed, wanting to grab the cup from her and drain it dry to the last drop, but he could not summon the strength to lift his arms.

"If you keep that down, I will give you a few sips more." Cinnamon-brown braids tumbled over her shoulder and curly gossamer wisps framed her soft oval face. She had high cheekbones and a dainty nose, long dark lashes and a full rosebud mouth made for smiling or, he suspected, singing hymns in the church choir.

He'd never seen anyone so beautiful. He waited while she turned away to put down the cup, hating that she had moved out of his sight again. This wasn't like him. He knew better than to get tangled up with a woman like her.

"The doctor ran out to check on another patient and to get a bite of lunch." She returned and folded the edge of the sheet lying across his chest. Her feather-soft touch soothed him, but he could not accept it. He could not get used to it. Unaware, she gave the edge of the sheet a final pat and straightened up. She reached for something, a book, as it turned out, a paperback serial. "I was reading to you while you slept. I hope you don't mind. Dr. Frost said it might help you to hear a friendly voice."

He swallowed painfully. Air rattled in his throat and didn't sit right in his lungs. When he opened his mouth a rattle came out and not the question he needed to ask.

"Are you uncomfortable?" Concern animated her eyes, kindness resonated in her voice. Lovely crinkles tucked the porcelain smooth skin of her forehead as she set down her book. She glanced at her watch pin. "I'm afraid you can't have more laudanum for at least forty minutes more."

Frustration clawed through him. He didn't want something to cloud his judgment. What he wanted was to get back on his feet. He tried to move but nothing happened. Not a muscle flickered. The effort of trying to speak left him dizzy and nauseated. He was as weak as a kitten. He drew in a wheeze of air and listened to the oxygen rattle in his throat. He couldn't just lie around. He had a report to make. He had to be sure she kept his secret.

"Badge?" He choked on the word. It came out garbled and more of a cough than a word. White-hot pain hit him like the sharpened edge of an ax and he squeezed his eyes against the blow.

"It's upstairs tucked in my hope chest." Her skirts rustled, her petticoats whispered and the stool groaned as she shifted her weight. He forced his eyes to open wider, fighting waves of pain as she whispered, "No one will think to look for anything there. Don't worry, Marshal."

He gulped, nearly blacking out.

"Don't worry. I will keep your secret." Her rosebud lips parted into an intriguing smile as she leaned in. "I'm very good with confidences. If there's anything you need, you let me know."

"Up." That came out more as a wheeze than a word.

She shook her head. "Sorry, not even your strength of will can do that. The doctor said you are not to move an inch, not until he's sure your stitches will hold. One of the bullets lodged close to your heart and nicked a lung. Very serious."

He swallowed, fighting the adrenaline coursing through him as he thought about being stuck flat on his back. He'd wanted to be a territorial lawman since he'd been five and a trio of them had rode into town. He could still feel the frayed edges of wood against his fingers as he'd clung to the fence in the orphanage yard watching the impressive men on their powerful horses riding straight and tall in the saddle, a symbol of justice and might.

"You have caused some excitement in town." She grabbed her book to mark the page with a length of purple ribbon. "Everyone is talking about the new deputy who drew so fast, not a single person on the street saw more than a blur and your gun firing. Too bad you didn't hit anyone."

"No." A sick guilty feeling sank into his stomach. How did he tell someone as obviously good and wholesome as Lila what he really was? If she knew what he was capable of, she would never speak to him again.

"And the newspaper said you were an expert aim, so that must be a great embarrassment to you." She clutched her book with both hands.

"Yes."

"Whenever anyone talks about the infamous bank robbery, everyone will remember the quick draw and the bad aim." She shifted on the chair. "The holdup is all any of the customers talked about all morning. Apparently it was some famous outlaw gang."

"I know."

"I suppose you would. All those wanted posters tacked all over the sheriff's office." A bell faintly jingled from the other room and her chair scraped as she hopped to her feet. She set her book on the cushion. "That's a customer. I've got to go. Don't worry, I'll be back."

He didn't answer. He didn't look as if he

could, poor man. The effort of waking had paled him even more. Her shoes dragged on the floor as she tripped down the hall. His gaze was like a magnet on her back trying to pull her back. Eunice had a ladies' aid meeting at the church, so there was no one to wait on the customer. She had to go.

"Lila, there you are." One of her best friends, Earlee Mills, smiled from behind the fabric counter at the far end of the store. In tow was her little brother, Edward, who pushed at a loose tooth as he studied the button display, held captive by one hand. Earlee didn't look inclined to let him go. "I heard all about the excitement. Are you all right? I saw the bullet hole right through the front window."

"It went into the counter, but all is well. I was providentially behind the counter instead of in front of it at the time." She flung her arms wide and gave Earlee a quick hug. "Oh, it's good to see you. I've missed you, all of you, so much."

"It's only been four days since church. We all saw each other then. And we have our sewing circle this week." Earlee looked sweet in a handed down blue calico dress that perfectly matched her eyes. Her hair tumbled down from her sunbonnet in golden ringlets. "Edward, remember what I told you?"

"Don't touch a thing," he repeated, pulling his fingers back just in time from a button made in the shape of a dog.

"My fault. I shouldn't have let go of you." Earlee rolled her eyes, good-natured as always and caught hold of her brother once again. "I just finished writing a letter to Meredith. That's where we're headed. The post office."

"Oh, I meant to stop by there yesterday but then all the excitement happened. At least I have something thrilling to write about. Meredith will keel over from shock, as my life is so boring." She paused, gathering up the words to tell the news about Burke, but they didn't seem to want to come.

"No, *my* life is boring," Earlee teased. "You can trade with me if you want. I'm stuck out on the farm and you are here in town, where all the action is."

"Action? Yesterday was the only action I've seen yet. Remember, if you trade lives with me, then you have to deal with Eunice."

"Oh, point taken. Think I'll keep the one I have."

"I knew you would say that." Laughing, Lila stepped behind the counter. "Did you come to get that trim you were hoping for?"

"No, I wish." Earlee glanced wistfully at the glass beneath the wooden countertop, where spools sat lined up in a long row of delicate laces, beautiful silk ribbons and colorful rickrack. "Ma needs another bottle of tonic. Her heart is troubling her again."

"I'm sorry she's ailing." Earlee's ma had suffered a severe case of small pox which had left her in a weakened state ever since. As the oldest girl, the responsibility of the children and the housework fell on Earlee's slim shoulders. Lila wished Earlee's situation could be easier. She bopped over to the medicine cabinet behind the cash drawer and sorted through the many bottles. "I'm keeping her in prayer."

"That would be a help. Thank you." Earlee cleared her throat and attempted to be stern — and failed. "Edward, what did I just tell you?"

"I'm sorry, Earlee. I can't help it. My finger just did it all on its own. Honest." The little boy didn't look very worried about getting punished. "There's a real bullet in here."

"Stop touching it." Earlee shook her head and tugged her brother away from temptation. "Did you hear Chance Bell got winged by a bullet? It went right through the wall of the hardware store. Someone else was shot right on the bank step. One of the bank's guards. Word is that he was winged in the leg and will be all right. Ma got word through her church group to pray for the deputy who got shot twice in the chest."

"He's here." She lowered her voice, wondering if Burke could hear her or if he'd drifted back into a healing sleep. "In the storeroom."

"Here?" Earlee's eyes widened as she opened her reticule and plucked out a fifty cent piece. "Is it the really attractive deputy? The newest one? He's even more handsome than Lorenzo Davis."

"I didn't think that was even possible until I saw Burke." She blushed, glad to take the coin and make change in the drawer. It gave her something to focus on so she could pretend to herself she wasn't blushing.

"Burke?" Earlee arched one dainty eyebrow. "You're on a first-name basis with him?"

"I am. I tended to his wounds after he stumbled into the store." She dropped a dime, a nickel and two pennies onto Earlee's palm. "Don't look at me like that. I had a responsibility."

"You like him."

"He's too old for me." Twenty-four to her eighteen. Six years was a lot. He was the manliest man she'd ever met, but in a good way. A mighty way. He was just like the Range Rider in her favorite novel series, but she couldn't tell Earlee that. "He will be strong enough to be moved soon, because Eunice is not going to let him stay here a second longer than he has to. Then I'll never see him again."

"You *do* like him." Earlee tucked away the money and gave her brother what passed for a scowl but fell far short. Edward lifted his forefinger off the wrapped butterscotch candy in the candy barrel. "What about Lorenzo?"

"Maybe I'll give up on Lorenzo." Lila ripped off a length of brown paper.

"But you've been in love with him since you were eight years old. That's a long time."

"Oh, he's never going to fall for me. I thought maybe after he forgave Fiona for ignoring him and falling in love with Ian, that he might turn his eye to me. But he's never going to, or he would have done so." That hurt, but it wasn't a surprise, either. "Things don't always work out the way you wish."

"What made you change your mind? Is it this new man? The deputy?" Earlee laid a gentle hand on her brother's shoulder.

"No." She didn't want to say anything until she was sure, but she'd spotted Lorenzo in church last Sunday watching a certain young lady with a wistful look, and that lady wasn't her or Earlee. She tied the package neatly with a string and handed it over. "I'm going to hold out for a dime-novel hero."

"Oh, I just finished reading the last book you lent me." Earlee tucked the bottle inside her reticule. "The Ranger Rider hero is utterly too-too."

"He always saves the day and he's a really good man down deep, no matter what." Fine, so she was thinking about Burke. How could she not? "I can't wait to see what comes on the train today. I'm expecting a new batch of books."

"Exciting. I can't wait, either." Earlee's smile faded as she kindly nudged her little brother away from the candy. He gazed at it with such longing. Treats like candy were not common in the Mills' house. Earlee clearly hesitated, worrying her bottom lip. "How many pieces for a penny?"

"A dozen." It was six candies, but Earlee was family to her. "Edward, did you want to pick out the pieces?"

"Really, Lila? Oh, I would!" Not expecting such a privilege, he hopped up and

75

down with excitement. "Can I have a but-terscotch one?"

"Absolutely." Lila grabbed a little striped paper bag meant just for candy and circled around the counter. "Here you go. Make your choice."

"Ma likes the peppermint balls." He bent his head to fish one of the cheerfully striped candies from the mix. "And Ramona does, too."

It took a while for Edward to pick just the right piece for everyone in his family. A customer came in and Lila waited on Lanna Wolf, who was in need of a new packet of needles. After wrapping the packet and add-ing the sale to the Wolf's account, Lila gave Edward an extra butterscotch candy for the road, hugged Earlee goodbye, refused the penny and dashed to the storeroom. Her patient lay asleep, a powerful man in spite of his wounds, a hint of natural color returning to his face.

Thank You, Lord, she prayed, grateful he was improving. Heroes should always re-cover to fight for justice another day. The door jingled, drawing her attention. It was the glass repairman come to replace the damaged pane in the front window.

CHAPTER FIVE

Earlee Mills couldn't stop her hands from shaking as she plopped onto the bench outside the post office and stared at the letter, just to make sure she hadn't imagined it. It was definitely real. She ran her fingertip over the stark handwriting that spelled out her name. Finally, after months of waiting and believing he had given up caring about her, Finn McKaslin had sent a letter.

"Earlee." Edward popped the butterscotch out of his mouth and held it by two sticky fingers. "Can we go home now?"

"Just one minute." She tipped the letter so he couldn't make out the return address. She didn't want anyone to know about Finn. A lot of people's opinions of him had changed ever since he'd been convicted of robbing a train last summer, but she had always carried a torch for the youngest McKaslin brother. She knew he was a good man down deep. Even good men made mistakes. "Why don't you watch the horses go by for two more minutes?"

"I'm hot. I want to play in the creek." Edward gave a gap-toothed grin, which always worked on Ma.

Earlee felt her strength weakening. It wasn't easy to say no to that cute freckled face. "I said two minutes. Is that really very long? Then we will be on our way."

"Okay." He popped the candy back into his mouth, wiped his sticky fingers on his trouser leg and turned toward the street. Fortunately a matched team of glossy black horses paraded by drawing a fashionable buggy with gleaming red wheels, which absorbed all of the boy's attention. "One day I'm gonna own me a buggy and horses like that."

"Yes, you will." She tugged a hairpin out of her coiled up braids and slit the envelope neatly open. Her fingers felt wooden and she stabbed herself in the scalp when she slipped it back into her hair. For months she'd had to accept that Finn wasn't interested in her. And why would he be? Fairy tales didn't happen to girls like her. She had to be realistic. He had only ever been in need of a pen friend, someone to help ease his loneliness.

There was a single sheet of paper and a

short note in his masculine script.

Hello, Earlee,
It's been a while since I got your letter. Honestly, I didn't know if I should write you back. It's something that's been bothering me the whole time and I may as well get it off my chest. I'm being self-ish writing you and looking forward to your letters. I am lonely here and un-happy, but maybe you shouldn't spend your time writing to a convict like me. That's what I am. I've come to accept it. After spending a month in solitary confinement or the pit, as we call it here, I can't be in denial any longer.

He was in a pit? Earlee tore her eyes from the letter, feeling as if she'd been struck. How horrible for him. A pleasant puff of warm breeze fanned over her face and stirred her bangs. She was free. She had never given it much pause before. Beauty surrounded her, bright blue sky, dazzling sunshine and the colorful excitement of the town street. The scent of the bakery wafted down the boardwalk, horses strutted by, and she could go anywhere if she had a mind to. Edward clomped over and dropped onto the bench beside her.

79

"Can we go now?" he begged.

"It hasn't been a full two minutes." She tweaked his nose gently to make him grin. The candy was tucked in the corner of his mouth and made him look a little chipmunk. "But I suppose I can walk and read at the same time, if you promise to warn me before I walk into a hitching post."

"I'm good at watching for stuff!" Edward bounded onto his feet, his boots thumping on the planks. "Hurry, Earlee!"

"I'm coming." She pushed off the bench and followed her little brother down the boardwalk. Her attention drifted back to Finn's letter.

I appreciated your description of town life and life on your farm. Your writing made me forget where I was for a few moments. That's a gift I'm grateful for but don't write me again.

Goodbye,
Finn.

"Earlee!" Edward grabbed her elbow.

She glanced up and skidded to a stop just in time. A teamster's loaded wagon and double team rumbled by. She wobbled on the edge of the boardwalk, heart pounding.

Finn had said goodbye. He didn't want

her to write anymore. Crushing disappointment settled like an anvil on her chest. She remembered him as he'd been in their school days, although he was several classes ahead of her. His dark hair tousled by the breeze, his good-natured grin, his easygoing friendly manner that made every girl in school swoon just a little.

"We can go now." Edward tugged her forward, shaking his head disapprovingly. "Girls."

"Boys." She ruffled his hair affectionately. She tucked away Finn's letter. That was the end of that. He didn't want her as a pen friend. If this were a story she was penning, the correspondence between the hero and the heroine would be the catalyst for a great romance, one of rare love and infinite tenderness, the kind of love that would last for all time.

But real life was not like a novel. She sighed and tugged another hairpin from her topknot. She had one more letter to open. She withdrew Meredith's envelope from her pocket and carefully unfolded it, trusting Edward to keep her from tripping as she bent her head to read.

Lila plunged her hands into the warm soapy water and grabbed one of the wet garments from the bottom of the tub. A hot puff of air breezed down the alley behind the store and across her face. She thought of the deputy asleep on the other side of the wall just feet away. She could picture him perfectly. There was something incredibly decent about Burke Hannigan. Definitely hero quality.

Lord, please save him. I believe he is worth it. She wrung the excess water from his shirt and scrubbed it on the washboard for a third time, although it did no good. The bloodstain had set. What was a Range Rider doing in Angel Falls? There were few more respected or awe-inspiring professions in all of Montana Territory — at least not in her opinion. And to think he had walked right into the store and into her life. She shook out the sudsy garment and leaned over the washboard again.

A faint ring of spurs sounded alien against the background noise of traffic over on the main street and the voices murmuring from the open windows of the neighboring buildings.

" 'Afternoon, missy." The warmth seemed to fade from the breeze as a shadow fell to a stop over her washtub. Sheriff Dobbs gazed down at her with his thumbs in his trouser pockets, dressed all in black, his tin star on his chest. "Is Deputy Hannigan still breathin'? Or was I right? He looked nearly dead the last time I saw him."

"His fever broke in the night, but he is still very weak."

"Then he's alive?" The sheriff seemed amused by that.

"He most certainly is." She shivered, even in the blazing heat of the day. She had never felt more aware of being alone. No one was in the alley. No dogs roaming, no kids playing kickball or chase or tag, not even persnickety Mr. Grummel from next door and his cantankerous donkey. She set her chin, determined not to be intimidated. "The doctor is sitting with Deputy Hannigan. Would you like me to fetch him for you?"

"Doc Frost is here? No, I don't like doctors." The sheriff rocked back on his heels, considering this information. He stared down the alley as if his thoughts, whatever they were, consumed him. "I came to get what belongs to the sheriff's office. Hannigan's things."

"You mean his clothes?"

"And anything you might have found in the pockets. Any papers, maybe his badge."

"His b-badge?" She lost her grip on the shirt. It tumbled out of her hands and plopped with a splash into the sudsy water.

"I don't want that to fall into the wrong hands." He tried to smile, but it fell short and looked more like a sneer.

"Of course." She shook off her hands, water dropping into the dust as she reached into her pocket. The five-point deputy's star glinted dully in the evening light as she held it on her palm. She'd removed it from his shirt a few moments before.

"That's fine, young lady." He covered her hand with his, his touch lingered a tad too long.

Lila's stomach turned. She jerked back, her pulse thumping like a scared rabbit in her ears. Dobbs turned away, spurs singing. He stopped to look the building up and down, studying the entrance and windows before moseying on his way.

Her pulse roared through her veins and she tremored with the force of it. This was more excitement than she felt comfortable with. At least Burke's secret was still safe. She'd kept her word to him. Relieved, she dunked the clean garment in the rinse water and plunged out the soap bubbles.

She could still see the sheriff taking his time ambling down the alley. Why was Burke working as a town deputy? The question crept into her thoughts as she wrung out his shirt and caught sight of one of the bullet holes. If he was a Range Rider, shouldn't he be out riding the range, hunting down outlaws and protecting trains? Or was he conducting an investigation right here in town?

"Howdy, Lila." Mr. Grummel called out from his cart as he drove by. "Eunice has you doing laundry again?"

"It's the deputy's clothes."

"Ah, that's good work you do. That poor man. Oy." Mr. Grummel pulled back on his reins and his donkey ignored him, stepping forward in brazen disobedience. "It's a wonder the bank hasn't been robbed before this. All these villains running loose. I don't know what's wrong with the world. It wasn't like that in my day. Stop, you stubborn donkey."

Mrs. Grummel poked her head out of the next door. "Albert, is that you? Did you pick up the package from the depot like I asked you to?"

His answer was drowned out by the squeal of the Bellamy kids from across the way. Three little boys, a dog and a ball tumbled into the alley, their calls, shouts and barks echoing against the buildings like a thunderstorm. The donkey brayed in protest.

A perfectly normal afternoon. Lila hopped up the steps to the small porch, where she

85

clipped Burke's shirt to the small clothes-line. Over the sights and sounds of kickball and the Grummels' conversation, she up-ended the washtubs neatly and stowed them on the porch, amazed that the afternoon could still feel so normal when she no longer felt exactly safe. That feeling did not fade until long after the sheriff was gone from her sight.

"How is the deputy?" The tray rattled as Lark set it on the edge of the counter.

"Better but still weak." Lila tallied up the last of Cora Sims's purchases. The tangy comfort of chicken broth steamed into the air. "Lark, you are a dear."

"Since Eunice is still at her meeting, I thought I would bring it down and save you a few steps." Lark sidled up and stole the pencil. "Go, take care of him. I can manage this."

"But Eunice —"

"What she doesn't know won't hurt her." Lark grinned as if she knew full well how hard it was for her big sister to say no to her.

It wasn't fair, but she loved her little sister too much to argue. "Let me finish up at the fabric counter. Miss Sims is still deciding."

"I can do it." Lark rolled her eyes.

Lila went around the shelves to the corner of the store where Cora Sims fingered the new shipment of calicos.

"I love a nice cheerful calico. I'm making new curtains for my sitting room."

"This would be very lovely." Lila hefted the bolt off the rack. The cotton was fine quality and soft to the touch. She breathed in the starchy, cottony smell as she set the fabric on the cutting counter. A few tugs of the material and it unrolled with a *thump, thump.* She admired the dark blue sprays sprigged on the light yellow background. "These will be very cheerful with the sun shining through a window."

"Exactly what I thought. I need twenty yards, please." Cora glanced over her shoulder to check on her adopted daughter, Holly. "I heard there was a bit of excitement in your store yesterday."

"So, you've heard all about Deputy Hannigan?" She gave a few more big tugs on the fabric and measured it against the ruler tacked to the counter, one long yard after another. "Word travels fast."

"I hear the deputy was a hero. He was running to the scene, spotted the robber getting away and drew his gun." Cora shook her head. "I'm not sure what violent thing will happen next. Not six months ago I was nearly assaulted on the street."

"And your reticule was stolen. I remember." Lila smoothed the cotton carefully and took out the scissors, which were snatched from her hand.

"Go on," Lark sang sweetly as she pushed up to the counter. "Miss Sims, if I remember, the sheriff hardly did a thing to that man."

"If it hadn't been for the bounty on his head, I wouldn't have gotten any justice. Rafe, my fiancé, was enraged." Cora waved her fingers in a friendly goodbye. "Take good care of our deputy, Lila. Don't look so surprised. I can smell that delicious broth from here."

"Does everyone know?" she asked as she wove through the store.

"That you're sweet on the man? Probably." Cora's answer sounded amused.

"I'm not sweet on him. Not really. It's my duty to take care of him. I take my responsibilities very seriously." She gripped the tray and went up on tiptoe to give Lark one last glance. It appeared as if she were doing fine folding up the cut fabric and chatting with Cora. No need to worry, and Lark was right. What Eunice didn't know wouldn't hurt. Eunice did not see Lark as capable, but how else was the girl to prove she was able to run the store?

Burke stirred, lifting his head an inch off his pillow as she neared. Had he been waiting for her? Her heart skipped a beat in hope, but she had to be practical. He had probably heard her footsteps and smelled the chicken broth she'd made for him. He was hungry, not interested in her personally.

"You're awake again." She slipped the tray on the barrel that served as a nightstand. "You look better."

"I feel better. Still can't get up off this pillow, though."

It was good to see a hint of the man she'd first met with humor twinkling in his striking blue eyes and dimples bracketing his lean, masculine mouth. A smile tugged into the corners. She wasn't fooled. "Have you been trying to get up on your own, while I wasn't here?"

"Guilty. If I had succeeded, I would be halfway home by now, although it might have caused a stir." He paused to catch his breath. "I don't know where my clothes went."

"Your trousers are drying on the clothesline, but I'm afraid your shirt needs more work to save it."

"Maybe I could buy one from you. I saw

a display of ready-made shirts in the store."

"We'll talk price once you are strong enough to stand. Until then, you are my prisoner, Deputy." She grasped the paper packet carefully so as not to spill the laudanum. "Open up."

"I knew this was coming, too." He made a face before taking the packet from her and dumping the acrid white powder onto his tongue. He seized the glass she offered and swallowed fast, but apparently not speedy enough to wash away the taste. "Bitter," he gasped, when he handed over the empty cup.

"This should help." She gave him a buttered slice of bread. His sun-browned fingers brushed hers and a jolt of sunshine spread through her as peaceful as a summer's morning. She tried to keep her gaze from noticing his ruggedly handsome and chiseled features overly much.

"Thanks." He chewed slowly, watching as she filled a spoon with the good broth. He swallowed. "Do you play nursemaid often?"

"I have some practice with it." She hoped he couldn't see the truth. She tried to tuck her emotions away and keep them out of sight. "I have a little sister, you know. Younger siblings are pesky, always needing tender love and care."

"I was the younger sibling, and something tells me you don't mind taking care of your sister so much."

"I wouldn't trade her for anything." She couldn't explain why her hand wasn't steady as she arrowed the spoon at his mouth. She grabbed the cloth napkin to hold it beneath the spoon, where a droplet of broth fell onto it. "How many older brothers and sisters do you have?"

"None."

"None?" Her frown wrinkled with confusion. But hadn't he just said he was the youngest? How could that be unless . . . Then realization dawned. She recognized the unspoken sorrow in his heart. She knew exactly what that loss was like. "I'm sorry."

"I had an older sister." He winced as if the pain were an old one but had never fully healed. He sipped the broth from the spoon and took his time swallowing.

"You don't have to tell me." She knew how difficult it was to talk about her ma's passing. "I understand."

"I was four years old when our house caught fire in the middle of the night." His gaze caressed her like a touch, lingering on her face. He seemed able to read her secrets written there. "A stray ember from the cookstove may have started the fire. I never really knew. All I remember is startling awake, choking on black smoke. The kitchen was roaring and glowing as if a fiery monster had been let loose in it."

"You had to have been terrified." She filled the spoon carefully, her hand steadier.

"I was. Ginna's bunk was across from mine and the fire was burning her nightgown. I couldn't see her because of the flames and the smoke. Pa took her out first, walking through the fire without thought for himself. Ma was there, too, but she couldn't make it to me. I remember her screaming in pain and telling my father to get me out first before her. So I was handed through the window to my sister and my life was spared in exchange for my parents'."

She didn't know what to say. She bowed her head, thankful at least one life had been saved in such a tragedy, although she wished there had been more. "I lost one parent to small pox. I cannot fathom losing two."

"Ginna took me into the wheat field and held me to keep me from running back into the house. She was seriously burned, it turned out fatally, but she never let go. She never complained about her own injuries. She had to have been in agony, but she walked me to the neighbor's house miles away and only when I was safe did she collapse."

"She loved you. That's a big sister's job." She remembered how curious she'd been about Burke and unsatisfied with the newspaper reporter's lack of information about him. She felt shamed, prying where only sadness dwelled. "Here, you must eat. You need to rebuild your strength."

He said nothing more as he sipped the broth from the spoon she held. Four years old. She remembered when Lark was that age, cute as a button and impossibly innocent. What an incomprehensible loss for a child so young. "Did you have other family to turn to?"

"No, I did not." His granite jaw tensed. "None that I know of, anyway."

"What happened to you afterward?" She refilled the spoon, concentrating on the task.

"It's not something I talk about often." He leaned back into the pillows, exhausted. "But I want you to know."

"You have been through enough with the fever and gunshot wounds." Concern shimmered in the swirls of green and blue of her irises when she shook her head. "No, you must not strain yourself more."

"I'm all right." His throat tightened. It had been so long since someone had been truly concerned for him. "I spent the next three years at an orphanage until I was hired out to work for room and board in the local fields for nine months out of the year."

"No one adopted you?"

No one had wanted him but he couldn't say the words, not to her. He didn't want her to think less of him. The wounds of that time had become fuzzy. He remembered the people in charge of the orphanage tried to do their best but were overwhelmed and underfunded. The families who had hired him had not been particularly kind to the small children working their fields. The boy he'd been, despairing and alone, had learned to cope. He took another sip of broth. "I came to like being on my own, and I like it now. No ties. Life is simpler this way."

"I suppose some men might agree with you." She appeared surprised at his answer and he wondered why. He wished he knew what she was thinking. "You are a lone wolf type, I suppose."

"That's me." He grinned so she wouldn't guess it wasn't by choice. "I don't settle down. Now it's your turn. Tell me about your mother."

"My ma was a lovely woman." The spoon wobbled, spilling broth onto the napkin. "Whoopsy-daisy. I am all thumbs today."

"You miss her still." He knew what that was like, yearning for those who were gone. "You tended her when she was sick."

"I did. Until the very end." The edge of the spoon bumped against his upper lip, spilling hot broth onto his chin.

"Good going, Lila." She rolled her eyes and leaned close to swipe the wet from his face. The tiny butterfly strokes of the cloth were the gentlest thing he'd known in two decades. She leaned back, folding the napkin. "Sorry about that. I get emotional about it even when I try not to be."

"It happens." He shrugged, forgetting about his injuries until the movement tugged at the torn flesh and cracked bone. He wheezed against the pain, pretending all that hurt him was the physical.

"Sometimes I think it would be easier if I never cared for anyone again." She refilled the spoon. Less unsteady this time. He slurped in the warm, tasty broth and felt stronger for it.

"That has been my conclusion," he confessed, swallowing. "Although you don't seem the type to live that way."

"I'm not. It might be easier to keep my heart safe, but I don't want to go through life with nothing to show for it. Loving someone and being loved is the only real living. Anything else is just existing, just passing time and I don't want to have to explain to God at the end of my life why I wasted all the opportunities He gave me to be loving." She dipped the spoon into the bowl, pausing thoughtfully. "If God is love, then I believe that is what we are all called to do."

"I've heard that argument before." He had a different calling and a path God had set him on. Burke envied the man who would win Lila's heart one day, who would have the right to brush those cinnamon-brown wisps from her eyes and kiss her innocent rosebud mouth. To protect her and cherish her and grow old with her in the security God meant true love to be.

Sharp, heavy footsteps pounded closer like the strike of a hammer on nails. Lila gasped, sat ramrod straight and spilled a spoonful of broth on her flowered skirt. The store owner's wife filled the doorway with flounced skirts and disapproval.

"Lila May Lawson, what are you up to?"

CHAPTER SIX

"Eunice! I mean, Ma." Lila gulped, dismay twisting her gorgeous face as she rose from the chair. The chair scraped harshly against the wood floor. Broth sloshed over the rim of the bowl and hit his sheet with a few fragrant drops. "The doctor told me to look after him."

"There is no chaperone, and do my eyes deceive me or is Lark running the store? You left a *child* in charge of the mercantile?" The pleasantly plump woman turned most unpleasant as she snatched the bowl from Lila. "I have serious doubts about your judgment, young lady. Now back to work. I want the entire store dusted. You are to send Lark upstairs to work on her needlepoint. And don't look at me like that, or I will have a talk with your father."

"Pa?" She winced and bowed her head. "There's no need to tell Pa about this. I was only trying to do what was right."

"I will be the judge of that." Eunice Lawson marched out of sight, herding Lila ahead of her and did not look back.

Burke swallowed, wishing he could have more of the soup and hoping Lila didn't get into trouble over helping him. She'd gone out of her way to care for him and few people had done that over the years.

He leaned back into the pillow and closed his eyes, hurting more than usual. Maybe he shouldn't have spoken of the past. It was gone. Nothing, not even God, could change it and it stirred up all sorts of longing for things he'd lost and could never find again.

After what he'd done in his life, no decent woman — no good, kind and gentle woman — was going to be able to love him.

He tried not to listen to the muffled boom of Eunice Lawson's unforgiving voice through the board walls, his sympathy for Lila growing. He didn't wait long for the strike of shoes on the boards or the charge of displeasure in the air as Eunice returned.

"I will not have the town whispering with rumors and speculation behind my back." Eunice towered over him, hands on her broad hips. "All it takes is one hint of unpleasant gossip and customers stop coming in the front door. This store is my husband's livelihood and I will not jeopardize it."

"No, ma'am. I understand." He felt ages old and tired. He felt every sore and stained spot in his soul.

"I know what you are." Her gaze narrowed as if she could see those stains hidden within him. "You are a grown man, twenty-five, twenty-six years old."

"Twenty-four, ma'am." His stomach coiled tight. He knew where this conversation headed. Only one outcome stared him in the face. Sadness crept in at the thought.

"I see how you look at the girl. She is far too young for you, mister. It is time for you to go." The woman turned on her heel and did not look back. "I'll have the sheriff make other arrangements."

"No, please." He struggled onto his elbows. The room spun. Sick dizziness swirled in his skull. "Have Jed Black take me to my boardinghouse."

"So long as you are gone today." She hesitated at the door, distaste curling her upper lip. "I see what you are, and I don't want you in this establishment an hour longer."

He collapsed onto the pillow, breathless, in pain of the type that laudanum could not ease. He stared at the ceiling, wanting to strain to hear the faint pad of Lila's foot-steps in the next room or the comforting sound of her dulcet alto. But that was unwise. Eunice Lawson wasn't entirely wrong. He did feel something for Lila — what it was he didn't exactly know, but it would be best left unexamined.

He squeezed his eyes shut against the fall of sunshine through the window. He preferred the dark, he told himself, willing it to be true.

What was Eunice planning to do? Anxious, Lila carefully folded up the delicate fawn-colored lawn she'd cut off the bolt to hold for Mrs. Olaff, keeping an eye on the front door where Eunice had barreled through a few moments ago. She might be back any moment, so Lila quickly tore off a length of brown paper and wrapped the fabric.

"I don't understand why I can't run the store." Lark sighed, disappointed, as she cut off a length of white string. "It was for a few minutes. I was doing fine. I didn't make a mistake adding up the purchases or anything."

"You are very good at arithmetic," Lila encouraged. Anger beat like drumrolls at her temples but she did not wish for it to show. It would only upset Lark more.

"Eunice will come to see that and then you will have my fate."

"I love the mercantile." Lark sidled close to wrap the string about the bundle and tied it up in a bow. "I can feel Ma here just like when I was little and I used to cling to her skirts when she was helping customers."

"I know." It was why she loved the fabric counter. Her mother had stood measuring calico by the yards and chatting with customers, who were her friends. Those who knew Lorraine Lawson instantly became her dear friend. She had loved everyone. Lila plucked up the package and hid it safely on the shelf behind a bulky ordering catalogue. Eunice did not have the same outlook on the family business. Lila put away the scissors. "I always feel close to Ma when I'm standing right here."

"I'm as old as you were when you started working here after school." Lark fingered an edge of yellow gingham. "Maybe if I can help out every day, Eunice could afford to start paying you."

"I doubt that will happen." She shouldered the fawn-colored bolt of material back to its place on the lower shelf.

The door swung open with a whoosh and the bell overhead rang jarringly. Eunice swept in, her shoes striking the floorboards like bullets. Silent fury reverberated from her as she focused her stern glare on Lila.

Oh, no. Her stomach dropped. She gripped the edge of the fabric shelf.

"I don't want one word from you." Eunice charged ahead, and the door whooshed open again. Two grimfaced deputies trailed in her wake. Jed Black glanced across the store, lifted his shoulders in a shrug as if to say there was nothing he could do. The deputies followed Eunice into the storeroom. Would her stepmother truly do something so uncaring?

"Eunice!" She rushed around the buttons display and past the cubicles of yarn. "We were only talking, Eunice."

The strike of her stepmother's heels on the floor did not pause. Oh, why did Pa have to be out on deliveries when this happened? Surely he could talk reason to his wife. Lila ran as fast as she dared, her skirts twisting and hampering her as she dashed into the hallway. Eunice stood with her hands on her hips and her chin set, watching the two deputies each lift one end of the pallet, but she could not see Burke. The men blocked her view of him.

She skidded to a halt. "You can't take him."

"Can't? Young lady, I can do whatever I

want. The deputy goes."

"At least wait for the doctor to come back from his rounds." She went up on tiptoe, straining to see any glimpse of Burke. She saw the bumps of his feet beneath the gray blanket, but that was all. "What if he starts bleeding again?"

"That is not my lookout." Eunice did not care. This man's life did not matter to her. "Back up, girl, make room. Think of this as your own fault."

Cool fear crept beneath Lila's skin and slithered there. She fell back, stumbling until her spine hit the wall, seeing the truth in her stepmother's eyes. How could Eunice be this cold? Lila bit her bottom lip. There was nothing she could do but watch the deputies shuffle by carrying their still burden.

She watched him go by. He'd turned ashen again. The jostling must be hurting him greatly. Her chest twisted in sympathy. If only there was something she could do, some way to help him. His dark blue gaze latched onto hers. For a brief moment the closeness forged between them returned. She read his resignation before he looked past her, breaking the connection between them. Distance settled and he could have been a stranger.

That was the way of a man who wanted no ties, she realized. He was friendly enough and very charming and he had shared with her a piece of himself, but leaving was easy. Ends were expected. He had never been the one getting attached.

She was. A little piece of her heart broke as the bell over the door jingled like a musical goodbye and he was gone from her sight. Maybe forever.

"I don't know how you could do this. Even you." Lila pushed away from the wall, tears stinging her eyes. She was too old to cry; she felt shameful at the burning she could not stop. She blinked hard, trying to will it away. What if something happened to Burke? Who would take care of him? Who could make sure he was safe and comfortable and fed? And why couldn't she stop caring about a man who did not want any ties?

"You had best set the storeroom to rights and tally up every item from the store we used on that man. He will pay the bill, or else." Eunice's set chin eased a tad. "I know you are angry with me, child, but this is for your own good."

"I am eighteen and I can decide that for myself." She stumbled down the hall, doing her best not to imagine Burke being carried through the streets of town. She grabbed an empty crate and gently placed one lamp into it to be cleaned up later and sold at a steep discount, used. Fury boiled beneath the surface, and she did her best not to let it control her. But it wasn't easy.

"It may not seem like it, but I am doing my best for you, your sister and your father." Eunice sounded strained, perhaps a little wounded, as she hesitated in the doorway. "I do not expect you to understand. That man is no good. Mark my words."

"You have a habit of judging people." A lamp shade rattled as she lifted the second lamp and settled it next to the first one. "It doesn't mean you are right."

"I am looking out for this family. I would have thought you would appreciate it." Eunice turned on her heels, pounded down the hall and disappeared into the store.

Lila closed her eyes. A verse from Ephesians flashed into her thoughts. *And be kind to one another, tenderhearted and forgiving one another, even as God in Christ forgave you.* She took the words into her heart. *Lord, help me to think kindly of Eunice. Help me to handle things the right way.*

That didn't stop her heart from breaking. She gathered up her skirts and settled onto the edge of the chair, gazing down on the bare spot where Burke had lain. The half-eaten bowl of broth sat on the small table. The dime novel she'd read to him was on the lower shelf.

Burke may be gone, but her sense of responsibility to him remained. She tucked the book into her pocket and stood, clear on what she needed to do.

Nausea roiled through him like motion sickness. Burke stared at the whitewashed walls of his room at the boardinghouse, listening to the tick of the clock he couldn't see and hearing the sounds from the open window he could not get up to close. On the street below, men called out, horses clomped by and wagons rattled over the ruts in the road. Dust wafted in along with the hot air and the even hotter sun.

Hours had passed, judging by the process of the patch of sunshine marching across the foot of his bed. The straw tick was a vast improvement over the hard pallet he'd been resting on at the mercantile, but being alone was not. He grimaced, mad at himself. All it took was a small bit of a woman's kindness and he missed it. What was wrong with him? He was tougher than that. He didn't need anyone.

What he needed was a drink of water. He

tried again to lift his head off the pillow, but the dizzy sickness rocked through him. Sweat broke out on his forehead and he collapsed the few inches onto his pillow. His tongue had turned to sand, the inside of his mouth to sandpaper and thirst had become a pain he could no longer ignore.

Be tougher, he told himself. Be strong. He could handle this on his own. If he rested a little more, then he could move enough to grab the dipper from the pail Jed had left by the bed.

Footsteps thudded up the stairway. A slow, heavy gait. He tried not to let hope leap into his chest. Jed had promised to come by and check on him. Not that he needed any help, but he wouldn't turn down a full dipper of cool water, either. Then he heard a silvery sound along with the footsteps.

Spurs. They rang like bells as the door squeaked open. Burke squeezed his eyes shut, gathering his strength and wondering if he had enough should he require it. His firearm was on the bureau top, too far away to do any good. He willed his heart rate to slow. He had to trust that God wouldn't send him on a mission he couldn't win.

As long as his cover wasn't blown, that is. As long as the sheriff wasn't questioning who he pretended to be, and then maybe he had a chance. He opened his eyes, aware that Dobbs watched him from inside the doorway.

"Look what the cat dragged in." The sheriff smirked. Not a whit of sympathy softened his cold gaze. Not an ounce of humanity gave life to his stony face. "I hear you got kicked out of Lawsons'. Where is your protector, now, boy?"

"Don't need one." His voiced sounded scratchy and dry.

"That's what you think." Dobbs moseyed up close. "I've been watching you for a while. I haven't made my mind up yet."

"You aren't the only one." The friction of the words in his throat made him cough. The cough drove sharp strikes of pain through his chest. Reeling, he swallowed hard. He couldn't lift his head. He hated being defenseless and weak.

Dobbs laughed, a short burst of mean. "I didn't know what to make of you. Almost didn't hire you, but when I saw you draw I thought I knew what you were."

"What's that?" His gaze slid to the right top drawer of the bureau. Five, maybe six steps away. How would he ever get that far if he should need to? He didn't dare try to lift his head from the pillow. He would conserve what little energy he had should he need it. "Who do you think I am?"

"I've been keepin' a close eye on you." Dobbs kicked the bed frame.

The shock of movement ricocheted through him like a blow. Burke clenched his teeth, determined not to let it show. Nausea gripped his stomach. His head spun slowly.

Dobbs knelt down to check under the bed and pulled out an empty satchel. He opened it and felt for anything that might be hidden in the lining. "You might be useful to me. No lawman has the kind of speed and accuracy you have. Only a man who lives and dies by his gun. A man who knows the way the world really works."

He tossed the satchel beneath the bed and stood. He opened the top left bureau drawer and pawed through the socks and handkerchiefs folded there. "When you went and missed Slim's gang not by an inch but by a mile, I knew I was right. You clearly weren't trying to stop them."

"No, I wasn't." When he'd spotted Slim's gang and his old nemesis, Cheever, his instinct had been to shoot. But he'd caught sight of Dobbs down the street, standing with his .45 holstered and his arms crossed on his chest, watching the show, and he'd realized there was more to his investigation than he'd first thought. Dobbs either knew about the robbery before it happened, or didn't mind that it did. Just in time, he swung his gun away and plugged two shots into the hitching post.

"You want to look good, be the big man in town. I see it, but I'm top dog around here. Don't you forget your place." Dobbs slammed the drawer shut and opened the adjacent one. He moved aside the folded shirts and studied the .45. "Well, I guess there are no surprises. I'll be talking to you again soon."

Footsteps tapped gently in the hallway. Dobbs stilled, tilting his head to listen to the unmistakable rustle of a woman's petticoats.

"Burke?" A knock rapped on the door frame, and he recognized Lila's voice. "I was told by the owner to come on up —" She fell silent. He could see the hem of her pretty blue calico dress enter the room and pause. "Oh, what are you doing here, Sheriff?"

"Nothing." The laughter crept back into Dobbs's voice as he backed away from the dresser. "Just checking up on the deputy. Guess I'll keep him around for a while after all, as long as he knows his place."

Spurs chimed with every angry strike of his boots. The door smacked shut, and he was gone. Burke listened to his retreating footsteps and tension drained out of him, leaving him weaker than before. Glad that was over.

"Why does the sheriff treat you like that?" A chair scraped against the wood planks and came to a rest at his bedside.

"He's establishing dominance. It's what bullies do."

"Are you all right?" Her skirts whispered as she settled into the chair beside him.

The thoroughly feminine sound comforted him and he opened his eyes. "I'm fine."

The basket she carried made a quiet thud as it came to rest near her feet. She was a vision in light blue sprigged cotton. Gazing upon her made his injuries ache less and the shadows inside him fade. Gratitude overwhelmed him when she lifted the dipper from the pail. Inviting droplets splashed from the ladle as she leaned in, bringing it closer.

Bless her. The refreshing wetness tumbled over his cracked lips and he slurped it in. Cool water sluiced across his sandy tongue, chasing away the grittiness and trickling down his throat. The agony that had been his thirst began to recede when he took another long swallow.

He shouldn't be glad to see her. His spirit

shouldn't be rejoicing that she was near. He couldn't help it. Her presence was like that cool drink of water.

"I'm tougher than I look." He watched her while she refilled the dipper. Soft cinnamon-brown wisps had come loose from her braid to frame her oval face and caress her porcelain skin.

"Will he guess who you really are?" Distress drew tiny crinkles around her green-blue eyes.

"That's not your worry, Lila." His heart could stop at her lovely innocence, if he let it. "Your stepmother isn't going to like that you're here with me."

"My stepmother doesn't need to know. I'm eighteen. I'm capable of making my own decisions." She brought the dipper to his lips again and tipped it.

He drank, grateful for the water and for her as his nursemaid.

"What did Eunice say to you?" she asked.

"Your stepmother was only looking out for you." He let his head drop back into the pillows. Now, if only the room would quit spinning.

"She said something hurtful to you, didn't she?" The dipper clunked lightly into the pail. "She had no right to say whatever it was."

"She had every right. I never said she was wrong." He felt awkward with her here, when he didn't think she ought to be. He may as well get it over with. Sooner or later Lila would start doubting and wondering, seeing the bad that had been there all along. The bad he couldn't pray away. "I'm no good for you, Lila."

"I don't know. You seem all right to me." Her forehead crinkled adorably. She appeared a little confused by his comments but her sweet smile remained on her soft red lips. She lifted the lid of the basket she'd brought. The scents of chicken soup and buttermilk biscuits filled the air.

"I went to all the trouble of cooking for you." Dishes rattled as she uncovered them. "At least wait until you are done eating before you reject me."

"I'm not rejecting you. I'm warning you."

"Is this about the 'no ties' speech you gave me?" She carefully filled a spoon with broth. "Because I heard it. I'm not going to fall in love with you, Burke. Honestly, my heart is already taken."

"By who?"

"That's none of your business."

The spoon brushed his bottom lip and he sipped from it. The soup was hot and bracing and good. Just what his body needed.

He couldn't send her away if he wanted to. He needed her and she knew it. Bless her for knowing it, bless her for coming. He had no one else.

"At least give me a hint." He swallowed, waiting for the next spoonful.

"It's not a real man so much as the idea of one." She carefully tipped the spoon against his mouth. "When my pa met my ma, he said it was true love at first sight. They were the other's best friend, missing half, soul mate. Pa said he couldn't breathe until she breathed, too."

"They were happy." He sounded surprised, as if anyone married could be.

"No, they weren't merely happy. They were joyous. That's what I want. I want a man who can be the other half to my soul, who knows my heart better than I know it myself and who is the champion of my dreams." She set the spoon in the bowl and reached for the plate of biscuits. "As you can see, that man isn't you."

"Yes. I fall far short."

"So rest easy, Deputy. I'm not setting my bonnet for you." She broke apart a buttered half of crumbly buttermilk goodness and set it on his tongue. "You are safe from the likes of me."

"Unless you lower your standards."

"I'm not interested in lowering them *that* far." She teased gently, because laughter was easier than admitting the truth. "And if no woman will ever claim your heart, I can't think I would ever be a danger to you. Unless you are not as tough as you claim."

"I'm tougher."

"Then I don't see any reason why we can't be friends." She spooned up more soup. "You seem to need one, Burke. At least until you are on your feet again."

"I suppose I can suffer through your friendship for that length of time."

"Good." She saw the glint of emotion in his midnight-blue gaze and the truth behind his words he could not admit to.

Neither could she.

CHAPTER SEVEN

Earlee couldn't get Finn's letter out of her mind. She padded through the grass, squinted into the early-morning sun and adjusted the buckets she packed. The grass felt soft beneath her bare feet and cool. The last vestiges of dawn painted the eastern horizon a faint pink. She breathed in the freshness of the grass, renewed by the night, and the hint of wild roses blooming hidden among the grasses. She savored the wide-open feeling of the prairie. She had to enjoy being outside while she could. Come September, she would be shut inside a schoolroom, if she could find a job, that is. She had a few more applications to fill out and mail.

"Good morning, Bessie." She set down the pail of fresh cold well water in front of the milk cow. Big brown eyes sparkled their appreciation and the Guernsey held out her soft brown head for a pet. Earlee obliged her with lots of strokes. "You are such a good girl. I brought you some grain, too. I know how much you like it."

In a show of affection, Bessie rubbed her poll against Earlee's skirt before diving into the grain bucket. That left only one bucket, empty, which she circled around and set beneath Bessie's full udder. She knelt to begin milking and leaned her cheek against Bessie's warm, soft side. Milk zinged into the tin pail and her mind wandered.

I'm being selfish writing you and looking forward to your letters, Finn had written. Selfish. That's how he saw it? Now that the initial devastation of his rejection had begun to fade, she could think about his words more clearly. *Maybe you shouldn't spend your time writing to a convict like me.*

Did he really think she would have begun corresponding with him if she thought it was a bad way to spend her time? It wasn't that long ago, before Finn fell in with a bad crowd, that he'd stopped to give her family a ride. He had cheerfully handed up each of the younger children into the wagon bed. He'd been kind to her sisters and brothers and respectful of Ma.

That's why she'd become smitten with him in the first place. He'd talked to her as if she were nobility and held out his hand to help her onto the wagon seat. A flash of recognition sparked in her heart when they touched. Kind was the true nature of the man, and she'd never forgotten it. Even when he'd been arrested for masterminding a train robbery, she hadn't believed it of him. He'd made the bad mistake of committing a serious crime, but to mastermind it?

"Earlee? Whatcha doin'?" Edward broke into her thoughts, his bare feet pounding through the grass. "Can I help?"

"Bessie's picket pin needs to be moved."

"I can do it!" Edward dashed off eagerly.

Bessie lifted her head from the grain bucket and mooed after the boy, apparently needing a pet from him, too.

With a smile, her thoughts returned to analyzing Finn's letter. *Your writing made me forget where I was for a few moments.* He may not want her to write him again, but he'd enjoyed her letters. He was rejecting her out of concern for her. He wasn't selfish; he cared for her.

"Earlee! Edward!" Ma called from the back doorstep. "Breakfast."

"Coming." Perfect timing. She squeezed the last of the milk into the pail and waved to her mother.

Ma waved back and disappeared into the

118

house. Poor Ma. This morning was a good one for her. She was up and assisting Beatrice with the kitchen work, but she tired easily. Ma was so delicate. There was no way she could ever discuss this situation with her.

So, did she send him another letter? Or did she do as Finn asked? She didn't know what to do. He'd clearly penned, *don't write me again.* She gave Bessie a pat on the flank and grabbed the bucket.

"I'll be back in a bit, good girl," she told the cow and carried the heavy milk pail toward the house. Edward finished moving the picket pin and came running after her.

In the wash of early-morning sunshine, Lila knelt before the penny candy barrel and opened the little striped paper sack. "What kind do you want?" she asked the children.

"The lemon ones." Little James McKaslin didn't hesitate. "That's my favorite."

"Then we had better get a lot of those. I'll pick all the best pieces." She counted out a half dozen of the biggest lemon drops and plopped them into the bag. She loved this part of her job. "What would you like, Daisy?"

The platinum blonde little girl pondered for a moment. "The striped ones, please."

"Good choice. Those are my favorite, too." She dropped an equal amount of peppermint balls into the little bag and handed it over. The children bent over their candy, each politely taking one piece before handing the paper bag to their mother to keep for them.

"Thank you, Lila." Joanna McKaslin hugged the wrapped bundle of fabric and notions. "What time do you think your father will be by with the rest of my order?"

"Probably sometime around three." Lila leaned against the counter. "We've been busy this morning, so Pa has a lot of deliveries today. Will that be too late?"

"Not at all. I'll keep an eye out for him." Joanna opened the door and watched over her children as they padded onto the boardwalk. The sounds from the street swirled in with the dusty breeze. The ring of harnesses, the rumble of voices and the clop of horseshoes rang like pleasant music as Joanna waved goodbye and closed the door.

"You spend too much time with the customers." Eunice looked up from the ledger open on the long front counter. "This isn't a social event, it's a business. Look at all the dust those people let in."

"There's no reason not to like Mrs. Mc-Kaslin." Lila headed straight to the fabric

120

counter to put away the bolts she'd taken down and cut for Joanna. "She's a good customer and a nice lady."

"She lived with that man before she married him." Eunice snapped the ledger shut. "I don't want a woman like that in this store."

"She *lived* next door to him. That's different than living with him." Lila did not believe Joanna was the type of lady who would do anything improper. "They are married now, so it's really not our business."

"We run a fine establishment. Our customers need to trust they will not be uncomfortable in this store." Eunice cared very much about profits. "The midmorning lull has died. Why don't you go out back and finish hanging the laundry?"

"I'll be happy to." She had been up early scrubbing the household garments, towels and sheets on the washboard and had made better progress than Eunice knew. Gladly, she shouldered the heavy bolt of candy-pink calico onto its shelf and hefted another light lavender one.

As she was setting the final bolt of light blue sprigged into place, the door chimed and Narcissa Bell paraded in with her mother. Definitely time to leave.

"Good morning, Mrs. Bell!" Eunice sailed

across the store, her tone falsely bright. "Whatever can I do for you?"

Lila ignored the sneering look Narcissa sent her way and turned her back. She would never forget what Narcissa had done to try to break up Meredith and her beloved fiancé. Shane had managed to keep Meredith's heart, but it was no thanks to their archenemy. Nor would she forget the names Narcissa always called Ruby. Lila was all too happy to trip out the back door.

The sun was bright on the porch as she overturned the washtubs. Next door, Mrs. Grummel was hanging up petticoats on the clothesline strung between her porch posts.

"Pretty morning, ain't it?" the older woman asked as she clipped the last waistband. "I see you've been to your washing early to beat the heat of the morning, too. It's likely to be a hot one. Don't tell me you have another load to do."

"No. I have a break from the store." Lila extricated the basket from behind the washtub and kept it level as she hopped down the steps.

"You poor girl. If I had to work for Eunice, I would find myself another job. Take care not to get overheated." Mrs. Grummel grabbed her clothespin bag and disappeared inside her building.

Another job. That had never crossed her mind. She hurried down the alleyway, going as fast as she dared without jostling the basket. She had never pictured working anywhere else but in Pa's store, where he and Ma had once been so happy. She swallowed the lump in her throat, stepped onto the boardwalk and dodged shoppers on their way to Main Street. The train rumbled on its tracks a few blocks over, black smoke rising above the storefronts like a billowing snake. Horses stood at the hitching posts jingling their bits and watching her scurry by.

Tiny airy tingles filled her at the thought of seeing Burke again. She wondered how he'd fared through the night with no one to tend him. She crossed the street, dodged a horse-drawn milk wagon and dashed down the boardwalk on Prairie Lane. The boardinghouse was quiet. A cleaning woman mopped the floor and didn't look up as Lila headed for the stairs.

Surely the doctor would have checked on him, she thought, as she tapped her knuckles on his door. He wouldn't have been left all alone.

No answer. Should she come back later? But what if he was in need of help? He could have succumbed to a fever again and could not answer the door. Boldly, she grasped the brass knob and turned. The door squeaked open and she peered in, seeing only a small slice of the room. There was no motion or no sound from within as she poked her head in farther.

"Burke?"

The smallest groan. Concern propelled her forward to see the man grinning at her. He was sitting up!

"I was hoping that was you." Whiskers stubbled the rock-hard angle of his jaw. "The doc just left. He said I'm doing better than expected. Probably because of your superior chicken soup."

"And don't forget the biscuits." Relief made her knees shake as she glided toward him. Her gaze roamed over him hungrily taking in the important details — his improved color, the faint flush of health in his cheeks, his bright eyes. She sank onto the chair beside him. "I'm so glad. I have been praying very hard."

"For me?"

"You were the one injured, right? Of course it was for you. My sister did, too." She set her basket on her knees. "Have you had breakfast?"

"Mildred, the owner, brought me tea and toast this morning." He adjusted his pillows and leaned into them, still sitting. His dark tousled hair made him look rakish. With his shadowed jaw, he could easily be mistaken for a dangerous outlaw. "Really early this morning, as it turned out, so I'm starving."

"Good. I predict you will make a full recovery." She pulled out one wrapped item after another. "I made you two sandwiches when Eunice wasn't looking. Egg sandwiches, since I was making breakfast at the time. Do you mind?"

"Mind? It smells great." He looked eagerly at the bundle. It was good to see him improved. She sent a thankful prayer Heavenward and handed him one wrapped sandwich. His fingers brushed hers as he took it.

Just ignore the skittles of awareness tingling inside your heart from that touch, she told herself. Ignore it and she could pretend it didn't happen. She straightened her shoulders and uncorked a small jug of cool tea. "I'm leaving you some cookies my sister made yesterday. An apple. A bowl of baked beans and some slices of ham. Here's another jug full of chicken soup."

"Lila, thank you. I can't believe you did this." He took a big bite of his sandwich.

"I couldn't let you starve."

"I appreciate that." He swallowed and

chased it down with a gulp of cool tea. The liquid trailed down to his stomach. Good. "What does Eunice say about you being here?"

"Nothing, as she thinks I'm doing the rest of the laundry on the porch, but I got up extra early to do it. She's busy impressing Mrs. Bell, so she won't notice I'm gone for at least five more minutes."

"I'm a bad influence on you."

"Yes, it's all your fault for getting shot." A dimple cut into her right cheek. "You could have chosen another store to stumble into."

"Yes, but the barbershop next door didn't look as if it had bandages. I intended to patch myself up and keep trailing the bad guys."

"The ones you didn't shoot on purpose?"

"Well, yes. I wanted to make sure they didn't try to gun down an innocent citizen on the street on their way out of town." He didn't figure she could understand the reason he felt strongly about protecting others. If she knew the truth, she would bolt off the chair and sprint out the door.

"Proof you are one of the good guys." She gazed at him with admiration shining in the swirl of her green-blue eyes.

"I'm not so good." The old shame remained, regardless of how hard he tried to push it aside. "I'm just doing my job."

"You are very dedicated."

"It's what I'm called to do." It was more complicated than that, but he didn't elaborate. Frustration ate at him because Lila shouldn't be here looking after him. He wasn't her lookout, he wasn't her concern.

"See what I brought?" She pulled a book out of the basket, the edges of the cover dog-eared from wear. "I was reading this to you when you were unconscious. I thought you might want something to pass the time while you are recuperating."

"I appreciate it, but it won't be long until I'm on my feet again."

"Yes, I know. You are invincible." She tapped the book before setting it on his bedside table. "Just like any passable Western hero."

"Passable?" He held back a chuckle. Lila could make him forget who he was and make him believe in the man he could be. He felt different when he was with her.

"Sure. I don't think you can compare to the hero in the book. He's really amazing."

"He's fiction." He squinted at the book. It was the same one she'd read to him. Did he admit it was his favorite series, too? "Fiction can't compare to the real thing."

"Too bad I haven't met the real thing."

"You will know him when you see him." He laughed. His healing wounds vibrated with pain but it didn't stop him. That's what she did to him, she made his world brighter. "You're leaving so soon?"

"I'll be back with your supper whenever I can slip away. You won't be rid of me easily."

"Did you hear me complain?" His throat filled with words of gratitude he did not feel comfortable saying. He bit back anger at himself because he didn't want to rely her. He didn't want to depend on anyone. "Tomorrow I intend to be up and about to forage for myself."

"Maybe I will come anyway. Someone has to watch over you, Deputy. You have agreed to be my friend and there's no getting out of it."

"I've been in sticky situations before and have gotten out of them," he quipped.

"Yes, but not with me." She lingered by his bedside for a moment, as refreshing as a summer's morning with her lustrous hair, green calico dress and her mouth as sweet as a strawberry. Her fingertips brushed his rough jaw and cheek, the slightest of touches, the briefest of contacts but the magnitude shocked him all the way to his soul.

"Be safe, Deputy." She swirled away with a whisper of petticoats and grace, taking all the sunlight with her.

He sat as if in darkness, his sandwich in hand, listening to her faint footfalls grow fainter. He no longer felt alone.

Laundry fluttered on the clothesline as she opened the mercantile's back door and hopped into the dim hallway. Seeing him briefly wasn't enough. She missed him. She didn't want to admit it, but she did.

"I am taking a break." Eunice slapped shut the account book and wiped the pen point on the wiper. "I expect you to run the store."

"Fine."

"Do *not* leave Lark in charge." Eunice corked the ink bottle with a pointed glare.

"I won't." She wanted to get along with her stepmother, she really did. "Go upstairs and relax. It's been a busy morning. I'll take care of everything."

"Fine." Eunice pushed away from the counter, her skirts billowing, and disappeared upstairs.

"Can I take a break, too?" Lark peered through the shelving, a little pale and tired-looking.

"Go ahead. I will take over the restocking —" The doorbell interrupted her with a harsh jangle as the door flew open and banged violently against the door catch. Pa stood in the threshold, his clothes torn, his hat missing, his hair standing on end. Blood ran down one side of his face and stained his shirt and sleeve.

"Pa!" She watched in horror as her father staggered. She caught his arm as Lark scrambled to grab the other. A blur of motion on the street outside was a horse and buckboard dashing down the street. "What happened to you?"

"I'm all right." He leaned on them heavily, struggling to catch his breath. Blood streamed down the left side of his face. A purple-red bruise marred the skin of his left eye, which had swelled alarmingly. The lid could barely open. Wet blood marked his off-center nose and his bottom lip, torn and puffy. "Thad is fetching the doc. I just need to sit down."

"Sit down? You need to lie down." She couldn't believe her eyes. "Let's get you upstairs."

"I don't need pampering, girls." He extricated his arms from their clutches, a strong man determined to walk on his own. "I'm no weakling."

"No, of course not, Pa." Shock washed

through her as she slowed her pace to match his. The door to upstairs seemed a mile away. Her poor father. Had the horses bolted? Had he taken a spill off the wagon?

Whatever had gone wrong, her father needed prayer. *Lord, please help him. Please take care of my father.* She tried not to imagine terrible things — a dangerous head injury, for instance.

"Pa, you didn't tell us what happened," Lark said, her face pinched with concern.

"I'm not sure you girls ought to know." He huffed heavily, as if angry. "It can be a rough world out there, and today I ran into some roughness."

"What do you mean, Pa?" Lila opened the door for him while Lark hovered in the background, her hands steepled anxiously.

"Some men jumped me." Anger made his voice harsh, something she had never heard in her life. He grasped the handrail and pulled himself up one step at a time.

"Jumped you? You mean they beat you up?" Lila couldn't believe it. How could anyone want to attack her father?

"Some men with bandanas masking their faces rode out of a gulley flashing their rifles. They told me to get down and hand over my horses and wagon." He became angrier with each step he took, panting with the intensity of his fury. "I had about ten rifles aimed at me, so I had to climb down and surrender the wagon. I didn't have any choice."

Shock trembled through her. Armed men had pointed their guns at her father? Anything could have happened. Anything. "I'm so glad you did as they asked, Pa."

"Me, too," Lark chimed in as she trailed them up the stairs. "Were they horse thieves?"

"They weren't after just the horses. They wanted the wagon, the deliveries. Everything." His wedding ring was gone, even his boots.

"Arthur!" Eunice spotted them and came running, horror stark on her face. "What happened? Lark, hurry and fetch the doctor. Lila, bring him right here onto the sofa. Oh, my poor Arthur."

"I'm all right." He wasn't a man used to attention. "Frost is on his way."

As if to prove it, a knock rapped impatiently on the door below. Without waiting for an answer, boots thudded on the stairs, echoing in the stairwell. Lila helped her father to the sofa. He looked broken, somehow, as if the attack had taken something from his soul. Her eyes stung, and anger at the thieves pounded crazily in her chest.

She stepped aside to make room for the doctor.

"Thad said it was urgent." Samuel Frost set his medical bag on the floor in front of the couch. "Arthur, what did you go and do?"

"Trouble found me." More blood streamed from the gash on his head.

"I'll say, but it doesn't look too bad. I say you got off lucky, considering. Lila, fetch me some water. Lark, I'll need clean cloths and bandages. Eunice, prepare the bed. Arthur is going to need some rest when I'm through with him."

Relief shook through her, making it difficult to walk but she made it to the kitchen. She skirted the table, grabbed the water pail. Pa would be okay. That's what mattered. That's what she had to focus on. Except for the fact that her stomach rumbled with fury. What gave thieves the right to hurt innocent people, especially her pa?

Cowards, that's what they were. Ten armed men jumping one unarmed man. Doing what amused them, taking what they wanted. Her jaw clamped shut so tight, her teeth hurt. It wasn't right. It shouldn't be allowed. This time the sheriff would have to do something. If not, she knew Burke would.

"The lawlessness in this town." Eunice marched down the short hallway, muttering to herself. "I've just about had enough of it."

For once, she and Eunice were in total agreement. She set the bucket down by the doctor's side.

"Thank you, Lila." Samuel Frost took a stack of towels and bandages from Lark and dunked the corner of a cloth into the water. "First, I need to clean away this blood and see what we're dealing with. Arthur, how is your eyesight? Do you have double vision?"

"I wish I didn't."

"Any dizziness? Nausea?"

"Yes on both counts. They struck me hard, Doc. With the butt of a Winchester."

Lila briefly shut her eyes, wincing against the thought of anyone treating her father like that. She gently nudged her sister down the stairs and closed the door tightly behind them.

"Why would someone do that to Pa?" Lark whispered shakily. The enormous space of the store echoed around them ominously. The sunshine no longer felt friendly. The world no longer felt kind.

"I don't know what makes some people

behave meanly." She wished she did. She thought of Burke. A week ago his wound had seemed extraordinary, the violence of the bank robbers an anomaly. What was happening to their town? Now Pa was injured. Her dear pa.

The front door chimed and two identical little girls, the Frost twins, tromped in like a whirlwind, followed by Molly, their new stepmother.

"You stay and help them," Lark whispered, too distraught to face anyone. "I'll get more water."

She hugged her sister, wishing she knew what to do to reassure her. Wishing she knew how to reassure herself.

"I'm sorry your pa is hurt," Penelope said.

"Real sorry," Prudence added. "But our pa is a real good doctor."

"Yep, he can make him lots better," Penelope finished.

"I'm sure of it." Lila couldn't help being enchanted by the girls. They both had identical black braids and golden-hazel eyes and fine-boned porcelain faces. One twin wore a green calico dress with a matching sunbonnet while the other wore blue. "What can I get you today?"

"We were about to take Samuel to lunch when Thad McKaslin came rushing into the office. Apparently he came across your father in the road," Molly Frost explained as she laid a gentle hand on each girl's shoulder. "I promised the girls a few pieces of candy to tide them over until their father is done."

"It will be my treat." Grateful for something useful to do, she grabbed a striped paper sack from behind the counter. "What would you girls like?"

"Cinnamon!"

"Butterscotch!"

Unable to resist the double level of cuteness, Lila knelt at the barrel and dug through the candy for the best pieces of each. "How about you, Molly?"

"Just one peppermint. I insist on paying you."

"Your penny is no good here." She dropped a few peppermint balls into the sack and handed it to the closest girl. "I was going to close the store for a bit, but you are welcome to stay in here. Or there's a bench on the back porch if you two want a little fresh air and shade."

"I may steer the girls and their soon-to-be sticky fingers away from your merchandise. Thank you." Molly's gentle smile was lovely as she led her beloved stepdaughters to the back of the store.

Lila went to turn the sign from open to closed and a familiar shadow filled the doorway, tall, wide-shouldered and as awesome as a dream.

Burke. She blinked. Surely she was imagining him. He could not be here, he could not be real.

"I heard what happened." He pushed through the door, substantial flesh and bone. He did not look well. All color had drained from his face. He swayed a little on his feet but didn't topple. Breathing heavily, he planted one palm against the edge of the counter and leaned on it, obviously willing himself to stay standing.

He had come. But why? And how? "You shouldn't be up. You shouldn't be here."

"How is your father?" Concern layered the rich tones of his voice, emotion that softened the hard lines of his face and his whiskered jaw.

"He's been beaten. The doctor is with him now." Whatever it took, she could not give in to the need for comfort — for his comfort. She must not think about laying her cheek against the dependable plane of his chest. She must not wish to be enfolded safely in his strong, sheltering arms.

"Who did it?"

"He didn't say." A tiny hiccup escaped. It

was a hiccup and not a sob. "This is peaceable country. I don't understand why armed men would hurt him and rob him."

"Things change and there are some folks that don't need a reason to do harm." Burke caught her hand with his, and sorrow lived there. "I promise I will do what I can to help your father."

"I know." The anger within her didn't abate, but her worries did. "Thank you. It's not right. Someone who would hurt someone else for gain is the worst sort of person."

"I agree." He gently tugged her close. His fingers curled at her nape and into her upswept hair. Nice. Soothing. Gently, he drew her against his chest and she didn't resist. She rested her cheek against his shirt and sighed when his mighty arms folded around her.

Safe. Sheltered in his arms with his jaw brushing the crown of her head, she felt safe. Drinking in his solace, she relaxed into him, listened to the reliable beat of his heart and held on tight.

CHAPTER EIGHT

You should not be holding her, Burke thought, but could he let her go? Not a chance. An emotion suspiciously like tenderness took root. She felt light and fragile in his arms. He breathed in her sweet lilac scent and listened to the quiet whisper of her breathing. He couldn't remember holding anyone since the last time his sister had held him in the wheat field. Lonely places within him ached with a razor-blade sharpness that cut him to the marrow.

He didn't deserve to hold her but he could not stop. The silken gossamer of her hair caught on his unshaven jaw and tickled his skin. The light press of her cheek to his chest tore him up. He swallowed hard, not believing he could be holding anyone so fine. That anyone so fine would want to be held by him.

Footsteps rang faintly through the store. Heavy, measured thumps. Sounded like the doctor's gait. Reluctant, Burke lifted his cheek away from her hair. When he wanted to comfort her, he had to straighten and put on his stony defenses. His fingers remained at the base of her neck and his other hand remained twined with hers. He could come to like being closer to her. Their gazes met and the dazzling wonder of her green-blue eyes filled with amazing light. Regard for him shone there undeniable and true.

He was not worthy of it. The right thing to do would be to step away and pretend he hadn't noticed her feelings for him. An honorable man would save her from the certain heartache he would bring her. A noble man would not yearn for her caring. When she stepped quietly out of his arms and unlaced her fingers from his, the bond of caring remained between them. Distance did not stop it. He wanted to gather her back in his arms and draw her to his chest. To one more time drink in the incredible and rare closeness of holding her.

It took all the honor he possessed to let her walk away.

"Dr. Frost." She hurried toward the medical man, her calico skirts swirled around her. She clutched the edge of the counter. "How is Pa?"

"I stitched up the gash in his scalp. I'm concerned about the blow he took to his skull." Dr. Frost snapped his medical bag shut. "For now, it doesn't seem serious, but if his symptoms don't improve or grow worse, send for me immediately."

"Absolutely." Her teeth dug into her bottom lip, worrying it.

Burke longed to draw her back into his arms to comfort her, but she'd moved several yards away. He wasn't sure he should try to walk with the store spinning so wildly. He let his eyes drift shut, fighting the dizziness he didn't want to admit to. *Lord, keep me standing upright. Lila needs help.*

"Deputy, I thought I told you to stay in bed." The doctor didn't sound too astonished to find him on his feet. "You won't heal right if you don't take care of yourself."

"I'm fine, Doc." He kept his eyes closed, not concerned with his own welfare. It mattered little.

The back door slapped open. Footsteps clattered, ringing in the quiet store. "Pa! Pa!" little girl voices called. "We've been waiting for you *forever!*"

"What are my girls doing here?" The doctor laughed, sounding happily surprised.

"Waiting for you," one high-noted voice informed him.

"And we're gettin' hungry," an identical voice added.

Should he risk it? he wondered. Bravely he opened one eye. The room had stopped spinning so he opened the other to see twins girls hanging on to both of the doctor's shirtsleeves. Both were cute as buttons in their braids and calico dresses.

"Thank you, Lila. We will be keeping Arthur in prayer." A kindly blonde woman waited in the bright fall of light through the open back door. When her gaze landed on her husband, she gentled. Love lit her softly, the way happy endings come in a fairy tale.

The twins dragged their father toward her and the family left together, their voices drifting after them as they discussed what to order at the diner and not to forget slices of apple pie for dessert.

Love had happened to other people. Not him. For him, love was something to lose, something that had failed to protect him from the world's harshness. He had no call for that kind of weakness in his life. So he was at a loss to explain why the echoes of the happy family lingered in his mind and why he pushed off the wall to settle his hands on Lila's shoulders.

He liked being near to her. He breathed in the faint scent of soap in her hair and the lilac sweetness that wrapped around his heart. The need to comfort her roared through him with a fury that shook his bones, violent and consuming and yet infinitely tender.

"I will find the men who hurt your father," he vowed. He brushed one fingertip over a lock of hair curling at her nape.

"You are a good man, Burke." She swirled to face him, lifting her chin so she could look him in the eye. Admiration softened the dear contours of her face. Caring polished her delicate features and made her impossibly more beautiful to him.

An answering caring threatened to rise up, but he caught it in time. What was he doing? Who did he think he was? He couldn't feel this way for Lila. He ought to move away from her, but he couldn't. His thumb traced the dainty cut of her chin, marveling at the satin softness of her skin. His gaze slid to her soft, rosebud mouth and deeper emotions left him weak.

Step away, Hannigan, he told himself. Don't think it. You don't even have the right to dream of kissing her.

Sharp, heavy footsteps rang in the stairwell. "Lila? I need you." Eunice's irritation sharpened her words and rang down the stairs and into the store with impressive force. *"Now."*

"I'm coming," she promised, but she didn't move away. She didn't break the connection of his touch. She had to feel this, too. Was she as vulnerable as he?

"I need to help with my pa's care, now that the doctor has gone." She didn't need to explain. He already knew she had to go. Was she lingering just to stay close to him?

He did not have the right to hope for that, too.

"Tell me. What can I do for you?" he asked with honest concern.

"You can try taking care of yourself for a change." She laid the flat of her hand against his jaw. "Go back to bed. Rest."

"No. Me? I'm fine."

"You can hardly stand up." The rough, masculine texture felt wonderful against her palm. He was substantial and tough and he'd come to comfort her. He'd vowed to find whoever did this to her pa. Impossible not to like him even more. "I worry about you, Burke."

"No need." His baritone rumbled gruffly, as if he were too tough to need a mere woman's concern, but she wasn't fooled. Something hid deeper in his voice, something she could not hear, only feel.

She knew no one had truly worried over

him in a long, long time. She was glad to be the one who did. In truth, she could not stop it. An endless supply of caring welled up from within her and she knew better than to examine it. If she were falling in love with anyone, then it could not be with Burke Hannigan. He had made that perfectly clear.

That didn't mean she couldn't take care of him. "Why don't you sit down? I'll drive you to the boardinghouse."

"Sure, but weren't your horses and wagon stolen?"

"We have another team. Driving horses for the family buggy, and Pa keeps a second wagon in case the first needs repairs." She looped her arm through his. She held her anger at the thieves and her caring for Burke in check. "Don't look at me like that. I'm a very good driver."

"I've seen a lot of women drivers, and experience has taught me to expect the worst." Humor looked good on him.

Too good. She had to be practical, businesslike and casual. She had to act as if she wasn't remembering how he'd held her in his arms. As if she couldn't remember in the least the joyous comfort of being enfolded against his chest.

She pointed to the back door. "There's a

comfortable bench on the porch. It's shady this time of day and a nice place to relax. Go sit."

"What did I tell you when we met? I don't like bossy women." He probably thought he could divert her with his incredible handsomeness and humor.

Not going to work. "Life is full of hardship and take-charge women. How sad for you."

"At least I'm getting a little sympathy," he quipped. "It might help my spinning head."

"Sit, and don't even think about getting up." She couldn't resist taking his arm and steering him in the correct direction. "Promise me you will rest?"

"I make no promises. Go to your father. You will worry less when you see him all patched up and looking better." He brushed the curls from her eyes but he didn't move to the back door.

She couldn't force her feet toward the stairs. She was anchored to him like a ship to the shore. Time halted, the demands of life melted away until there was only the kindness luminous in his midnight-blue eyes and the synchrony of their hearts.

"Lila!" Eunice called, her annoyance echoing down the stairwell like a thunderclap. "Do not make me call for you again."

"Go." He withdrew first. It was like being torn apart. His features pinched as if he were in agony, too. His tender silence said what words did not.

Her heart rolled over, touched beyond measure. The silence of true feeling remained with her as she shuffled forward, loath to leave the man she would not, could not love.

"I don't know what to do about the deliveries." Pa sat up, his frustration palpable as Eunice rushed to plump his pillows. His wounds didn't look nearly as serious with the blood cleansed from his face, his nose straightened and his gash stitched. He appeared almost like his old self. "Our customers have been so good to us. I don't want to leave them without their groceries for supper."

"It is a worry," Eunice agreed. "Lie back, Arthur. You are going to follow the doctor's orders if I have to force you to do it."

"All right, Eunice." Pa patted his wife's hand, patient as always. The doctor was right. Pa wasn't badly injured. In a few days, he would almost be as good as new. "I wasn't thinking of taking the wagon out myself, but someone has to."

"I can." This was her chance to help her

father. He'd had a very bad day. The last thing he should worry about was losing business, after losing his horses, wagon and merchandise. Lila took the tray Lark carried into the room. "I know how to drive, and it wouldn't take me long to redo the morning's orders and to pack up the afternoon deliveries."

"That's not going to happen." Eunice jerked the tray from her, still terribly upset and trying hard to please Pa. It must be difficult being the second wife, the necessary and convenient woman a bereaving widower had married when he hadn't loved her. Lila settled on the foot of the bed.

"No." Pa's eyebrows furrowed together. "I won't have it. Those bandits are still out there."

"We could hire someone." Eunice set the tray on the bedside table with a clatter. "I hate to have such an expense, but you are right, Arthur. We can't disappoint our customers. We don't want to lose their business."

"Which is why I should go." She leaned against the foot post. "Let me, Pa. Please?"

"I'm not sure." He rubbed his forehead, as if he had a raging headache and thinking was difficult.

"Then at least let me do the deliveries in

town." She used to ride along with him when she was a little girl. "I know how it's done. Nothing will happen to me with so many people out and about on the streets."

"I don't like my daughter doing a man's work." He relaxed into his pillows. His black eye, bandaged nose and puffy lip made him look bedraggled, but he was still his patient self. He thought a moment and nodded, a sign he was about to relent. "What do you think, Eunice?"

"Who will run the store? I can't leave your side, Arthur. The doctor said you have a concussion and need to be watched. I won't risk your health."

"Lark can do it." Lila spoke fast before her father could frown and her stepmother could object. "She's never made a mistake so far when she's helped in the store. If she feels overwhelmed or needs help, then she can call up to you, Eunice. Otherwise, you will have to hire someone or close the store. Neither is good for profits."

She waited breathlessly, praying a one word prayer. *Please, please, please.* She hoped the Lord was listening. She wanted to do this for her father. To take one burden off his mind.

"Yes, if Lark would like to." Pa held up one hand when Eunice protested. "It's only for an afternoon."

The rapid sound of thuds came from the kitchen down the hall. Lila could imagine Lark hopping up and down with glee. She must have been able to overhear the conversation.

"Thank you, Pa. You won't regret it." Lila launched forward to carefully kiss his cheek. She did not want to jar his poor head, since he had to be in more pain than he was admitting. "I'll start filling the orders."

"Tell your sister to run and tell one of the Dane brothers to bring the spare wagon and our buggy team by." Pa managed a one-sided grin. "Lila, you are quite a young woman. It's good to know I can count on you."

"It's good to be counted on." She squeezed his hand before she left. Lark waited for her in the hallway, skipping in place with joy.

"I'll run to the livery straightaway." She hurriedly tied the strings of her sunbonnet. "I promise I won't let Pa down. He's counting on me, too."

"Yes, he is." She opened the door for her little sister. Her not-so-little sister, these days. Lark stood tall and slender, looking ladylike as she remembered not to run down the stairs. Halfway down she slowed and walked gracefully, so like their ma it put a lump in Lila's throat.

Now that one wounded man was tended to, there was another one to deal with. While her little sister went out the front door, Lila trailed out the back. She pushed open the screen door and poked her head around the door frame. Was he still there? The sight of Burke sitting with his eyes closed surprised her. He was snoozing. She resisted the urge to remove his hat, lie him down on the bench and find a pillow for his head. Doing those things would wake him, and he looked like a man who needed a nap.

What had it cost him to climb out of bed? He was barely strong enough to sit up, and yet he'd walked here to comfort her, regardless of the pain he had to be in. He'd done that for her.

Don't read too much into it, she warned herself. She spun on her heels and quietly closed the screen door. Maybe Burke would do the same for anyone he knew. Maybe he was simply being a good friend. He *was* a Range Rider, after all, a man of exemplary honor.

The instant she waltzed into the storeroom, she spotted one of the new crates that had just come in on the morning train, the top off, showing a handful of titles from their latest book order. She let her fingertips rest on the spine of one volume of her favorite series. She had already plucked her copy of the newest installment and it was waiting for her upstairs on her nightstand. The character in the books would definitely push himself beyond all limits just to be helpful. But it seemed to her in comparison that Burke's caring toward her went beyond an employee's devotion to his job.

Didn't she just tell herself not to read too much into his actions? The man had an impossible hold on her, but one thing was sure. He was a very, very good man.

She grabbed an empty crate and filled the first order, humming.

He'd just turned fifteen at the start of summer. In the hot evening sun, Burke situated the old gun against his shoulder and ignored the sting of the morning's beating that had broken the skin on his back. He concentrated on lining up the notch on the barrel with the five-inch piece of scrap two-by-four sitting on top of the stump.

"How long are you gonna stay with them folks?" Olly talked around a plug of tobacco.

"You mean the farmer and his wife? 'Til the end of the harvest." Harvest felt like a long time away.

"Do you like stayin' with 'em?"

"No, but I've stayed with worse. Much worse." Burke let the kiss of the late-July breeze ruffle his hair and tug at his battered hat brim. It waved through the seed-heavy tips of the wild grasses and sent daisies to nodding as he let out a breath, fastened his gaze on his target and squeezed the trigger. The old rifle let out a ringing blast and a burst of fire. The lead bullet thudded into the wood and set it flying into the grass. Bull's-eye. He shrugged. "Got nowhere else to go but the orphanage. If I go back now, they'll just find me some other farm to work."

"You ought to strike out on your own." Olly spat juice into the grass as he chased down the chunk of wood. He held it up in the air. "Dead center. Don't no one shoots like you do."

"It's not like it can do me any good." He stood the rifle upright on its butt and poured gunpowder down the barrel — just enough, not too much. "It's not like I can earn a living at it."

"Sure you can."

"Me? No. I wish." The plug of tobacco Olly had given him soured his mouth and made his stomach sick-feeling. It was hard talking around a wad stuck into his cheek, so he spit the whole thing into the grass, hoping his buddy wouldn't notice. They'd met at the swimming hole back in April, where Burke had come to wash off the grime from long days of sowing oats, wheat and corn. They'd been fast friends ever since in what little spare time Burke had. He gave the barrel a shake and a tap.

"My pa does." Olly set another chunk of wood on the stump. He carried his polished Winchester carelessly, as if he was used to packing a firearm, a man of the world.

"Is he some kind of gunslinger?" Burke fed a bullet into the muzzle and used the ramrod to push it deep into the barrel.

"You could say that." Olly kicked at daisies and sent their heads flying into the grass as he made his way back from the stump. "See if you can shoot that one dead center."

The chunk was smaller, maybe three inches. A challenge. "You're on." Burke raised the hammer, slid a cap over the hollow pin. He settled the rifle against his shoulder and carefully sited.

A rattle of a wagon bouncing over road ruts startled him awake. Burke blinked. The bright memory of the dream broke apart and faded like smoke as one of the brothers who ran the livery stable pulled a pretty pair of quick-stepping bays to a stop.

"Whoa, there." Walton Dane climbed down. "Deputy, you have been the talk of the town, at least until today. Now poor Arthur is. A shame what's happening to a peaceful place like this. Some say it's the railroad's fault."

"Others might say it's man's fault." Burke tried to boost himself off the bench seat, but nothing happened. He swept off his hat, rested his back against the cool brick wall and breathed in enough air to make his head stop swimming. "Doing wrong is a man's choice."

"We didn't used to see many men like that in these parts." Walton paraded onto the porch. "Now we've got 'em on the town's payroll."

Hard to miss the venom in Dane's words. He tried to stand again and he made it off the bench. He broke out in a weak, cold sweat.

"You had better watch yourself, Deputy." Dane yanked open the screen door. "Folks are hoppin' mad about the sheriff. One day they just might run him out of town. That might go for you, too."

"No one is running me anywhere." He hated the physical weakness trembling through him when he needed to be strong.

He had a job to do, a sheriff to stop.

"We'll see." Dane shouldered through the door, leaving behind an air of disdain that was hard to ignore.

Folks were starting to think he was in league with the sheriff. He couldn't let it bother him. He wouldn't be a good Rider if he didn't. He did his best to ignore the pain slicing through his ribs, maneuvered forward and made it to the screen door.

"Coming through!" Lila sang in her dulcet alto, three crates stacked high in her arms. She peered over the top of a small bag of flour. "Go wait for me in the wagon. I'm taking you home, mister."

"Is that so?" He manhandled the crates from her so smoothly, she didn't have time to protest. Too bad his wounds didn't have time to hurt. Humor made the pain matter less. "Remember, I don't take orders from a woman."

"You must be getting used to it by now. Give me back my crates."

"Not a chance, sweetheart." The light drained from his eyes as he took the first step off the porch. It hurt so much. He stumbled into the alley blindly and gave thanks when his vision cleared. He hoped Lila couldn't see his knees shake or hear the groan of keen-edged pain he did his best to bite back. So far so good. He wasn't bleeding or lying on the ground, so he gathered every scrap of willpower he possessed and hefted the crates up into the wagon bed and lost his eyesight again.

"Move aside, Deputy." Dane returned, carrying a stack of six and plopped the boxes down like they weighed nothing at all. "Lila, do you want a hand up? I'll get the rest of the orders."

"I can climb up myself, thanks." She waltzed up next to him in the shade of the wagon, her presence restoring his vision and easing his pain. She tied her sunbonnet ribbons into a bow beneath her chin. "Time to get you home, Deputy."

"Home? No. I'm staying with you." The need to protect her rose up fiercely within him, greater than any pain and mightier than any weakness. "I intend to keep you safe."

"Unnecessary. I'm perfectly safe if I stay in town."

"You never know what might befall you." He grabbed hold of the side of the wagon to keep steady. "It's better to be safe than sorry."

"What if I'm a risk-taker? What if I like to let the winds blow where they may?" She swung up onto the wagon seat before he could help her.

Sunshine slanted into his eyes and outlined her with blazing gold, and against the bold blue sky she could have been a dream he had wished into his life. Emotion choked him as he followed her shakily onto the seat. "That's risky talk for a fabric counter clerk. I think you need me."

"I need you?" She tugged up the brim of her sunbonnet. The sage-green color brought out the luster of her bright hair and the compelling green in her irises. She arched one slender eyebrow. "You are entirely wrong, Deputy. It's you who needs me. I fed you, remember?"

"I do. I'm grateful. You are a good cook." His throat felt doubly thick. The words sounded clumsy as he reached for the reins.

"I saw that wince. Burke, I don't want you to strain yourself. You could have died from your wounds." Her hand settled lightly on his arm. All humor faded as she searched his face. Honest caring radiated from her, the most beautiful thing he'd ever known.

All he wanted was to have her gaze upon him with caring and kindness for the rest of his days. If he could have her, then he would cherish her with all the might he possessed.

He could never be worthy. He waited for Dane to latch the tailgate before he snapped the reins. "I'm too tough to die."

"That's your opinion. I have a different one. Since it's a free country, I'm going to keep it. You won't change my mind."

"If only I were strong enough to try." He did his best not to fall off the seat. He had a hard time focusing on the alley ahead. He kept the horses walking slow and hoped his dizziness would fade. "I can be stubborn, too. I'm going to do my job. You won't stop me."

"Your job? Driving my father's delivery wagon is your job?"

"Close enough. While I'm laid up and no use to the town, I may as well spend my time protecting ladies and their wagons when I can." He hoped she could not guess why his voice sounded strained or why he could not look at her as he chirruped to the horses to keep them walking.

"Yes, I'm glad you can make yourself useful," she said lightly. "As long as you don't fall off the wagon seat."

"I'm getting the swing of driving while dizzy."

"There ought to be a law about that."

"I'll be sure and take it up with the sheriff."

The back stoops and windows of the alleys passed in a blur. He was able to focus enough to see a donkey pulling a cart turn off Main and head in their direction.

"Lila!" Mr. Grummel called as he approached. "I heard about your father. Oy. At least you have the deputy beauing you. Smart girl."

"It's nothing like that, Mr. Grummel!" Lila explained, but the older man held up his hand to wave off her words, chuckling. She frowned. "Some people leap to the oddest conclusions."

"That they do." He eased the horses to a halt at the intersection. When Lila smiled up at him, it made him forget about the past, leaving only the here and now where there was no reason he couldn't care about her, no reason they couldn't be more than friends.

CHAPTER NINE

"I'm sorry this is so late." Lila handed over the last crate on the daily order. The prairie winds pleasantly swirled her skirts and ruffled the tendrils that had worked their way out of her braided up-knot.

"I'm surprised you were able to make it at all." Joanna McKaslin took the crate gladly. "After my husband heard what happened to your father, he planned on driving into town tomorrow to fetch the order. Is it safe for you to be driving on the roads alone?"

"I'm not alone." For the thirteenth time that afternoon she gestured toward the wagon seat where Burke sat holding the reins. The breeze ruffled the ends of his dark hair. Dressed in black, his face shaded by the dark brim of his Stetson, he could have been any woman's dream come true. Not that she was dreaming.

Fine, she was dreaming, but only a little bit.

"He insisted on coming along with me. Since I couldn't get rid of him, I decided to make the out-of-town deliveries, too," she explained, praying she wasn't blushing.

"Deputy Hannigan." Joanna smiled her approval. "I don't pay any attention what some folks have been saying about him. I'll never forget how he stopped to help us in town last month. James had been stung by a bee and the deputy went to the trouble of asking the clerk in the nearest shop to make a poultice for him to take the pain away. That man has a kind heart."

"Yes, he does." He also had a stalwart spirit — or a stubborn one, depending on how you wanted to look at it. He'd insisted on driving through town, patiently negotiating traffic and residential streets although he looked ready to tumble off the seat. Would he admit he was in pain?

Never. She watched him like a hawk, but she'd only caught the tiniest grimace twice. He'd blithely talked her into the out-of-town deliveries, since he was armed and he didn't figure any robbers would want to raise trouble with the town's deputy. He sat powerfully, as if not a thing was wrong with him, but she knew better.

"Have a nice evening, Joanna."

"You, too, Lila. My family is keeping your

father in prayer."

"Thank you so much." She crossed the shady covered porch and hopped onto the sun-blasted pathway flanked by flowers blooming merrily in border beds. Bees buzzed and the distant sound of children's laughter came from somewhere behind the house.

Burke held out his hand to help her into the wagon. Maybe he did look a little better. The fresh air may have done him some good. She plopped onto the seat next to him and arranged her skirts. The dappled shade overhead was refreshing. She could not admit to herself it might be the company.

"That was the last delivery." He snapped the reins. "The next stop, home?"

"Are you anxious to be rid of me?" She tugged at her sunbonnet as the matched bays plodded forward. The wagon rattled and lumbered along the dusty driveway toward the country road, bouncing her on the seat. She pushed her bonnet off her head and let it dangle by the strings down her back. The breeze fanned her face and her hair. Much better.

"Yes, I am anxious to be rid of you, but you already know that." Humor hooked the corner of his mouth, betraying his real feelings. "I'm a lone wolf. Spending an entire afternoon with a lady is more than I can do."

"You need toughening up, Deputy." She knelt down to unbutton her right shoe. "Maybe I can help you with that."

"Do I look like I need help?" The hook of his grin widened. "I'm too tough for that."

"Good, because your afternoon with me is not over yet." She loosened her shoelaces.

"What does that mean? That was the last stop."

"I packed a few snacks when I was crating the orders." She slid her foot out of her shoe. Her summer weight stocking felt too hot, so she shucked it off. "Why don't you take the next right when we hit the road to town?"

"Are you going to leave that off? Because if you are, I don't think it's decent that I see your bare feet. Your stepmother might come after me with a broom."

"It's just my feet, and besides, didn't you just say you were tough?"

"There's tough and then there's stupid. Put your shoe back on."

"No, I'm dying in this heat. The thermometer at the bank said it was ninety-five when we were in town last. It's gotten much hotter since." She bent to undo her other shoe. She didn't list the reasons why she was so uncomfortable. Her corset bound her tightly, a layer of clothing she could not take off. Her petticoats were the lightest cotton, but also added to her discomfort. Did her feet have to be hot, too? "Just don't look."

"I'll try to restrain myself." He chuckled as he reined the horses onto the main stretch of road, desolate and dusty this time of day. "But if your stepmother finds out, I'm blaming you."

"Much better." She tugged off her other shoe and wiggled her toes. "Turn right up there. It's not a driveway, but the wagon won't tip over."

"You've been here before?"

"It's the best spot to wade the river in the entire county."

Tall grasses gave glimpses of old wagon tracks as they danced and swayed. He urged the horses off the road and onto the bumpy ground. The wagon wheels lurched over clumps of bunch grass as the horses picked up their gait. Rich shade beckoned beneath the arching rustle of old cottonwoods and the lush grass looked invitingly cool. The music of the river sang above all the other sounds. Sunshine on water glinted with promise.

It was hard to believe strife could happen anywhere in the world with beauty like this, hard to believe Slim's gang and Cheever lurked in this peaceful prairie valley. He knew they were probably behind the attack on Lila's father. They hadn't gotten away with a lot of money from the bank, and they had to eat. The delivery wagon was full of groceries and supplies. His promise to her weighed heavily on him. He would catch Slim and Cheever. Arthur Lawson deserved justice.

Lila hopped from the seat, not bothering to wait for his assistance. He suspected his tough act hadn't fooled her nearly enough. She knew he was in pain. She was a dear sight as she landed with her bare feet crunching in the grass. She reached up, arms slim and elegant and plucked the pins out of her hair. The coil of her long braid came loose and slid down her back. She tossed her head innocently, lifting her face to take in the kiss of the cooler wind off the river's surface. Her thick lashes brushed her ivory skin as she closed her eyes briefly, savoring the sensation of the wind.

His pulse tumbled. He lost the ability to think. He forgot how to breathe. Never had there been a more arresting sight. He memorized the moment, the curve of her cheek, the faint smile on her lips and how alive she was, crowned by the sunny sky and surrounded by daisies. One day far in the future he would want to remember this moment, remember her.

He stumbled down and tied the horses, unable to look away. He laid his hand on the grip of his .45 tucked in the waistband at his back. The trouble had happened far out of town, nowhere near here, but he could keep her safe. In a blink, he would lay down his life to protect her, his Lila, as sweet as the wildflowers brushing at her skirts.

"This way." She circled around a thistle flower where a big honey bee drank and skirted in the other direction to avoid the crown of a gopher hole. A jackrabbit darted through the foliage, terrified by the invader in a calico dress. Across the span of the river a doe lifted her head from grazing to stare at them warily.

"Divine." She sank both feet into the clear water, holding her skirt safely out of the water with both hands. "Oh, it's so cool. You have to feel this."

"I haven't gone wading since I was fifteen years old." The summer his life had gone from miserable to worse. The summer he'd grown up in a hurry. He'd lost more than his innocence that year, things he'd never been able to get back. "Kids play in the river."

"Don't you dare call me a kid." She flicked one long braid behind her shoulder and lifted her skirts higher. The snowy white lace edging her petticoats flashed against the silvery water's surface. "You are far too much of a stick-in-the-mud for your own good. Always playing the hero."

"Hero? Hardly. Maybe I'm the villain. You just don't know it." It was the truth and he held his breath. What would she say? Would she believe him?

"A villain? I don't think so."

Maybe she couldn't see it now, but she would. He sank onto a nearby boulder at the grassy edge. Eventually she would be able to see the real man he was. He couldn't hide it forever.

"I know what you are, Burke Hannigan." Water sparkled around her. She marched toward him, splashing rainbow droplets with every step. "You are in danger of suffering heat sickness. A little fun isn't going to hurt you."

"It might. You never know. I'm not used to frivolity."

"Yes, but something tells me you aren't opposed to it." She knelt at his feet and untied his boots. "At least give it a try. Since you are on leave from work, what else do you have to do?"

"Riding shotgun with you isn't as easy as a man might guess." He resisted the syrupy feelings gathering deep inside. "I can untie my own boots."

"Let me do it." She tugged on the second pair of laces and they fell free. "I don't want you to bend over too far and tear your stitches."

"My stitches are fine."

"I know." Mesmerizing tendrils tumbled forward to shield her face. Her affection warmed the air like summer and it made forgotten seeds take root within him. An answering affection he had no right to took root along with wishes he had no chance at.

She tugged off his boots and then his socks. He should stop her but he couldn't. He could not turn down her care and her closeness. When she rolled up his trousers to his knees with ladylike tugs on the fabric, he did his best to hold back his heart. He truly did. It fell anyway.

She cared for him. It was not right, it would not last, but for this moment he could not reject it. He needed it more than air to breathe, more than any sustenance. When she offered her hand to help him up, it was more that she offered. More that he accepted.

"You have gone gray again." She slid her arm around his back, as if to support some of his weight.

She probably had no notion what that meant to him, how she stole a piece of him. He didn't need to lean on her, he was too proud and independent to do it now that he was back on his feet, but he loved her for it. He loved her.

"The rocks are a little slippery and the water is —"

"Cold," he supplied, startled by the icy bite of the current. The wetness sluiced over his toes and lapped around his ankles. The gray stone river rocks bit into his soles, but she was right. He cooled down ten degrees. He grabbed the brim of his hat and tossed it into the grass.

"There's a boulder over there." She pulled him upstream into the tug of the current. Silt clouded upward like dust with every footstep. "I'll get you sitting down and then I'll fetch the treats from the wagon."

"You have been spending too much time with your stepmother." He grabbed hold of her braid and tugged, gently, before draping his arm around her shoulder. Not to lean on her, but to draw her close to his side. Being with her was nicer than anything he'd ever known. "You are not in charge here."

"Oh, and you are?" She planted her feet, forgot about her skirts and they dropped into the rushing water. Not that she noticed. "Because you are the man, I suppose?"

"Why? You act like that's the wrong answer. Of course I'm in charge because I'm the man."

"I can't believe my ears." Mirth made her eyes twinkle like emeralds. "The hero in the Range Rider books would never say something like that."

"I'm no hero," he protested lightly.

"But you have your passable moments. This isn't one of them. I think I've discovered the reason why you are a lone wolf. No one woman would have you."

"Yes. You've stumbled on the truth." His foot slipped on a stone, and he was glad she was there to steady him. He hated the weakness that left him shaky as he eased onto the sunny rock. Water gurgled around him and to his left the river spanned wide and dangerous. But here, in the dappled shade of the cottonwoods with both the horses and the country road in sight, Lila was safe. He could relax and let his guards slide down. "No woman has ever wanted me."

"I'm not at all surprised." She towered above him, blocking the sun, lithe and willowy and full of life and beauty. "The article in the newspaper warned you were not about to be caught by any lady in this town. Pete, who owns the paper, wasn't kidding."

"I get that everywhere I go. If there's a town newspaper they want to know if I'm single and willing." He raked a hand through his hair.

"But you're too much of a lone wolf." She waded away from him, her skirt hem floating in the water. "Haven't you been tempted even once?"

"Once." The truth rolled out, impossible to stop.

"Ooh, now I have to know more." She bounded up the bank, her alto bobbing on the breezes. "What was her name?"

"Sorry, but that's on a need-to-know basis."

"And don't I need to know?" She swirled through the daisies and went up on tiptoe to lug a few items from beneath the wagon seat. "I'm curious about the woman who could bring down your defenses."

"She is quite amazing." He leaned forward to dip his finger into the cold water. "I have never met anyone like her before."

"Do tell. I'm listening." She splashed into the glinting water, startling a dragonfly hovering nearby. Her skirts billowed around her as the current tugged and flowed. "Did she steal your heart?"

"As close as anyone has ever come," he confessed.

"Not that you would release it completely, ever really let anyone in." With a small basket hooked over one arm, she dipped the water bottle into the rippling water, filling it. "Or did you?"

"If anyone could, it would be her." He didn't feel comfortable saying more. No one's kindness could mean as much to him as Lila's had. His throat tightened with the feelings he could not speak. They remained wedged beneath his Adam's apple, a lump he could not budge.

"What was she like?" She handed him the small jug, deliciously cold from the water.

"She is pure caring." The deeper reaches of his consciousness could still remember the lilting softness of her voice reaching him through the fever and nightmares. For a time, she'd been his anchor, the only one he'd known in his adult life. "She has brown hair, but no ordinary brown. It has layers of color. Cinnamon. Auburn. Russet. Ginger. Chestnut."

"She was beautiful."

"To me, she's the most beautiful of women." The lump in his throat expanded, straining his words, making it hard to speak. "She has eyes that are the color of a northern sea, an eddy of ocean green and stormy blue sky that can make even a man like me dream."

"I have brown hair. I have green-and-blue eyes." She narrowed her gaze at him and plucked open the basket. Fresh strawberries spilled out of an ironware bowl and tumbled over onto a neighboring stack of sugar cookies. "You aren't being serious."

"How do you know?" He grinned, hiding his heart because she would not believe him. He didn't blame her. A sweetheart like her would not be interested in a man who had made bad choices in his life. Some choices could not be reversed, some acts could never be redeemed. The river's whisper and the melody of larks and Lila's sunny presence kept him in the light, away from the past.

"Have a strawberry. They were brought into the store fresh this morning." She held the basket out to him, refusing to stop taking care of him.

"I've told you a secret." He plucked a ripe berry from the bowl. "Now it's your turn."

"You didn't tell me a secret. I think you were playing a joke on me. Not a mean joke, but you managed to avoid my question quite nicely."

He pushed off the boulder, ignoring the protest of his healing wounds and the rush in his head from standing too quickly. "I answered your question the best I could. No one in twenty years has been as close to me as you."

"Oh." She gave her braid a toss, lifting her chin so that her gaze met his. Whatever she felt remained shielded and the saucy uplift in the corners of her mouth gave no clue. "Is that only because you were shot and couldn't escape me?"

"Yes, that's exactly the reason why. The only reason why." He held the berry to her lips. "Ladies first."

"Surely you had friends growing up?" She took the strawberry from him and popped it into her mouth.

"For a time in the orphanage, but it was difficult. The other children were always coming or going and the lucky few were adopted. I was hired out to a different place every year."

"No friends." She set the basket down on the boulder. "I can't imagine what that must have been like. My friends, the seven of us, have mostly been together since we were very young. They have been my pillars. When I lost my mother, they helped see me through."

"I'm glad you have them." He pulled her into his arms.

She rested her cheek against his sun-warmed shirt and her soul stilled. She listened to the steady beat of his heart as his iron-strong arms wrapped around her. Complete peace. Total bliss. Feelings filled her that were purely romantic, as poetic as if they had come straight off the pages of a novel. Not even Earlee, who was gifted with paper and pen, could have written a scene more moving than the joy she felt in Burke's arms.

And he was alone. He had no one, except for her. She breathed in the sunshine and soap scent of his shirt and let her eyes drift shut. "Who did you have to see you through? Wasn't there anyone you could turn to?"

"No one." His cheek caressed her forehead with one tender stroke, then two before he drew away and released her. "You will have to do."

His shadow fell across her, engulfing her, cutting off all light from the sun above. She could not stop her feelings from rising up buoyant to the surface. Unspoken affection darkened his gaze that was so deep she could see past his defenses. She could hear what words could not give meaning to.

"Thank you for everything you've done for me." His baritone dipped, tiered with feeling. He cradled her jaw with his calloused hands. No man could be gentler. "You saved my life when I was shot."

"I applied bandages and pressure." She couldn't help leaning her cheek against the rough pads of his fingers. The well of emotion she felt for him deepened fathom by fathom. "It was nothing."

"You read to me. You put cold compresses to my forehead." He leaned a wisp closer so that she could see the lighter blue flecks in his irises and each individual whisker stubble. "You stayed with me every time I felt most alone."

"I don't have much else to do." Her humor fell short.

He did not smile. He did not chuckle. "Tomorrow when your pa returns to his delivery driving, make sure he takes a gun with him. It would be best if he didn't go alone. It would be worth the cost to hire someone."

"I'll tell him." She felt cold, although the sun blazed and baked through her cotton dress. "You are going back to work tomorrow, aren't you?"

"I have a job to do." He leaned his forehead gently against hers. The contact was more poignant than a kiss. She could feel his regrets. She knew he was preparing to tell her goodbye. He cleared his throat. "I won't forget what you did for me, Lila. I will never forget."

"You think this is the end, that we won't have the chance to see one another again?" She could feel tension move through him. "I thought we were friends."

"We're not friends." He nudged her jaw, tilting her face to his. His lips slanted inches above hers and hovered for a fraction of a second. Then his mouth brushed over hers with a light, feathering kiss. A kiss so sweet it brought tears to her eyes. A kiss that stilled her soul.

When he broke away, he stared out at the horizon for a moment, as if warring with his internal thoughts. He did not move but held on to her for a few minutes more. She recognized the wish moving through his heart because the same wish moved through hers.

"No, we are not friends," she agreed. It was a good thing she wasn't falling in love with him because that kiss alone could have made her tumble irrevocably, inexorably. "I think we will always be a good deal more."

She swirled away from him to pluck a

cookie from the basket, wishing he was a settling-down kind of man. Tucking away her tender feelings, she splashed through the water and kicked up a cool spray.

He chuckled, not quick enough in his weakened state to dodge it, but his good-natured laughter rang above the merry bird-song and burned itself into her memory, a sound she still could hear hours later long after the sun had set and darkness fell.

As she sat in her room finishing her letter to Meredith, she remembered Burke's booming laughter and his kiss, her first kiss.

Now that was definitely like something out of a book. She dipped her pen into the bottle, tapped off the excess ink and continued writing with a smile on her face and in her heart.

CHAPTER TEN

"My pa is looking to hire another gun." In dream, Olly dropped a pinecone on the top of the stump.

They were target practicing again in the stuffy heat of a muggy August evening, his only free time off from fieldwork and chores around the farm. Burke set the gun on its butt. He pulled the last bullet from the leather pouch tied to his belt. Tonight he needed to melt more lead.

"It's a real job. You interested?" Olly swung his sleek Winchester by the barrel as he strode through the grass, crushing daisies beneath his boots.

"Interested? Sure." Burke sited carefully. "But I can't walk away from my fieldwork just for one day's work. The farmer would tan my hide and there's no one to stop him from hitting me. If he kicked me out, I'd have to go back to the orphanage."

"It's not work for only one night, stupid."

Olly spat a stream of tobacco and laughed with a mature confidence. He was grown up for his years. They might be the same age, but Olly was older somehow. Rough language slid easily off his tongue, and he knew a lot of the world. "This is a legitimate job offer."

"With pay?" Burke squeezed the trigger, the flash bang of the long rifle knocked him back a foot but the pinecone shattered into a hundred pieces. Perfect hit.

"Pay, room and board. Long term. It's gun work. You would be providing security for my pa." Olly leaned his Winchester against the rough bark of a skinny pine and untied his pack. "You would stay with us. Pa would pay you a dollar a day."

"A whole dollar?" That was thirty dollars a month. Over three hundred a year. He would be rich. He put down his gun, raked a hand through his hair and tried to imagine having so much money.

He could buy a fine driving team and maybe a shiny buggy to go with it. Or he could buy his own land, maybe it wouldn't be a big place, but he didn't need much. A little shanty with a roof and a cookstove, maybe his own milk cow. His own horse and buggy, his own house. Maybe he could save up enough to go back to school. He had the notion of becoming a Range Rider one day, and he figured he needed a lot of schooling for that.

Excitement jumped in his belly, and he felt hungry for those dreams. Desperate to have them.

"I've never seen anyone shoot the way you can." Olly pulled out a silver flask. "That's talent. Real talent."

"It's just shooting." He shrugged. It came easily to him, as simple as breathing. His talent didn't seem like anything special, but if it could get him out of the farmer's house and earn him money, he wasn't going to argue. His back was still scabbed and tender from his last beating. "You are serious? Thirty dollars a month?"

"As serious as a judge." Olly uncapped the flask and the strong scent of alcohol carried on the wind. Whiskey, Burke knew because the farmer drank it. Olly handed over the alcohol. "All you have to do is keep a sharp eye out and make sure Pa and his men stay safe. Are you in?"

"Yeah. Why not? Anything is better than what I've got." He took the whiskey, feeling good about his decision. He would sneak back to the farmer's house, pack up his clothes and bedroll and he would be free. A man on his own. He lifted the flask and coughed when the burning whiskey hit his tongue. It tasted the way kerosene smelled, but he choked it down. He was a man now and he was in control of his own destiny.

Burke woke with a start, blinked away the dream and sat straight up in bed with the taste of betrayal on his tongue. The sun was bright, traffic sounds clattered through the open window to echo in his rented room. He'd slept longer than he'd intended, judging by the slant of the sun on the floor. He pushed off the covers, ignored the trembling weakness when he stood and the pain in his chest when he moved and poured water from the pitcher into the washbasin.

His hand was steady enough this morning to shave. As he scraped at his whiskers with the sharp edge of his razor, he realized he hadn't trusted another living soul since that first taste of whiskey with Olly. The mistakes of his past stood in his way and he couldn't be the man Lila needed. If he could have just one prayer answered, then that would be it.

He set his razor on the rim of the basin and splashed water over his face. Yesterday's happiness clung to him. He couldn't remember having a better day. He hadn't been that happy in ages. He grabbed the towel off the bar and dried off. But yesterday's sparkling moment of happiness didn't belong in his life.

He got dressed. He bit back a groan of pain as he slipped into a white shirt. He buttoned up, trying to stop the musical lilt of her laughter rising up in his memory. She'd refused to believe he was a villain. She was wrong.

If God was merciful, He would never let Lila know the truth. Burke tugged on his trousers, sat down to put on his boots and bowed his head instead. *She isn't in Your plan for me, this I know, but keep her protected. Find for her the man who can make her happy beyond imagining.*

He reached for his belt and holster. The man who stared back at him in the mirror radiated hard, cold purpose. The besotted fellow who laughed in the river yesterday had gone and was no more. Burke pinned on his tin star. Work waited for him. He buckled on his holster. Work was his life. It was the only thing that could redeem him. Today was the day he made Dobbs and everyone else see the man he used to be. He hated that Lila would see it, too.

"I didn't make a single mistake tallying the sales yesterday, did I?" Lark asked anxiously as she peered around the edge of the shelf she was dusting. "I double-checked every total."

"You did it perfectly." Lila swiped away the figures on her slate with a rag. "Not a penny off, and you remembered every sale price. Eunice will have to admit you can handle the store on your own now."

"I want to be like Ma." Lark went back to stocking. Hidden behind the aisle of pots and pans, the honesty of her hopes rang as clear as a bell. "Maybe it can be the two of us running this store one day. It can be the happy place it once was when Ma was alive."

"It's a good plan." So easy to remember those happy days when their mother rushed around this space, humming to herself as she restocked or did the books or cleaned, tossing loving looks to Pa all the while.

That was the kind of love she longed to find. She refused to let her thoughts spiral back to yesterday afternoon. Do not think about his kiss, she warned herself as she snapped open the accounts receivable ledger.

The door swooshed, the bell sang merrily and her dear friend Kate Schmidt waltzed in with her sleek dark hair tamed by a ladylike knot. "How is your pa?"

"He's at the sheriff's office filing a report." Lila circled the counter to hug her friend.

Burke rolled into her mind. Pa was probably talking with him right now.

"It's a shame he has to do that. I don't suppose Dobbs will do anything." Kate headed straight for the far end of the store.

"Burke will look after him. I know he will take care of Pa." Lila slipped behind the fabric counter. "A man like him, why he could even get our horses back."

"I hope so." Kate shook her head. "First the bank and now this. Pa isn't going to let me drive alone anymore, at least until those men are caught. He came with me. He's over at the feed store."

"I know how you love to drive." Kate lived far west of town in the foothills of the Rocky Mountain range and now that she had her own horse, she was always out in the cute little cart her father had made her. Lila knelt to retrieve the colorful flosses she'd saved for her friend. "Does this mean you won't be coming tomorrow?"

"No, I'll be there, although I won't be able to stay as long as usual." Kate ran her fingertips over the beautiful threads. "Oh, these are perfect. Just what I wanted."

"I slipped them in as a special order, but Eunice hasn't found out yet." Lila tore off a length of brown paper to wrap the pretty flosses in. "Is this for a new project?"

"Always." Kate loved to cross-stitch. "You'll be able to see it tomorrow. Ma has a few things she wants me to pick up while I'm here. Oh, Lila, look."

They turned together to the front windows. On the boardwalk across the street a tall, lanky young man with very nice shoulders marched along with great purpose.

"Lorenzo." Kate sighed. "I am always going to have a crush on him. He's dreamy."

"I suppose."

"You *suppose?* You were always sighing right along with me. Something is wrong." Kate didn't take her gaze off the man as he stopped to chat with a shopkeeper out sweeping his walk. "You can't be feeling well, Lila. Maybe you should have Eunice check you for a fever."

Lila bit her lip. How did she begin to describe her association with Burke? The closeness, the kiss, the laughter and then the feeling of goodbye? She couldn't fight the suspicion that she wouldn't see him again.

"My dear sister has chosen someone else!" Lark popped up to comment. "She's in love with the new deputy."

"Lark!" How could her own sister betray her like that? "It's not love. I'm not like that with him." She bit her lip. Did what she just say make any sense? She didn't think so. "I mean, it's not like that with him. I'm not in love with him."

"No, you are calm as could be talking about him." Kate's mouth quirked up at the corners, as if fighting a smile. Across the street Lorenzo nodded goodbye to his friend and continued on, stalking out of sight. Kate sighed. "Maybe he has replaced Lorenzo in your affections?"

"I've decided to give no man my affection." She couldn't say more or that when Burke's work in Angel Falls was done, he would leave town forever. She grabbed a basket from the stack by the door and handed it over. Pa stormed into sight on the boardwalk, shoved open the door with a clatter and pounded into the store.

"Pa!" She'd never seen him glowing red with anger. His battered eye had swollen shut, the skin a shocking purple-black.

"I'm fed up." His puffy lip twisted with rage. "Forgive me, girls, but that sheriff burns me. I can't remember the last time I've been this furious."

He slammed his fist into the counter, vehemence heaving through him. Lila jumped. Lark gasped. Kate stared wide-eyed as he took a deep, calming breath.

"Papa." She laid her hand on his forearm.

"What happened?"

"Dobbs, that's what. He refuses to investigate." Pa gentled his voice, regaining control. "He says it happened outside of town, so it's not his job."

"I'm not surprised." Everyone she knew had a complaint about Dobbs. "Why don't we find Burke? I know he cares. He can make this right."

"Hannigan? Ha!" Pa spit out the word and jerked his arm away. "He was the worst. Standing around in the sheriff's office, a newcomer to town, questioning me on what happened."

"He has to do that if he is going to investigate." She ached for her poor father as he pressed the heel of his hand to his forehead and accidentally bumped the stitches marching along his hairline.

He winced. "That wasn't what he was doing, Lila. I know you are a good girl and you don't know the ways of the world. Eunice and I have seen that you don't, but believe me when I say the deputy was less than helpful."

That made no sense at all. She remembered the bliss of Burke's kiss and this concern about her father. "Did he try and tell you that you shouldn't go on your deliveries alone until he catches the thieves?"

"No. In fact, he questioned that it even happened at all. Can you imagine? He called me a liar to my face." He flushed with anger again and he pushed away, marching through the store. His hurt and indignation knelled in the hard strike of his boots. "You are never to talk to that man again, Lila. If he comes in this store, no one waits on him. Understand? You send him away. And don't forget to account for the supplies he used while he was here. I've decided to agree with Eunice and to bill him after all."

The door closed behind him with a bang, leaving them alone. Eunice's muffled voice of concern murmured through the ceiling above. Lila stared in disbelief at the closed door, not able to understand exactly what had happened. Burke wouldn't have been cruel to her father. He wouldn't have been disrespectful. Something was wrong.

"I've never seen Papa so angry," Lark whispered, worried again.

"It makes no sense." Simply thinking of him made her stronger. She knew he would make things right. "Pa must have misunderstood."

"He seemed fairly sure about what happened." Kate plucked a box of canning lids off the shelf. "I hate to say it, Lila, but if what he said about the deputy is true, you need to be careful. He might be cut from the same cloth as the sheriff."

"Impossible." Tenderness filled her as she hefted a five-pound sack of white sugar from a shelf for Kate. "I know him better than you do. He isn't anything like Dobbs."

"I pray that you're right," Kate said in her gentle way. "Looks can be deceiving."

"I'm not deceived." She thought of the badge still tucked away in her hope chest. She remembered how Burke had driven the wagon so she could make her deliveries although he was still in pain. His honor, his goodness and the tenderness of his kiss assured her. Burke would never do anything wrong.

If only she could speak to him, she knew she could make everything right. Her father's ultimatum kept her from leaving Lark in charge of the store and going straight to him. She would not disobey her pa.

She realized Kate had quietly gone about her shopping and carried a partially full basket to the front counter. Lila opened the sales book to a new page.

"Burke is one of the good guys," she assured her friend.

Kate nodded as if she wanted to believe it but didn't.

"That was a good touch, Hannigan." Dobbs moseyed over to the bar.

The saloon was quiet this time of day and stuffy with the stale odors from the night before. Dank cigar smoke and spilled whiskey tainted the air as he sidled up on a stool. The barkeep nodded to Dobbs and hurried over with a bottle and two shot glasses, which he filled.

"Good to see you, Sheriff. Deputy." The barkeep nodded, set the bottle on the counter and backed away warily.

Warily. That was interesting. Burke had to wonder why. He made a mental note to talk to the man after hours when Dobbs wouldn't be around. He waited for the sheriff to reach for his glass first.

"Accusing Lawson of stealing his own horses and goods for the attention." Dobbs rasped out a grating chuckle. He downed the whiskey in one swallow. "You should have seen the look on his weak face. That storekeeper is getting on my last nerve."

"I can see why." The glass felt cool as he dragged it on the bar in front of him. He was no longer a fifteen-year-old boy impressed by whiskey. He let it sit. "You told

Arthur to get out of your sight and he went."

"Spooked like a scared jackrabbit." Dobbs upended the bottle and poured another generous shot. "Got no backbone. None of 'em do. How about you, Roger? Do you got a spine?"

The barkeep startled. Tension crept into his jawline.

"That's what I thought." The sheriff barked out another harsh chuckle. "Chickens. I got no respect for 'em."

Dobbs was busy gulping his whiskey, so he didn't notice how Burke pressed his lips tight against the glass so none of the liquid did more than wet his upper lip when he tipped it.

"You've got me wondering who took the horses." He set the glass down.

"Why do you think I would know?" Dobbs plunked down the bottle. "Do you know what I think, Hannigan?"

"I'm curious." He ran his finger around the rim of the glass.

"I think you play the good guy when it suits you, but you're as black as sin underneath." The sheriff knocked back another double shot. "I caught up with a few friends of mine the other day. One of them says he knows you."

His pulse kicked up a notch. He didn't let

it show. "Cheever?"

"Guess I know why you didn't shoot him that day in the street." Dobbs knocked back another shot, emptying the glass. "It ain't nice to shoot a friend."

"True." His mouth soured as time rolled back. Memories he would rather stay forgotten surged into his thoughts, filling his head with images he could not stop and blotted out the present. The past came alive as the scent of the whiskey on the bar mixed with the scent from the bottle on the hot August evening. In the Cheever cabin, fifteen-year-old Burke had tossed his bedroll and mended satchel on the floor. Dust clouded upward and he coughed.

"This your friend?" Old Man Cheever reeked of cigar smoke and whiskey. He had a grizzled, unkempt appearance. His untrimmed mustache and beard gave him a wild look, or maybe that was the dead gleam in his eyes.

"Pa, this is Burke." Olly spat out a stream of tobacco juice on the floor. "He's the best shot I ever saw."

"That so? I hear you need a job, boy." When he grinned, four teeth were missing as if he'd taken a hard fist to the mouth. One tooth had a jagged, broken look to it. "I'll give you a dollar a day, the first month up front."

"Really?" He hadn't expected that. Thirty whole dollars. He stared in amazement as Olly's father reached into his pocket and pulled out a thick fold of paper money. He'd never seen so many greenbacks in his life.

"Hold out your hand." Mr. Cheever laid a twenty-dollar bill on it and a ten. "There you are. Thirty dollars. What kind of gun you got?"

"A long rifle. I picked it up for painting an old lady's house on my time off five weeks ago. I haven't had it long." He stared at the money. He was rich. And there was more to come. He could earn it. Think how that would improve his life. No more beatings. No more farmers who couldn't care less about him. "I could get better. I just need to practice more."

"Boy, you aren't seeing the larger picture here. No way am I letting you do security work with a gun that's no better than garbage. Here's a Winchester. Brandnew." Olly's pa shoved the fold of money into his shirt pocket and grabbed a rifle among many leaning against the wall by the open door. "This is yours."

"I can't afford it. Yet."

"It's my gift to you. Welcome to the gang." He tossed it over. "You hungry? Did you get something to eat?"

"Not enough." His stomach rumbled at the mention of food, but he couldn't take his eyes off the rifle. The black barrel was sleek and shiny, not a scratch on it. The stock was polished walnut and smooth as silk. He ran his hands over the gleaming wood and glossy steel. He'd never owned anything so nice.

"There's some rabbit stew and corn bread left from supper." Olly held out a plate. "Eat until you're full. There's plenty."

Burke had been hungry for so long. He'd been fed, but he hadn't been fed until he was full. The farmer had called second helpings an indulgence, but Burke figured the man and his wife were cheap. They didn't want to spend a penny more than they had to to feed him. Unable to let go of the rifle, he tucked it in the crook of his arm and grabbed the plate. On it was a thick chunk of buttered corn bread and a full bowl of steaming stew. His stomach growled and he ate standing up, shoveling spoonful after spoonful into his mouth.

"You've got a home now, boy," Old Man Cheever said. "You've got a place to belong. Don't you worry."

Burke swallowed hard, stopping the memory before it could carry him any further into the past to a place he could not bear to recall. He pushed away from the bar. "Cheever is my oldest friend. His old man gave me my first Winchester."

"So he told me." Dobbs hopped down from the stool, not bothering to pay. "He also said you went missing one night after a heist."

"Missing? Things went south, and I got left behind." Burke hopped off the stool, bitterness darkening him. "I was shot. Too injured to move."

"They thought you were dead." Dobbs pushed through the swinging doors into the blaring heat. Dust swirled in the air, stirred by a strong wind and traffic on the side street. "Imagine their surprise to see you alive with a tin star on your chest."

"A man's got to make a living." He could feel the sheriff's quandary. If he pushed too hard to make the man believe him, then it might backfire. He had to sound casual. "I spent a stretch of time in prison. They commuted the term when I convinced them I was reformed."

"God bless parole." Dobbs chuckled.

"I keep my nose clean most of the time." He shrugged as he took his time moseying down the boardwalk. "Now and then an opportunity comes along to help out an old friend or a new one."

"To think at one time I feared you might be too squeaky clean to be of any use. Glad I was wrong." Dobbs slapped him on the back.

Pain shot through his chest as his wounds protested. Burke covered his groan with a barking laugh. "Me, squeaky clean?"

"I thought you might be investigating me, boy." Dobbs appeared relaxed about that now. "I haven't been able to stop all the complaints against me. I know a man or two who wrote to the governor's office."

"There's a whiner in every crowd."

"You just gotta know how to silence 'em." Dobbs's gaze narrowed.

Burke's guts cinched. He figured the sheriff still had his suspicions, but at least he'd made a step in the right direction. A buttery blur on the boardwalk across the street caught his attention.

Lila. She handed over a small sack of flour out to her father, who was waiting on the wagon seat, with the wind swirling her skirts and trying to steal tendrils from her braids. The sunshine dimmed as she swiveled and saw him stopped in the middle of the boardwalk, with Dobbs patting his shoulder again.

"I'm gonna trust you, boy." The sheriff

growled. "If you cross me, I'll make you sorry you was ever born."

Burke nodded, his throat too tight to speak for Lila's face wreathed with confusion and emotions he was too far away to read, but he could feel.

Did she know he hated what he'd said to her father? Surely she could piece together that he was investigating Dobbs. And why was he upset about it? He had to let her go. He'd been able to fool himself yesterday thinking he could ignore the past, but today was a new day. The past was alive and littered with things no one could forgive.

"Looks like a storm's blowin' in." Dobbs marched on a few paces. "C'mon, boy. Don't go moonin' after that calico. She's out of your league."

He couldn't argue with that. He drank in one long last look before he strode away, knowing she watched him the whole length of the street.

CHAPTER ELEVEN

"Ian's grandmother is such a dear," Fiona McPherson stitched on the gingham tablecloth she was hemming. "I'm so glad she lives with us. She is a blessing to my life."

"A new husband, a new grandmother." Lila paused with her needle in midair. They were tucked on Scarlet's roomy porch where the wind rattled the leaves shading the Fisher family home on the quiet end of Third Street. "You finally have the family you deserve."

"I am blessed." Fiona sighed, the dear that she was, her dark curls framing her heart-shaped face. Her wedding ring glinted in the light. "These past months being married to Ian have been the happiest I've ever known."

"It shows." Kate smiled as she poked her needle through the fabric stretched across her embroidery hoop. "I'm praying each coming year of your marriage is more joyous than the last."

"Me, too," Ruby chimed in as she worked loose a knot in her thread. "You and Ian seem made for each other."

"A fairy tale come true," Earlee agreed as she pinned a section of a skirt she was cutting down for her sister. "Speaking of fairy-tale loves, has anyone heard from Meredith lately?"

"No," Lila admitted. "I got sidetracked and only finished a letter to her on my way here."

"I wonder what sidetracked her," Ruby said, not so innocently. "Or should I ask, who?"

"The handsome new deputy." Scarlet's crochet hook stilled. "I saw them driving through town together."

"Burke was helping me with my deliveries." Lila's face heated. She had to be shining like a strawberry, which made her remember how he'd handed her a berry when they had been at the river together. He'd practically fed it to her, and then his kiss . . . She blushed harder.

"Somehow I don't think he was only helping her." Ruby tossed a light blond braid over her shoulder, sweet as could be. "I think he was beauing her."

"Maybe there will be another engagement

soon," Earlee speculated. "First Fiona, then Meredith. Are you next, Lila?"

"Hardly, as my father has forbidden me to see Burke." There was more, but she wasn't ready to talk about it or to dim their merry gathering with unhappy talk.

"Burke, is it?" Fiona plucked a pin from her work and dropped it into her pin box. Her needle flashed as she worked. "You and the deputy are on a first-name basis. That's a good sign. You're being awfully quiet, Kate."

"I've got my floss in a twist." Kate bent over her hoop, fiddling with the beautiful blue floss.

"Does anyone else notice how red Lila is turning?" Earlee squinted as she threaded her needle.

"Why are you forbidden to see the deputy?" Ruby asked as she went back to stitching a patch on her father's work shirt. "Doesn't your pa approve of him?"

"Is it because he's older than you?" Scarlet stopped counting her stitches to ask.

Lila studied her friends' curious faces, all glowing with expectant happiness for her. They had the wrong idea, all but Kate. Worry dug fine crinkles into Kate's brow. Her friend would never admit it but she didn't approve of Burke. She knew how it looked. She was confused by his behavior, too.

"There's no engagement in our future." She may as well nip those hopes in the bud before her dear friends started planning an engagement party. "I only just met him and besides, he's not the settling-down type."

"That's what I think, too," Kate spoke up in her gentle, caring manner. Her shoulders relaxed a fraction, as if she had been more than worried. "I'm sure he's nice enough, but a man like that has a past."

"Ooh, it's like an adventure novel," Earlee spoke up, delighted. "The rugged, dangerous hero breezes into town and captures the heroine's heart."

"But then he rides out of town after all wrongs are righted," Lila finished. "I read the same stories."

"Because you lend me your books," Earlee quipped.

"Those kinds of stories don't end in marriage," Lila pointed out, quite practically. No one might guess how much it hurt to admit. When he was gone, the tenderness of his embrace and the beauty of his kiss would stay with her always. "I'm not in love with him and I won't fall in love with him. We're just friends."

"That's how it started with Ian and me,"

Fiona pointed out sweetly.

"And remember Meredith and Shane?" Earlee added. "Do you see a pattern, Lila?"

"I see a bunch of romantics on this porch." She rolled her eyes and went back to basting the tucks in the waistband of the calico apron she was sewing. Another item for her hope chest, which was getting quite full. She noticed Kate hadn't said anything more but had bent her head over her work. "Kate and I spotted Lorenzo in town yesterday."

"Lorenzo." Scarlet sighed. "I've caught brief glimpses of him in church this summer, but that's all. How is he going to fall in love with me if he never gets the chance to see me?"

"Or me?" Kate joined the conversation quietly.

"I know he's not about to fall for me." Ruby sighed, too. "I don't think he even knows my name."

"You might be surprised," Lila spoke up, remembering catching Lorenzo Davis watching Ruby a while ago. "After all, someone has to end up with him. He'll get married eventually."

"Maybe when he has stopped pining for Fiona," Scarlet speculated. "Fiona, you broke his heart."

"I didn't mean to. I was never interested

in him. I was never interested in anyone." She laughed, a musical happy sound, proof that her life had transformed from sadness to joy. "Remember how I wasn't going to marry anyone? I was going to move far away so I would never have to see my parents again."

"You didn't have to move so far to escape them, and we're glad." Lila reached out and covered Fiona's hand with her own. Understanding between all of them settled silently, a lifelong love of friendship that God had blessed them with. A blessing she would never take for granted.

"Who wants some lemonade?" Scarlet asked, setting down her crocheting. "I made sugar cookies to go along with it."

"Me!" Fiona and Kate called out.

"Me!" Earlee and Ruby chorused together.

"I'll help you," Lila offered and secured her needle in the pinned seam. At least the conversation had safely turned away from Burke. She hoped it would stay that way. With the secret memory of his kiss to smile over, she followed Scarlet into the house.

Something in the vicinity of his chest tugged hard, like a lasso tightening. Burke didn't have to turn down the street to know Lila was near. The sight of her captivated him, left him unable to think, much less breathe. She strolled along the boardwalk swinging a woven sewing basket. Carefree and lovely in a light yellow cotton gown, she was as breathtaking as a sun dawning. Her simple bonnet tied with a matching yellow ribbon hid most of her cinnamon-brown locks except for the unruly bouncy curls that framed the graceful curve of her face.

Softer emotions threatened him. He clamped his jaw. Maybe he would turn back around on his patrol so she wouldn't spot him. The taint of his past clung to him as he headed in the other direction past the feed store. It would be best to keep away from her. It would be doing her a kindness.

"You're not foolin' me one bit." A strapping man in a muslin shirt and denims pushed out of the store's front door. Devin Winters's hands fisted in what appeared to be anger. "I heard what you did to Arthur."

"I didn't do a thing." He planted his feet and resisted the urge to check over his shoulder to see if Lila was in hearing range. "You are misinformed."

"Hardly." Disdain soured Mr. Winters's face. "Arthur doesn't lie and he didn't beat himself in the head. You know that as well as I do."

"I was merely making on observation is all." The back of his neck tingled. That always happened when Lila was near. Her presence tugged at his soul in a way he could not deny. He swallowed hard and faced the shopkeeper. "Have you had any problems lately? Anything stolen? Is there something I can help you with?"

"Nothing I would want to talk to you about. If my wagon needs a repaired spoke or my horse throws a shoe, I'll give a holler." Scorn laced his words as he turned and went back into his shop.

Burke hardly noticed. Horses and their drivers, teamsters and their wagons and pedestrians on the boardwalks hurried by, yet he saw nothing but Lila. Her skirt snapped with her gait. The low melody of her voice rose and fell as she talked quietly with her friend. Above all the noises on the street, hers was the only thing he could hear, the only sound that kept him riveted. Air stalled in his chest as he watched her tap along the opposite boardwalk, growing smaller with distance.

Utter sweetness. Her kiss had been just as pure as she was. The memory of being with her and splashing together in the cool river refreshed his dusty soul. He wished he could call out her name, cross the street and have the pleasure of talking with her, the way a courting man would. But he could never court her. Love whispered through him and he kept his boots rooted to the planks of the boardwalk. He did not call out her name. He did not rush across the street.

Who knew a man like him could love anyone?

As though hearing his silent question, she chose that moment to glance over her shoulder. Time stood still. Nothing moved and no one else existed but the two of them. Their gazes caught and held. Wholesome longing filled him up. Was she feeling this, too?

She broke away before he could tell. She swirled down the street, swinging her basket and talking with her friend. Had nothing passed between them? He hung his head. The pain burrowing into his chest was no longer a physical one.

"Those strawberries look too good to pass up." Cora Sims, the good customer that she was, set her full basket on the counter. "I must have at least a half quart."

"I'll let you pick your own." Lila gestured toward the counter. "Go on back and take which container you would like."

"Thank you kindly." Cora efficiently circled around the counter, probably used to doing so a dozen or more times a day in her dress shop. "You wouldn't happen to know anyone looking for a job, would you?"

"Not outright." Lila opened the sales book, inked her pen and lifted the first item out of the top of Cora's basket. "I could ask my friends just to be sure. Why, do you know of an opening?"

"I plan on hiring a store manager to assist me when I get married next month." Cora chose one of the little buckets of strawberries and wove around to the front of the counter. In the back of the store, Eunice cleared her throat in protest and a bolt of fabric hit the cutting counter exceptionally hard. Cora gracefully pretended not to notice. "I want to start someone now to train them. Ideally, I would like to hire you, but I know that's impossible."

Across the store, the bolt of fabric hit the counter with another hard *thump, thump.*

"Can you imagine? My parents would forbid it." She tallied another purchase with a fast scratch of her pen. "I'm afraid I am in this store for life."

"As you ought to be," Cora agreed warmly. "But if you have a friend just like you, I would hire her in an instant. It comes

209

with generous pay and a room, as the renter in the upstairs apartment above my store just moved out. I still plan to work at the shop, just not long hours. I would give whoever I hired a lot of say in how she did her job."

"Sounds wonderful to me." Realizing she had spoken without thinking, Lila blushed. She wondered what Eunice would thump around on the counter next. "Will this be on your account?"

"Please." Cora waited politely while Lila wrapped up her purchases and handed over the pail of strawberries.

"Have a nice evening," she wished and followed Cora to the door. She opened it for her. Hot humid dusty air breezed in as Cora stepped out. Since it was the end of the business day, Lila cheerfully turned the lock and flipped the sign in the window around to Closed.

"What do you think you are up to, young lady?" Eunice's terse tone reverberated against the walls of the empty store. Her heels tapped a staccato rhythm, drawing closer. "You are not in charge of this store, Lila. You are given rules to follow for a reason."

"I know." She added Cora's total in her head, double-checked it and scribbled it down in the ledger.

"Then explain this," Eunice demanded.

A thick fold of fawn-colored fabric landed on the counter in front of her. The material she'd saved for Mrs. Olaff.

"How many times do I have to tell you? Every yardage of material that is cut has to be paid for immediately." Eunice held her hands out helplessly. "This is not your store, Lila, as much as you would like it to be. Which customer do we bill?"

"I will take care of it." She tore off a length of wrapping paper. "I will take it over to Mrs. Olaff this evening."

"And you will explain to her the policy again. That woman thinks she can have her way just because her husband is the super-intendent of the county schools. She is not above having to pay for her purchases."

"I was trying to do her a favor." She carefully wrapped the beautiful fabric and tied it with white string. Immediately, she regretted her words.

"Your allegiance must be to this business, Lila."

Help me to show compassion, Lord. She thought of all the kind things her step-mother did for Pa. She thought of how Eunice had taken charge of the household when she and Lark had struggled with it after Ma's passing. Eunice had straightened out the chaos the store had been in, for Pa had gone through a hard grieving period. No one was perfect, and Eunice gave the family her best.

The back door opened and boots strode in the hallway. Pa strode in, sweeping off his hat to fan himself, a little dusty from his afternoon on the country roads. "It was a relief to have the Pawal boy ride with me. He's a strapping kid. The two of us didn't have a lick of trouble."

Time had passed so quickly. She was no longer the little girl helping her mother in the store, just as she was no longer the schoolgirl helping out after school.

Pa stopped in his tracks. "Is something wrong?"

"No, I was just apologizing for making a mistake." Lila plucked the package from the counter. "Eunice, I won't go against your rules again."

"Thank you." Eunice lifted her chin with great dignity. "Supper will be on the table in one hour. Don't be late."

"I won't." Lila unlocked the door and bolted outside. Pa didn't look upset as he scratched his head, bumped into his stitches and winced. She watched him for a moment through the glass. His swollen lip had gone down, but his black eye had become a sickly swirl of yellow and green. He had asked her to get along with Eunice long ago and it was a promise she must keep somehow. Lost in thought, she turned around and nearly crashed into someone walking by.

"Lila?" A familiar deep-noted voice rose with surprise. "Are you all right?"

"Sure, but I would be better off looking where I was going." She took a step and watched Burke hesitate before his confident stride slowed to match hers. She thought of how he had treated her father. It hurt that he hadn't made things right.

"I see you have a last-minute delivery." He gestured toward the thick fold of material clutched in the crook of her arm.

"Oh, the package." She had forgotten about it. Seeing him again jarred her. The kiss, the closeness and how he'd treated Pa. She felt awkward. "My work is never done. What about yours?"

"It's ongoing and never-ending, although my deputy shift is over and I'm headed home." He stood straight and strong, his wounds all but forgotten.

Pure stubborn male will, she suspected. "Home? Isn't the boardinghouse temporary?"

"My room, then." He shrugged. "I haven't

had a permanent home for a long time."

She shouldn't be talking with Burke. Too late she remembered her father's ultimatum. How did she tell Burke about it? They reached the end of the block and stepped onto the cross street together. Plumes of dust kicked up beneath their shoes. "What about Miota Hollow? The newspaper said you were from there."

"Part of my cover story. I'm from a little town east of the Montana and Dakota border." He walked along like a perfect gentleman in a leather vest, crisp white shirt and black trousers. He appeared nothing like the renegade who had guarded her on her delivery route. Nothing like the man who had kissed her with infinite tenderness. This Burke could have been a polite stranger. His tone dropped, so that only she could hear his admission. "I call Helena home, for the little time I spend there. I keep a room in a boardinghouse to come back to."

"Another rented room?"

"I told you. I don't let anything tie me down. Even a rented room is a little too permanent for me." A note of sadness rang in his tone. For a moment, his casual manner slid away, revealing the man beneath.

She wondered about the sadness. What

would it be like to always roam from town to town and assignment to assignment? He formed friendships only to leave them. It had to be lonely.

Remembering her promise to her father, she put her sympathy for him aside and her caring. She could be casual, too. She could pretend there had been no kiss with this man who wanted no ties, this man who hadn't helped her father. She cleared her throat, hoping to sound breezy. "Today I'm a little envious of your no-ties philosophy."

"Why's that?" He sounded distant again, remote. Back to business.

They stepped onto the boardwalk together. She flicked a braid over her shoulder. "Eunice."

"Ah, the stepmother." Understanding softened the harsh edge of his voice. "That isn't a surprise."

"No. I'm sorry, but you will be receiving a bill in the mail."

"For the supplies I used over my stay at the store. I expected as much." He nodded in grim acceptance. "I guess I didn't need a letter of credit from another store and a job reference after all."

"You made such an impression, more than any letter could." Humor deepened the green and blue swirl of her eyes.

"I wonder if your stepmother would consider a new career," he quipped. "I could hire her to deal with the really scary outlaws."

"No banks in the territory would ever be robbed again." Her gentle retort made them laugh together, the merriment rising above the quieter sounds of the street. It was after five, most of the shops had closed up. The streets were nearly quiet. The boardwalk stretched two more blocks, empty except for a merchant far down at the end sweeping his part of the walk.

"I'm sorry for what I did to your father." He blurted out the apology on the dying wisps of her laughter. He fisted his hands in frustration and remorse. "I wanted to back up Dobbs. Make him see I had a dark side."

"Oh, that makes sense." The unhappiness returned. She sighed, clutching her package more tightly. "You really hurt Pa. He felt betrayed and humiliated."

"I know how that feels, and I hated doing it to Arthur." He refused to hang his head, but the past whispered reminders of the man he used to be. The man he would always be. Burke began to believe he could never escape it. That no amount of sacrifice and service would ever free him from his guilt or his penance.

"When this is all over and before I leave town, I'll explain everything to him. I'll apologize." He wanted her to know that he intended to do the right thing. "Arthur doesn't need to go through life thinking he deserved to be treated badly, after your family took me in."

"That would mean a lot." They had reached the block's end and she drew to a stop. "He thought well of you before. He talked highly of your wagon repairing skills."

"I've had a lot of practice. This isn't the first time I've come to town posing as a new deputy." He brushed an errant curl from her cheek. The warmth of the afternoon they'd spent together crept into his cold soul. He'd never known sweetness like her. "I need my badge back. I should have gotten it before now, but Dobbs has searched my room twice by my guess. I think it's safe to take it back."

"What if he searches you next?"

"Is that a bit of worry I hear?" His hand lingered against the satin of her ivory cheek and the silk of her hair. Soft feelings weakened him. He didn't want to love her, but he did. *Lord, help me.*

"Worry, oh, no. Curiosity, yes," she quipped.

"I don't believe you for a second." He

could read the truth in her eyes, the same truth he was trying to avoid. Feelings came into being, sometimes no matter how hard one tried to ward against them. His love for her wasn't something he could express or act on but it lived lasting and steadfast, the strongest emotion he had ever known. He swallowed hard, hoping his affection did not show. "I worry for you, which is why I need my badge back. It's why I can't see you anymore."

"And I can't see you." She laid her fingertips over his, gently increasing the contact of his hand against the gentle curve of her face. "Pa has forbidden it and I cannot go against it."

"I wish . . ." It was one sentence he could not complete. A roil of emotions too many to name twisted up inside him. He was not a free man or a redeemed man. If he was, then he would never leave her side. He could fight for her, provide for her, protect her in all ways. Commitment fired up in him all-consuming.

Help me to walk away from her. He did not have the strength on his own. He had to do what was right for her. He swallowed hard, taking a moment to cherish the soft fall of sunlight burnishing her hair and the brush of it against her cheek. Her green-blue gaze met his with the same tender feelings that rooted in his soul.

For one moment filled with longing, he saw the future he could not have with her. He envisioned their little house in town and coming home to her as his wife. Supper would be on the table and a cooing baby in a bassinet. He wanted it so sorely he could almost feel her arms wrapping around his neck tight to welcome him. His entire being yearned for the beautiful dream of a life spent with her.

A dream he could never have. The past choked him. It was time to part paths from her but he could not walk away. Not yet. Her soft rosebud lips softened slightly, as if she wished for another kiss. He wanted nothing more than the sweetness of brushing her lips with his, but he could not allow it. He could not stay on this perilous path. He had to get off it. He had to end it. He tilted her head gently and pressed a chaste kiss to her forehead.

Her disappointment rolled through him. He was disappointed, too. He hadn't meant to fall in love with her, but he was in control of his decisions. He would do the right thing.

"Leave the badge behind the stack of washtubs on your porch right before dark."

He gave her flyaway tendrils one final nudge so he could admire the color of her eyes one last time. "It's been nice knowing you, Lila."

"The honor has been entirely mine." She blinked hard and in that moment love blazed brightly in her gaze. For one precious moment it shone unmistakable. He wanted to watch forever, to feel the connection of being cared for, but it could not last. She tucked her feelings away and left, tapping down the side street with her package to deliver and taking the last of the sunshine with her.

CHAPTER TWELVE

It was right before nightfall. Dusk was made darker by the black storm clouds blotting out the stars and stretching as far as Lila could see out her bedroom window. Humid, uncomfortable heaving wind gusts exploded through the screen, scattering Lark's drawings as she lay on her stomach on her bed and ruffled the pages of the open book on the nightstand.

"Whatcha doing?" Lark asked, her pencil rasping against parchment.

"I think a storm is on its way." Distant lightning crackled along twisting cloud bellies, illuminating them with a purplish glow. "I need to bring in the bench cushions."

Lark mumbled something, her pencil darkening a portion of the page as she worked. Lila left her sister to her sketching, listened in the hallway for her parents' voices rumbling softly from the parlor as Eunice read something aloud to Pa, probably from the church magazine she was so fond of. Seizing the opportunity, she quietly opened the door and tiptoed down the stairs. The weight in her pocket pulled on her conscience as she padded through the dark, echoing store.

She'd had to speak to Burke to tell him goodbye. She had to speak to him to tell him she couldn't speak to him. Technically, that wasn't breaking her promise to Pa, but it felt wrong. She unlocked the back door, careful to open it slowly enough so the hinges would not squeak.

The instant she stepped outside, the muggy air closed around her like a damp blanket. She eased across the dark porch, groping. Her eyes took a moment to adjust to the inky darkness. Noises echoed eerily between buildings as she plucked the cushions from the bench and tossed them inside. She felt like a heroine in the new Range Rider novel she was reading, caught in the dark of night in an echoing alley with only shadows to guide her. She even felt watched, too, as if she weren't exactly alone.

Burke had dominated her thoughts all evening long. Having to end things with him distressed her. She missed him already. She missed knowing she could never laugh with him, walk down the street at his side or look forward to another wagon ride with him holding the reins.

I'm sure this is Your will, Father. Her prayer felt small against the angry stretch of the bruised sky above and the silence settling in the alley. *Please help direct my heart. I know I should not love him.*

A gust of wind knocked over something on Mrs. Grummel's porch. What sounded like a tin watering can rolled with uneven metallic thuds and then clunked to a stop. With the wind kicking up, a storm was definitely on its way. She knelt by the stacked washtubs. A strange shadowy flutter in the dark at the metal rim caught her attention. She reached behind the stack. Something was hidden there!

Sunflowers. She pulled the bouquet gingerly from behind the relative shelter of the tub. The wildflowers were furled up for the night, their delicate yellow petals the exact shade of her dress. Burke. Why had he done it? She reached quickly into her pocket and seized the badge. Out of the corner of her eye she saw a movement in the inky darkness.

Burke. She couldn't see him, but she knew. His presence changed the night, changed her. She tucked his badge where the flowers had been and straightened. Affection that no storm or hardship or ultimatum could diminish burned inside her. She could not stop it. Maybe nothing could. It wasn't smart and there was no way a relationship could work out between them, but she wished. She hoped.

Across the alley, a shadow parted from the others and took distinct shape. She recognized the assertive tilt of his Stetson, the mountain-wide shoulders, the strength in his tall muscular frame. It was too dark to distinguish his features but she could feel his kindness like a candle in the night, a single flame burning brightly. He raised one hand in both hello and goodbye, and she raised hers, too. The gulf between them was wide. The space between their hearts was not. Still feeling the faint tingle of his earlier kiss to her forehead, she walked backward to the door.

Precious seconds ticked by and she wished she could make time stop, but the wind gusted with a sudden icy chill. The sky overhead broke apart in a blinding flash of white-tailed lightning. Thunder crashed so loud it drowned out the sudden clamor of hailstones pummeling the ground.

He rejoined with the shadows. She backed through the door. They were apart again, but strangely not separated by heart at all.

Burke ducked out of the hail into the Steiner Saloon. As thunder cannoned overhead and ice stones hailed on the roof with a deafening clatter, he wove around empty tables and couldn't forget Lila. He tried to. She stayed front and center in his thoughts, the willowy shadow on the back porch clutching a spray of sunflowers. He knew she cared for him. He had felt the existence of her affection as surely as if she'd said the words aloud.

"What'll it be?" the barkeep asked, shining a tumbler with a hand towel. Dobbs had called him Roger. "Whiskey?"

"Not tonight." He sidled up to the bar and pulled out a stool. He wasn't a drinking man. "I came to talk to you."

"To me?" Roger's towel stilled. He carefully set the tumbler on the bar. The dim lamplight could not hide the tic in the bartender's jaw. "So now you're doing Dobbs's dirty work?"

Dirty work? Burke settled on the stool and leaned his forearms against the edge of the bar. "What if I were?"

"Tell him I don't have it all, but I can get it by the end of the week." Roger tossed his towel on the bar, distaste curling his upper lip. "No need to say it. I know Dobbs will be mad, but it's his own fault. I told him when he threatened me there wasn't a whole lot to spare. Wait right there."

"Threatened you?" How about that. He'd stumbled onto his best piece of hard evidence yet after two months of subtly asking questions around town. Burke shook his head. God never failed. God always led him exactly where he was meant to be. He glanced around the saloon, taking in the half dozen tables, beaten up chairs, the floor clean but scarred by cigarette butts, matches and one too many brawls. He'd been in many saloons like this over the years and the memories tortured him.

Lightning flashed, starkly illuminating the room around him with a brief blinding whiteness. Time reeled, taking him backward in time to the glare of the lantern shining in his face. Memory seized him and he was fifteen-years-old again.

"Here's where you sit lookout." Old Man Cheever blew out the wick, and the sudden change to blackness pressed upon Burke's eyes. "You protect us. That's all you gotta do, boy. Just follow Olly's lead."

"I'll show him the ropes, Pa." Olly spoke up with importance. Experience puffed up like pride in his voice. "Don't worry. We've got your back."

"That's my boy." He disappeared in the thousand shadows and shades of the night. When he spoke again, his voice came as if disembodied. "That's the sign. Rifles ready. Here she comes."

"Now the fun starts, Burke." Olly stretched out on the rocky high ground and dropped the pail of ammunition between them. "Get yourself a good view of the road below."

"I see it." Excitement quivered through him as he lay belly down. A rock jabbed his ribs and he swept it away, impatient to get his polished new rifle positioned. He lined up the site with the dark roadway below.

No one came or went. There was no sign of Mr. Cheever or his other employees. He wondered what they were moving that needed security. It was too late at night and there weren't enough men to move cattle. Maybe it was gold. This was mining country. Maybe Mr. Cheever had a lot of nuggets to move. That would explain why he was so secretive.

A faint drumming of hooves and the rattle of rigging rose above the sounds of the plains. Six horses broke into sight pulling a small stagecoach. Two men sat on the seat, one with the reins, the second with a rifle.

Thunder cracked in his ear. Burke jumped, realizing Olly had taken a shot. Adrenaline hammered through his blood, making his own gun shake. He watched with horror as the rifleman on the seat below slumped sideways and fell bonelessly off the side of the stage.

"You killed him!" Hoarse with terror, his words carried no more sound than a whisper. "You just . . . killed him."

"Looks like it." Olly beamed. "I hit him square in the chest. Pa'll be real proud of me."

Burke gulped. He hardly paid attention to the chaos below. On horseback Mr. Cheever rode firing at the driver.

"Take him down," Olly shouted in his ear. "I left him for you."

"I c-can't." He tossed the gun at his so-called friend, sick over the weapon he'd been fawning over not an hour earlier.

"You have to." Olly tossed it back. He picked up his Winchester long enough to site and fire. "Awww, winged him," he said, disappointed.

Range Riders who had been protecting the stage surged forward, their badges glinting faintly in the moonshine.

"Shoot, dummy!" Olly hollered. Peppering gunfire exploded through the night.

A peal of thunder rattled overhead, shaking the rafters, drawing Burke back to the present. He blinked, startled to realize he was sitting in the bar in Angel Falls.

"This is all I got." Roger slapped a thick envelope on the bar. "Tell that —" He paled. "Dobbs. What are you doin' here?"

"I came for my money and not a moment too soon." Dobbs took the closest stool. "Hannigan, you weren't helpin' yourself to what was mine, now were you, boy?"

"No, Roger thought I was working for you, and I guess I am." Burke swallowed hard, but the bitterness of the past remained thick on his tongue. At least Lila was out of his thoughts where she belonged, where he wanted.

Where she would remain.

Morning rain pattered on the boardwalks and puddled in the street to make mud. Lila lifted her skirts to the tops of her polished black shoes and crossed the intersection carefully. Her soles squished in the mud but not a drop landed on her pink calico. A horse splashed through the wet and muck.

"Lila," a familiar rumbling voice called out.

She knew who the rider was before he

spoke. She stepped safely onto the board-walk on the other side of the street and whirled. A Stetson shaded Burke's face. He sat astride a stunning black mustang. Sil-houetted against the dark sky and silver rain, he could have ridden right out of the story she'd been reading.

"I can't speak to you." She hated the distance between them. No smile softened his features, as if he hated it, too. "I'm sorry."

"Then we won't talk." Burke reined his horse over, swaying slightly in the saddle, his posture and command that of an ac-complished horseman. She didn't see how anyone could look at him and merely see a deputy. She saw nobility, honor, might. He could not hide who he was, not from her.

"Don't say a word," he orderly gently. "Ever since I decided to stay away from you, I keep running into you. This morning I saddled up to ride out of town and you are the first person I come across. It's either bad luck or Providence."

Providence, she decided. At least that was what she hoped.

"I'm following a couple leads on my day off." He glanced casually up and down the street. No one was out in the humid heat where the threat of lightning kept most folks close to home. "The sheriff is sleeping off his bender from last night, so I thought it was a good time."

She nodded, wishing she could speak. Seeing him strengthened the well of affection rising up within her. Burke leaned to lay his gloved hand tenderly against the curve of her face.

They needed no words. She could feel the love in his touch. Respectful and sincere, it traveled as if on a current from his heart to hers. Could he feel the same from her? Did he know? She wanted to hold back, she wanted to be sensible but her love for him overpowered reason. All she wanted, all she could ever want, was him.

It was not meant to be. She pressed her cheek against his palm. What if this was her only chance at true love? What if the one man who matched her soul was Burke? He would leave and take her only chance for happily-ever-after with him. And then what? She thought of all she would regret if she continued down this path. She thought of the rest of her life alone and unmarried, running the store with Eunice and how all she would have of Burke would be his memory.

Tears stung behind her eyes but did not fall. She wouldn't allow them to. Bourne away on emotion, she covered Burke's hand with both of hers and drew it to her lips. She kissed his knuckles, nerves needling at her boldness. Could he feel what she could not say?

"Me, too." His midnight eyes darkened to a stormy black, but tenderness shone in him as he bent his head to kiss her lips. No kiss could ever be more loving or respectful. She clung to him, wishing the moment could last forever. On tiptoe, she wrapped her arms around his neck and held on but she could not stop the moment from ending. She fell back on her heels, Burke straightened and his saddle creaked.

"I wish." The tenderness of his gaze deepened. A muscle jumped along his jawline. Regret lined his face as he tipped his hat to her. "I just wish."

The wind gusted, driving rain into her face and blurring her vision as he rode away, a lone rider dressed in black, outlined by the storm. She swiped at her eyes, the pesky rain, so full of pure love her ribs ached from the pressure against them.

Maybe there was a way, she thought. *Let there be a way,* she prayed.

"Lila!" a friendly voice called out, as dear as could be. Shoes drummed on the slick boardwalk. "Wait for me!"

"Earlee." She gave her face a final swipe drying away the last of the rain — not tears. She was too strong for that. She firmed her chin and genuine joy smiled through her at the sight of her friend hurrying closer. "What are you doing out in this weather? It's a long walk from your family's farm."

"Pa let me take Hilda." She gestured to the sway-backed, gray-muzzled mare hitched to a cart tethered in front of the druggist's storefront. That could only mean one thing.

"How is your ma?"

"It's a struggle for her." Earlee looked miserable, as if she hated being helpless to help her mother get well. "She is determined to hold on, and we're all glad to have her with us."

"I pray for her every night." Lila wrapped her friend in a comforting hug. When she stepped back, Burke was merely a small dark smudge against the long stretch of road. She missed him already. "Do you have some time or do you have to rush right back?"

"I have time and a list of errands to run." Earlee linked her arm in Lila's. "Where are you headed?"

"To the post office. I have the monthly bills to mail." She patted her skirt pockets.

"How about you?"

"I need to check the mail, too." Earlee's golden blond curls bounced as she walked. "I saw something interesting on the way here."

"You did? Ooh, tell me."

"I saw a friend of mine kissing this incredibly handsome deputy right in the middle of the street."

"Earlee!" Lila turned beet-red. "Were you watching?"

"I tried to look away, honest I did. But I couldn't believe my eyes. Does this mean he is courting you?"

"Burke?" she sputtered. "No. Definitely not. He's not exactly the marrying type."

"It looked like it to me." Earlee couldn't contain her delight. "He does have that dangerous thing about him. Dark, handsome, oozing charm. I see why you're in love with him."

"I'm not —" She led the way around the corner. The rain drove against them, making her squint. "Maybe it's time to confess it out loud. I am in love with him. Oh, Earlee, what am I going to do?"

"Maybe he loves you enough to change his mind about settling down. Never underestimate the power of love." She thought of her own dilemma and Finn's letter that kept haunting her mind, his goodbye she could not forget. "Deputy Hannigan seems like a nice guy. I know what folks are saying about him. I've heard the stories about your father and he's spending more time with the sheriff after hours."

"He's not like Dobbs. He's a good man," Lila insisted. Sincerity defined her, pinching her eyes and tensing her from head to toe. It was as if she could will it to be true.

"I know what it is like to see the good in a man others think are bad." She swallowed hard. Did she share her secret and her heartache? "You see the good in him."

"There is so much good. I'm certain of it." Conviction gave power to her words. "I can't say how I know, but I do. Eunice thinks he's a terrible man. Pa has forbidden me to talk with him. They won't understand and there is nothing I can do to make them."

"I know how you feel." She thought of Finn so far away, incarcerated and suffering. By his own fault, she knew, but it was hard not to remember the kind young man he'd once been. She cared for him. She did not want to, but she did. "I've been corresponding with someone my parents would not approve of if they knew."

"Corresponding?" Lila appeared shocked.

"I know nothing about this."

"I've kept it quiet. I'm not ready for everyone to know." She stopped beneath the land office's awning, where the slap of rain did not reach them. "There is a lot of good in the man, but I'm afraid all anyone would see is the bad and they wouldn't approve."

"It isn't as if you can tell your heart what to do." Understanding softened Lila's tone. "Even when you know it's impossible, your affections remain."

"Exactly." Earlee thought of Finn's life of labor and hardship. He was paying the price for his crime. It would be a shame if the laughing, good young man she'd once known died in that place. Maybe her letters would help to keep the goodness inside him alive.

A relationship between them would be impossible. He had a long sentence and he had never shown her anything beyond platonic respect, but her love for him could make a difference. Wasn't that what her faith taught? That love could give light to the darkest of places where even hope dared not grow? And where love could shine, then hope could follow.

She could hear the letter she intended to write to him unfolding in her head. She would tell him of funny stories from the

236

farm, because there were so many, tales meant to make him laugh. She could give Finn a reason to laugh and remember the man he used to be. It was the right thing to do.

"Isn't that Cora Sims's store?" Lila skidded to a halt in front of the town's nicest dress shop. "You wouldn't happen to be looking for a job, would you, Earlee?"

"I am, actually. I have a few applications for teaching jobs to mail. That's one reason I came to town." The fall was fast approaching. There would be harvest time on the farm, canning and preserving and the cellar to fill and then she intended to teach. Her family could desperately use the income. "I have my teacher's certificate, remember? Why do you ask?"

"I have to speak with Cora first, then I'll tell you. Come in out of the rain and wait while I do?" She phrased it as a question with a desperate silent plea.

"Sure. I love to look at all the pretty gowns she has on display," she agreed, thinking of the verse from Psalms her mother had read to her this morning, as she did every morning. *Wait on the Lord; be of good courage, and He shall strengthen your heart.*

It's true, she thought, God's timing was

impeccable. Her burden lightened, she trailed Lila into the store.

CHAPTER THIRTEEN

"Eunice, is Pa back from his deliveries yet?" Lila peeked around the storeroom door where her stepmother sat in a chair marking the new shipment of buttonhooks against the invoice tacked on a clipboard.

"No. He's a bit late and I'm worried." Eunice's chin went up. "I heard you practically give away the penny candy to the Worthington girls. They are a wealthy family. They can afford to pay."

"They are good customers and Meredith's sisters." The bell sang above the door in one soft note, as if someone had opened it gently.

"I don't care who they are." Eunice set down her pencil. "I do not want to have this discussion again."

"Fine." She'd been worrying over her decision all morning. The noon hour had been busy. A break in the rain had sent customers flocking into the store eager to get their shopping done without being rained on. She may as well ask the one question weighing on her mind while the store was quiet again. "Is there any chance you will ever pay me a wage?"

"A wage? Whatever do you need that for?" Eunice picked up her pencil and made a mark on her clipboard. "You have everything you need right here. Your father provides for you."

"Yes, but I am requesting a wage." She knew it was a losing battle, but she had to ask. She had grown up in this store. She did not want to leave. "Please. It would not have to be much."

"Your father relies on me to keep this store running at a profit." Eunice looked at her as if she'd sprouted two heads. "I can't imagine you would want to interfere with your father's income."

"No, I certainly would not." The bell jingled once and was still. A second customer? This was not the time to discuss the issue further.

"That's a good girl. Don't forget to keep the floor clean. Customers are dragging in all kinds of wet and mud." Eunice turned her back, absorbed in counting the merchandise.

This was the way it had to be, she realized.

The store echoed around her. No customers roamed the aisles or selected purchases off the shelves. Odd, considering she'd heard the door.

A bouquet of sunflowers lay on the front counter. Raindrops dampened their satiny pedals like dew. She ran a fingertip over one closed bud and smiled. A shadow fell across the window. Burke stood on the boardwalk, hands on his hips, boots braced powerfully. The impact of his dark blue stare speared through the glass and it was as if they stood side by side. She felt the brush of his kiss to her forehead, the comfort of his hand against her cheek.

Just one chance, she found herself praying. *Just one.*

Burke lifted his hand in a slow wave. She missed him even before he strode from her sight. The need to hear his voice tore through her with a terrifying power. She wanted to rip open the door and run after him. To be close enough to see the lighter blue flecks among the midnight-blue and the hint of a day's growth on his granite jaw. She wanted every minute she could find with him. Overwhelmed, she gripped the counter where his flowers lay, hurting so much she could not breathe.

The back door rasped open and Pa's voice

rumbled low in the hallway as he spoke with his wife. Lila curled her free hand around the green stems to give her courage.

"Was that the deputy I forbade you to see?" Pa asked, his tone low and ominously quiet. His footsteps stopped behind her.

"You said I couldn't *talk* with him." Lila clutched the flowers, drew her spine up straight and faced her father.

"It was what I meant, and you know that. Daughter, I am disappointed in you." Hurt pinched in the deep crinkles in his face. He looked smaller, more vulnerable than she'd ever seen him, even after the death of her mother.

"Please allow me to talk to him." She wished she could tell him why. "I want to see him."

"He brought you those flowers? He's courting you?" Pa looked horrified.

"No, not courting. He is more than a friend, less than a beau." She loved her father. She did not want to hurt him. "You were young once. Surely you can guess how I feel."

"He's a bad man, Lila. The way he treated me." He shook his head. Only the faintest wisps of color marked his eye. The thin scab on his lip was the only visual sign of the beating he'd suffered. His hat hid his stitches. "He's spending a lot of time with Dobbs. He's one of those charming men who are friendly until they have lured you in close or have no use for you. You need to stay away from him."

"I can no longer do that." The door from upstairs inched open and Lila saw her sister listening in, perhaps sensing what was to come. "I've been offered a job and I've decided to take it. It comes with lodgings, so I will be moving out, as well. This is my formal notice."

"You can't mean that. You can't walk out on your responsibilities here because of a disagreement over a man, a man who isn't good for you." Pa's jaw tensed. His color flushed. "Lila, you will not take that job."

"It's for the best," she insisted, although the move would not be easy. Eunice came out to see what was going on. Her stepmother looked as displeased as Pa. Lila had to be honest. "I'm not happy here. I love this store. I love you, Pa, and I respect everything you are trying to do here, Eunice, but our differences can't be solved. I hope you can understand in time."

"Lila, you can't go," Pa pleaded.

"It's time for me to move out. I'm not happy about it, either." She stopped to brush a kiss to his cheek. "If I don't do this now, then I'm afraid life is going to pass me by."

It was time to grow up. Her parents would understand eventually. She spun away, already going through her possessions and how best to pack them. On the stairs she stopped to give her sister a hug. "Now it's your turn."

"He's not the kind of man who will marry you," Eunice called out from the base of the stairs, her pronouncement echoing against the ceiling like thunder.

"He's not why I'm doing this."

She had always lived in these rooms. The parlor sat quiet, everything in its place. She remembered being a little girl running around the couch to show Ma the pretty bow she'd tied in her rag doll's hair. She could hear the echo of Lark's toddling footsteps and Ma's musical alto as she lavished praise and gave both daughter and doll a kiss on the cheek.

Nothing stayed the same. Life rolled forward inexorably like a wave in the ocean too mighty to stop. If she did not show courage now and seize this opportunity Cora had given her, there may not be another. She may spend her days wishing she'd had the courage to follow where God's wave would have taken her, sitting in the mercantile always wondering what if. If she was going to be the heroine of her own life, then she needed to make a change.

Fiona was married. Meredith was engaged and teaching school. Her friends had followed their dreams. Now it was her chance to live hers.

Burke strode out of the alley after a productive day. He'd left Lucky, his mustang, bedded down in a warm corner stall at the livery. With the evidence written down in his back pocket he had enough for a territorial judge to issue a warrant. All he had to do was telegraph his superiors in Helena. He whistled as he marched down the street. When he looked up, he couldn't believe his eyes.

Across the way, Lila struggled with a heavy crate in her arms. All thoughts of work flew right out of his head. He bolted out into the muddy street and the rain, which had returned with the thunderheads. "Hey, pretty lady. Where are you going with that box?"

"Wouldn't you like to know? It's good to see you." Sorrow dimmed the wattage of her smile. "Thank you for the flowers. Again."

"Do you know what they mean?" He took

the crate from her, surprised at how heavy it was. Her father should have given her the wagon if she had this large of a delivery. "Sunflowers always move to face the sun. That is what you do to me, heart and soul, make me move to face you."

The admission cost him, so he said nothing more. He studied her out of the corner of his eye, pretending he wasn't. He shouldn't be giving her flowers or carrying her delivery. He wanted to keep his distance, but he didn't like being apart from her. "Maybe next time I should go for something fancier."

"No, I rather like the sunflowers." She blushed shyly, a light pink color traced across her nose and cheeks.

In the silence between them, hope beat crazily in his chest. She turned down the cross street and he matched her pace, taking the outside edge of the boardwalk so she could walk beneath the shelter of the striped awnings and jutting roofs crowning each store front.

"You're speaking to me." He broke the stillness between them.

"Yes. My father isn't pleased, but as I no longer live under his roof he can't forbid me to." She watched him through the long curl of her lashes.

"Wait. You don't live above the store?" He skidded to a halt. "You moved out?"

"Moving." She pulled a key ring from her skirt pocket. "Here we are. Would you mind carrying that up for me? It's really heavy."

"Yes, as it is full of books." He caught the door she held open with his elbow, so she could slip up the stairs first. The enclosed landing made a tight turn and kept rising. Another door whispered open and he stood in a pleasant room with polished floorboards and white plastered walls. A green length of calico covered a sofa with neat tucks. A length of yellow cloth draped a round table at the other end, near to a small cookstove in the corner.

"Welcome to my home." She gestured toward a built-in row of shelves near the door. "The furniture came with the rooms and is worse for the wear, but I can spruce things up. I will have it cozy in no time."

"It already is." He set down the box. "Why did you move out?"

"I stayed at the mercantile because it was a family business. It was expected. But in truth, Eunice and I do not see eye to eye and we never will. It will always be her store to manage, since that's the way Pa wants it. It's her right as his wife." She knelt to fish a book out of the box and slip it onto a shelf.

"I've been staying there because it was easy, because I can still remember my mother in that store and because I was afraid to make a change. I would have to stand up to my parents, face their displeasure and be on my own."

"You aren't alone." He set a book on the shelf, his arm brushed hers. "You have family. You have friends. You have me."

"I know." She couldn't resist turning toward him. "I have been praying for God to fix my mundane life, and I wonder just how long He has being trying to do that. But would I budge off the fabric counter stool? And if I did, I didn't go far. I was the problem in my life. I can see that now. I was waiting for it to come to me. I think you might just be God's last ditch effort to get me to figure this all out."

"Me?" He chuckled, shaking his head. Shadows deepened around him like twilight. "I don't think God would use me for good."

"Too late." She knew the truth. "You stumbled in bleeding and almost dying. You were the answer to my prayers, although I'm sorry you were shot."

"Thanks, I think." Then he took the book from her hands and set it carelessly on the shelf. Moving in, moving closer, as ominous as the dark clouds visible through the window behind him.

"I wouldn't have discovered who I really was without you." She splayed her palm against his chest. The reliable thud of his heartbeat made her smile. Sturdy and stalwart, that beat. Just like the man.

"You give me too much credit." Sadness weighed in his voice, dropping it a note lower. "I'm a bad influence on you. Everyone says so."

"Eunice. My father, sure. But they don't know about the other badge you carry." She loved the man. She wished she could step back into denial where it was safe. Where as long as she didn't love him, she wouldn't get hurt. It was too late for safety. "Although you could be right. I quit my job. Moved out of my father's house. Who knows what I might do next."

"It's not a joke, Lila." Although the curves of his mouth threatened to hook upward. "They aren't wrong. If all goes well, I leave next week."

"So soon?" She swallowed hard to hide the wince of pain. It slashed through her like a saber. Maybe if she sat very still, the agony would stop.

"Yes. I have what I've come for." An apology marked his features. He could not mask his infinite caring. "I wish I could stay."

"I do, too." Her affections wobbled on the edge. She held on to them tightly, afraid of where they would take her. "You could stay now. For supper. I could fix something."

"No, let me. I will be right back." He cradled her chin in his hand. His face became stone, his gaze remote and he tore away from her with a grimace he could not hide. Sorrow cloaked him. "We have this time. Let's make the most of it."

His abiding strength shone through as he tipped his hat. He turned crisply, striding away like a Western hero straight out of her dreams. He was her dream, she realized. Everything she had ever wanted in a man, everything she prized, everything she loved.

She must not let her heart fall any further for him or she would never get it back. She listened to the door click shut and his boots ringing down the stairs, growing more distant until there was only silence.

What are you doing, Burke? he kept asking himself that question as he dogged down the boardwalk in the rain. The delicious scents from the meal the diner had packed up for him permeated the air, undeniable proof of what he was about to do. He was beauing Lila. He shouldn't be anywhere near her, but he was acting like a courting man.

I know I don't have that right, Lord. He wanted God to know he was perfectly clear on what he deserved and what he didn't. He wasn't making assumptions. His boots splashed through a puddle on a low place in the planks and he shifted the box he carried so he could see his way better. He'd been honest to Lila about having to leave, but he felt as if he were doing something wrong. That was usually a sure sign that he was.

He was being selfish. He wanted time with her. For once he wanted to know what it was like to be loved. It had been a lifetime since he'd felt accepted, since someone had looked at him as if he were somebody in their view. *Forgive me for wanting that, Father. I am not strong enough to stay away from her.*

Thunder grumbled, rumbling as if in answer. He wasn't a man who could forgive himself for that weakness. He wanted to see her gaze up at him with love quietly alight in her eyes. He wanted to walk into her rooms and feel as if his existence mattered to her. She chased away the loneliness which had trailed him since he was four. Being with her made the sorrow of the past twenty years vanish.

"I saw you from the window." The door swung open. Lila's skirts snapped in the fierce winds. "It's raining so hard, you're drenched. Hurry in."

"Another storm is on the way." He shook off what water he could like a dog, which made her laugh. He thought of the lucky man who would have the privilege of listening to her soft, musical laughter, the man who would be able to take her as his wife. Terrible jealousy rolled through him mixed with complete despair. He didn't dare ask God to let him be that man. They both knew it couldn't happen. The Lord would never allow it.

"That smells good. Did you go to Dolly's?" She led the way up the stairs, lithe and graceful. She spun at the landing and closed the upstairs door after him. Cool air blew through the windows and snapped white curtains. Rain beat on the roof with wet fury as he surrendered the food carton to her.

"She makes the best fried chicken." He managed to speak past the lump gathering like a fist behind his sternum. "I got something else, too."

"Let me see." She dug through the packaging and came up with a book. "Oh, you bought it! I was going to give you my copy after I was through."

"I figured this way we could read it together after supper."

"You have the best ideas, Deputy." The lamplight shining from the table's center revealed her completely. She felt open to him, unguarded spirit and emotions. He was vulnerable to her in a way that frightened.

No barriers stood between them. There was no past and no worries about the future. Nothing but the present moment with her gentle regard and his ardent devotion. He swallowed hard, taking a step forward. He could not stop. His future would be barren without her, but he would be satisfied with this moment to hold in his memory forever. He would always see her like this, polished by lamplight, wholesome beauty and calico innocence with raindrops drying on her long cinnamon-brown braids.

Lightning scored his eyes and flashed like gunpowder. Lila jumped, twisting toward the window where thunder boomed in answer, rattling the glass panes. The liquid hammering of the rain had changed tunes. Hail fell like snow and hit like steel.

"Let's eat in front of the window and watch the storm." She handed him a plate. "I love to watch the lightning."

"Whatever you want." He did not take the plate but unwrapped the bundle of fried chicken for her. "I'm happy as long as I'm with you."

"My feelings exactly." She filled her plate with chicken and buttermilk biscuits, hashed potatoes and buttery green beans. She left the thick wedges of cherry pie for later. "You aren't like the Rider in the books, are you? He has a woman fall in love with him in every town he rides into."

"I've never had a way with the ladies." He grabbed the other plate from the table and dropped two drumsticks on it. "Truth is, you're the only one I let close to me and that was because I was shot and bleeding. I was too weak to ward you off."

"Yes, I had you at a disadvantage. What was a man to do?"

"Exactly. I was unable to use my typical woman-repelling powers on you in my injured state."

"Your unconscious state, as you were asleep most of the time you stayed with us." She grabbed a cup of cool water and settled in front of the large window seat. The wind blowing in brought welcome coolness. The hail fell at a slant away from opened glass. "I'm not sure I believe you. Surely you have left a broken heart behind, at least a time or two."

"Never." He eased down beside her, sitting straight, his shoulders braced, his jaw set. "There has not been anyone but you. I've tried to stay away from you. I couldn't."

"I tried, too." She squeezed her eyes briefly shut. She did not want him to see how much his admission mattered to her, although she feared he already knew.

"I love you, Lila." No man in the world could be more gentle as Burke when his calloused hands cradled her jaw. He gazed at her with reverence she could not measure but her heart responded to.

Don't fall deeper, she told herself desperately trying to keep from being forever lost in his eyes and in his soul. But it was no use. He leaned in slow and deliberate. His mouth claimed hers with a kiss that became a wish. A wish for a future. A wish for forever. A wish their time together would not end. Her heart was no longer hers.

When she broke away, she was not the same woman she'd been. She was stronger, better. What she felt for Burke was an infinite devotion that words could not define.

"I love you, too," she whispered, the admission too small for the greatness she felt within.

He nodded, as if he understood, as if the greatness was within him, as well. He took her hands in his, linking their fingers, their hearts forever one. He bowed his head to begin the blessing. Perhaps Heaven leaned in a little closer to listen.

CHAPTER FOURTEEN

"Lila!" Lark sailed into Cora's shop with a chime of the over-the-door bell and exuberance. "It's strange to see you behind a different counter."

"It's strange to be here, but nice." Definitely nice. Her first morning at her new job had gone smoothly. Cora was a joy to work for and she'd been so pleased with Lila's performance that she'd left to run errands. Lila glanced at the only customer in the store who was industriously matching ribbons and buttons to a sample of delicate pink lawn and didn't yet look as if she required help.

Glad to have a few moments to chat with her sister, Lila skirted the counter, swished around a table displaying the newest velvets and wrapped Lark in a hug. "I've missed you."

"Are you terribly sure you like it here? Eunice is making me clean beneath the fish barrels." Lark wrinkled her nose.

"You said you wanted more responsibilities." Lila had a hard time letting go of her dear sister. "I've shared your pain, so I won't belittle it. Eunice can be a tough taskmaster."

"I think she misses you, too." Lark clasped her hands behind her back and studied a beautiful polonaise and poplin dress tailored with overskirts, tucks and imported lace.

"I'm sure she does miss how well I did all the cleaning," Lila quipped.

"Ma had to do it, so I will, too." Lark squared her little shoulders, petite and sweet and sparkling. "I came to see if you want to go to the bakery with me. It is your lunchtime yet?"

"Cora will be back in a few minutes. Wait here a moment, okay?" She caught her customer looking up. "Is there something I can get for you, Mrs. Fisher?"

"Yes, dear." Scarlet's mother, a stately woman dressed in the finest bonnet, tailored gown and imported slippers gestured to her in a kindly way. "I am ready with my choices. Cora has promised to have this frock finished for my daughter by week's end. You will remind her, won't you?"

"I'll be happy to, although I knew she was working on it this morning."

"Excellent."

She felt in her element among the pretty fabrics as she slid behind the display counter to write down the rest of Mrs. Fisher's order. "The mother-of-pearl buttons are a lovely choice. They match the silk ribbon perfectly. This will complement Stella's complexion."

"You are all growing up so quickly." Mrs. Fisher sighed, helpless to keep time from turning. "It was only yesterday you were all five years old, I'm sure of it."

"My pa says the same thing." She took the samples and double-checked them against what she'd written down. "Say hello to Scarlet for me."

"I will, dear."

"Have a nice day." She tucked the information into the top of the order book, where Cora would be sure to see it. The doorbell chimed, humid air breezed in and voices erupted on the boardwalk. Cora, back from her errands, chatted amicably with Mrs. Fisher.

"You look happy," Lark observed. "I'm glad you're here, even if I miss you."

"I'm glad, too, even if I miss you." She tweaked her little sister's nose. This felt right being reliant on herself, forging her own path through life. It seemed so much time had passed since she'd prayed for a little excitement, and God had answered her generously. There would be so much to learn here and so much to do. It would be a whole new adventure managing this pretty store.

"Whew, it's almost pleasant out there. Not too hot at all." Cora breezed in with an arm full of packages. "It's your turn, Lila. Be sure and take the entire hour."

She grabbed her reticule and led the way through the store. The clean windows sparkled, she'd washed them for Cora earlier in the morning, and something caught her eye. A tall, scarecrow-lean man rode a black horse through town. His wide-brimmed hat shaded his face. His clothes were nondescript, a brown shirt, black trousers and boots, but she'd seen him somewhere before. The back of her neck tingled at the memory.

"C'mon, Lark." Fear beat like a hummingbird's wings behind her ribs as she hauled her little sister onto the boardwalk. Shoppers littered the way ahead. Horses and wagons provided obstacles that hid the lone rider from sight. The sun glared in her eyes and reflected blindingly off store windows as she tugged Lark after her.

"Hey! Lila. The bakery is that way." Lark

pointed across the street.

"Hurry." She'd lost sight of the rider and horse. She perched on the street corner on tiptoe straining to see beyond Emmett Sims's teamster's wagon. Nothing. No sign of him. She'd lost him.

"What's wrong?" Lark's forehead furrowed. "You're completely pale."

"Come with me. Don't ask why. Just come." She squeezed her sister's hand in reassurance, checked for traffic, waved to Mr. Grummel driving by grumbling to his donkey and led the way across the street.

Last night's storm kept dust from the air and mud in the wagon ruts, which squished beneath her shoes. She smelled fried chicken from Dolly's Diner as she towed Lark down the intersecting street to the sheriff's office. What if Burke wasn't in? What if Dobbs was there alone?

She was strong enough to handle that man. She steeled her spine and forced her feet to carry her forward. The door was open to the breeze and angry voices rumbled inside.

"I don't care. I say it is your jurisdiction." Lorenzo Davis stabbed his forefinger with angry jabs in the sheriff's direction. "You are the only law around these parts. You had better do something."

"Don't tell me what to do, boy, unless you want to end up with more trouble." Dobbs laid his hand on the grip of his holstered Colt. "Is that what you want?"

"I want you to find whoever stole my cattle. One hundred head missing. My father shot in the leg. Fencing bashed and broken." Lorenzo swept off his hat and slapped it against the edge of Dobbs's desk. "My family pays taxes to this town and this county. I expect you to find my cattle."

"Ain't gonna happen." Dobbs stood. "What do you think, Hannigan?"

"I think you're looking for some sympathy, Davis. There's no proof your cattle are missing." Burke strolled into sight. His attention faltered when he spotted her. His eyes shielded and he laid his hand on his holstered gun, just as Dobbs did.

"Proof?" Lorenzo fumed, disdain for the men dripping in his voice. "Do you know what I think? You are behind the crimes happening around here, Sheriff. Deputy, you ought to be ashamed of yourself."

A muscle jumped in Burke's jaw, his only reaction as Lorenzo stalked off, hat in hand. Fury darkened his eyes and he looked mature, no longer the schoolboy she'd once had a crush on but like the powerful rancher he was always destined to be. He nodded at her. "Lila."

"Lorenzo." She stepped aside to let him pass. The sweetness of her crush on him had faded to nothing, because she knew now that's all she had ever felt for him. Admiration, an innocent adoration, but it had no depth or no potential for any. It was like a leaf blowing on a wind compared to the anchoring, iron effect Burke had on her as he approached.

"What a surprise to see you here. Hi, Lark," he added. "What are you two fine ladies doing in this end of town?"

"I don't know," Lark spoke up. "Lila wouldn't tell me as she dragged me here."

His chuckle was the music of her dreams. "I was just about to come look you up, Lila. Wondered if you wanted to spend another evening with me."

"Yes." She felt the sheriff's gaze, not exactly a curious or a comfortable one. Uneasy, she grabbed Burke by the wrist. "We were just about to go to the bakery. Come walk with us."

"I'll lock up, boy," Dobbs called out, not ashamed at listening in. "Go on with your gal. I've got things to do."

"Thanks, Dobbs." Burke joined her on the boardwalk. A gust of cool air ruffled her bangs bringing back memories of the evening spent in her sitting room. They had watched the storm roll in. A dazzling display of lightning snaked across a velvety black sky, accompanied by a symphony of thunder and hail. Afterward, they had sat in companionable silence curled up on the sofa, he at one end and she at the other reading.

Peace filled her at the memory. She laid her hand on his wide shoulder, went up on tiptoe and whispered what she had seen in his ear. His eyes went black. Tension hopped along his rocklike jaw. An emotion strangely like sorrow pulled at the corners of his hard mouth.

"I'll take care of it," he promised. He caressed curls away from her cheek, his touch light and unnecessary, but it was the connection he needed. She needed it, too. The power of his emotions coursed through her, a current with no end. His sadness touched her. She didn't know why.

"Keep a watch for him whenever you can. Take notes if you see him again. Maybe even if you see anything out of the ordinary. Would you report it to me?" His thumb grazed her chin. Tenderness mixed with the sadness. "I'm gonna have to turn down lunch with you."

"I understand." She laid a hand on his chest, one final connection to him, the man she loved, before she tugged Lark with her. They left him standing on the busy board-walk, a motionless shadow, a man alone.

Hold until the unit arrives on train tomorrow. Stop. The warrant had come through on the sheriff. Burke read the telegram in the shadow of Lucky's stall. His black gelding snorted, clamped his velvety lips around the bottom of the page and jerked.

"Sorry, this isn't for you, buddy." He leaned against the wall where cracks of sunlight filtered between the gaps of the boards and lit up the page. *Want to get Slim's gang also. Stop. Wait for instructions.*

"Looks like our time here is nearly done." Misery cut through him. He'd never minded moving on. The drifting nature of his work suited him. No ties, no loss, no permanence. He could go like the wind, never stopping too long to really think about what he couldn't have in life or how much he wanted it.

How much he wanted her. Lila. In all his wanderings he'd never met a woman who made him wish he could put down roots, tie up his heart and live a real life. To have a home, a wife to love, a family of his own.

All things he could lose. All things he could not keep.

It's a moot point, Hannigan. He scrubbed a patch of straw away with his boot, lit a match and set it to the folded telegram. The flame caught and licked greedy, devouring the paper. Lucky nickered in his throat, not fond of fire of any type, but he'd seen this before.

"Easy, boy," Burke assured him as he knelt, letting the embers of the page tumble onto the exposed earth. When the flame approached his finger, he let it fall. A few more moments and his orders were nothing but smoking ash. He ground it out well with his boot heel, made sure all embers were out and buried in the dirt.

Lucky snorted loudly in relief. He spotted Burke grab the currycomb and nodded his approval.

"Got to get you looking your best for our dinner with Lila." His time with her would be coming to an end. He grimaced, hating how much it hurt to think of leaving her. It was for the best. She didn't know his real story. She didn't know the man he'd been.

He fit his hand into the leather strap of the comb and began to brush Lucky's flank. The horse stilled, he stroked the metal teeth of the comb along the grain of the mustang's soft black coat. The past floated to the surface, memories he could no longer hold back.

"Shoot, dummy!" Olly hollered over the *crack, crack* of gunfire booming through the night. "Pa could get shot while you're being a big chicken."

"I'm no chicken." Horror unfolded below. A Range Rider rocked back in his saddle, blood blossoming on his shirt. The moonshine captured him perfectly as he collapsed backward onto his horse's rump, still firing. One of Cheever's men shouted in agony, a victim of that last bullet, before the powerful-looking man with a square jaw and integrity radiating from him tumbled off his horse and fell lifeless to the ground.

"Shoot, or else!" Old Man Cheever shouted his threat and raised the hairs on the back of Burke's neck, where the muzzle of a rifle pressed. "Shoot or I shoot you."

"I can't." He watched in horror as another Rider fell, badge glinting dully in the moonlight. He lay with eyes open in surprise, mouth twisted as if with determination, but the life had gone from him, slipped away in an act of cold-blooded violence.

Nausea twisted his stomach at the carnage below. The driver and his gunman, dead. Two of Cheever's men, dead. Three Range Riders, dead. Air chocked in his throat. Terror clawed wildly in his chest. Gunfire flashed in the draw below. There was one Rider left and Burke knew without asking what Olly's pa would make him do.

"Hold yer fire, boys!" The old man hollered to his men. "Let the kid make his first kill."

"No," Burke choked. Sickness bubbled in his stomach. The acrid taste of it soured his mouth. "I won't."

"You will." The barrel dug into the flesh behind his right ear and below his skull. "Pick up your gun. *Pick it up.*"

The hair on his scalp prickled and tried to stand straight up. He'd never heard a threat like that, so menacing and terrifying. His hands shook. He picked up the polished, brand-new Winchester. It felt cold in his hands.

"Take aim." The gun boring into the flesh between his neck and skull gouged deeper. "It's you or him, boy. You decide. Now, *aim.*"

Burke swallowed hard. He didn't want to die. Numbness crept through him until his finger couldn't feel the trigger. His sight blurred as he lined up the shot with the lawman's chest. The Rider took advantage of the cease-fire and, caught without cover, turned to face him with gun raised. He didn't fire.

"Don't do it, son." A warm, steady voice. A plea in calm eyes. "I can help you."

"There's no hope for this pup." The old man laughed. "No one is gonna help you but me, boy. Don't listen to a lawman's lies." He spat.

He knew Cheever was right. No one cared, no one would help him. He also knew that the outlaw wouldn't, either. He was alone, like always. He would always be alone. The hope for anything more was gone.

He couldn't shoot. His finger didn't move and he didn't want it to. Maybe he was going to die anyway, and he wasn't going to have to explain to God, if there was one, that his last act had been to gun down an innocent man.

"Shoot." The old man's hand closed over his in an instant. Fast as lightning, Cheever's forefinger pressed his against the trigger. There was no stopping the inevitable.

No! Burke's soul cried out in horror. In the fragment of the second it took the rifle to fire, he shifted the barrel hoping to miss the heart. The shot deafened him, the gun's butt kicked hard against his shoulder and the Rider fell.

"He's down!" one of the gang called out victoriously below. "Good job, kid."

Revulsion twisted through him. The Winchester tumbled from his hands. He never wanted to touch that rifle again. Vaguely he was aware of men stepping out from behind rocks and tree trunks, applauding before heaving open the coach's doors. Olly's pa stood up and stuffed a plug of chew into his cheek. "That wasn't so bad, was it, boy? You're a wanted man now. There ain't no goin' back. Decent folks won't want you near them. You are no good. You are a marked man."

The Rider he'd shot lay like a lump at the side of the road. He'd tried to miss his heart but it looked as if he'd failed. Shock rattled him. Disgusted at what he'd done, he rolled over on his side and retched. He'd taken a life. His soul bled, torn apart, and he swiped sweat from his face. Realized too late it was tears.

"You did good, Burke." Olly slapped him on the back. "I hesitated with the first one, too."

Old Man Cheever spat out a stream of tobacco juice. "The second one is easier."

It had been. Burke hung his head, the near decade-old rip in his soul smarting. Lucky reached around to dig his teeth in Burke's shirt.

"Sorry, buddy." He returned to grooming,

the rhythmic motion calming, but nothing had been able to erase the stain on his conscience. He'd been young, he'd been vulnerable and he'd been forced to do it. Every shot he'd taken with that Winchester had been with a rifle at his back or a gun pointed to a hostage's head, but he'd done it all the same. At the time he had believed Cheever was right. That no one would want him, there would never be a normal life for him. But now he wanted it, Heaven knew he did.

What was he doing beauing Lila? He knelt to curry down Lucky's front legs and belly. By not telling her about his past, it was as good as deceiving her.

I know what to do, Lord. He straightened and switched the comb for a brush. *I just don't want to do it. I don't want to end things with her, not yet.*

The horse in the neighboring stall nickered. Down the aisle another horse answered. He brushed Lucky's forelock and tail. It didn't matter what he wanted. It was time to do what was right.

When he was done, he gave Lucky a pat and set aside the brush. He wouldn't think about losing her. He wouldn't allow himself to imagine the loving light fading from her beautiful green-blue eyes when she looked at him. If he did, then he couldn't get through it. He'd chased felons through treacherous mountain passes in the dead of winter. He'd tracked soulless outlaws in the heat of summer through the badlands with no sleep and a single canteen of water. He'd been shot, dragged from a horse, survived fistfights, gang fights and his past, but he wasn't tough enough to face losing her.

One step at a time, Hannigan. He blew out a breath, grabbed Lucky's lead and guided him down the aisle. The oldest Dane brother didn't hurry looking up from his forge.

"Got the buggy in back," was all he said with a cold drip of disdain before jamming a horseshoe into the fire with a big pair of tongs.

While Burke hitched up Lucky, he kept his mind on his job. He'd done some good in this town. Because of what he'd tracked down on Dobbs, an innocent man in the territorial prison would go free and another would receive a lighter sentence. Roger, who had been threatened into giving part ownership of his bar to Dobbs, would no longer live in fear. Lila's father might get his wagon and horses returned. Lorenzo Davis might get some of his cattle back. There were more long-term wrongs that Burke wasn't able to track down the evidence for, but his boss was aware of them. Once Dobbs was indicted, more folks would feel safe enough to speak up.

He buckled the last of the rigging and hopped into the buggy. Lucky lifted his head, feeling the bit, his ears pricked and swiveling, eager for the command to go. When Burke released the brake and chirruped, the mustang stretched out into a snappy walk, glad to be out and about in the wind and sun. The sky was a clear robin's-egg blue, although white thunderheads gathered in the south. The last of yesterday's storm had evaporated from the streets as he reined Lucky down Second.

Jed Black, his fellow deputy just starting his evening shift, didn't tip his hat as he patrolled the boardwalk. Their friendship had been strained recently. Burke tried not to let that bother him as he adjusted his hat to cut the sun, but it did. It always did. One would think he had been on the outside looking in for so long, he would get used to it. He hadn't.

He drove past the feed store. Devin Winters was out sweeping in front of his shop. The shopkeeper took one hand off his broom to shake his fist in anger. There was no mistaking the contempt on the man's face. No doubt the story about Lorenzo's experience in the sheriff's office had gotten around town by now, another story added onto the others. To them he was showing himself to be a bad seed, just like the sheriff, and they weren't all that wrong. He tightened his grip on the reins, steeled his spine and prepared himself for what he had to do.

CHAPTER FIFTEEN

It was like being in one of her favorite novels, Lila decided as she turned the sign over in the front window. Her official first day as a store manager had successfully ended and her unofficial job as Burke's assistant was still going strong. She kept an eagle eye on the street as she grabbed the dry mop and began to clean the day's dust from the polished oak floor. The skirts of the nearby display rustled as she guided the mop beneath the table.

She noticed Scarlet's sage-green straw bonnet out of the dozen others crowning the heads of women hurrying about the last of their errands. She unlocked the door and swung it open just as Scarlet swirled to a stop beneath the shop's swinging sign.

"I had to come see!" She tugged at her bonnet ribbons as she waltzed in. "Ma said you were doing a spectacular job, and she's right. You look as if you belong here."

"I feel that way." She eased the door shut and whirled her mop into the corner. "No pickled herring barrel to clean. No Eunice. I can sew or read if all my other work is done between customers."

"That's nice." Scarlet gestured toward the small front counter, where a paperback novel sat, pages ruffled. "You look happy, Lila. I'm glad for you. You have no notion how much I've been praying for you."

"And I for you." Her dear, dear friend. What would she be without Scarlet and the rest of the gang? She had grown up with them as her closest friends and they were a big part of who she was. She was a better woman because of them. The Lord had blessed her greatly that first day in Sunday school when they had met as small children and again the day Meredith first came to school. And finally, when Ruby joined them. "There have been so many changes lately, it feels like ages since we were all together."

"I think we should meet in your new rooms for our next sewing circle gathering." Scarlet stopped to admire the display of rich velvets in a dozen different colors. "I have enough lace made for a hat. Ma was right about this fabric. It would be perfect for brim lining."

"You have a new project to start on and I

—" She glanced toward the window. A lone horse and driver pranced down the street, but it wasn't the bank robber. Her heart skipped because it was Burke.

"You're in love with him, aren't you? You don't have to say it. I can see that you are." Scarlet studied the ends of her bonnet's ribbons. "I think he's a bad man and I'm worried for you."

"He's not bad. He's a good man. One of the best." She watched the black mustang stride closer and then Burke on the buggy seat, holding the reins. Dressed in black, he appeared as dangerous as a bandit. A five-o'clock shadow darkened his angled jaw and his capable hands drew the horse to a stop at the hitching post. Dangerous, yes, but how could anyone not see the integrity radiating from him? "You don't know him as I do, but if you did I'm sure you would agree."

"Everyone has some good in them. That's not in question." Scarlet turned to watch Burke hop down from the seat. "It's a matter of the bad. I don't think a man like that is good for any girl."

Scarlet's heart-shaped face pinched in a perfect picture of loving concern. Her soft red locks floated with the hot puff of wind as she opened the door. "Don't be mad at me," she begged.

"I'm not. I love you, Scarlet." She was beginning to see what love really was. An action, not an ideal. A concern for others instead of one's self. Standing for what was right, regardless of how hard that may be.

Burke's boots tromped on the boards. Her soul turned to him. She was helpless to stop it. He walked in larger than life, her very own hero.

"I should go." Scarlet squeezed her arm gently as if in a plea. Her skirts rustled as she wove around Burke without saying hello to him. In time, she told herself, Scarlet would understand. One day everyone would know the Burke she esteemed.

"I'm almost done. Two more seconds." She gripped the mop, guided it along the far wall and back again. "There. Now I can go."

He didn't smile. The lines of his face were harsh and his midnight stare remote. Tension corded the tendons in his powerful neck.

"Is everything all right?" She stowed the mop in the little closet by the counter, withdrew her bonnet and closed the narrow door. "You look as if you had a difficult afternoon."

"Nothing I can't handle." His attempt to

smile failed.

She could feel his pain in the stillness. She thought of what Scarlet had said and what others had to believe about him. The story of Lorenzo's cattle had spread like wildfire through town.

"You don't have to handle it alone." She touched his shoulder. Beneath her fingertips, he was as strong as a mountain and felt just as distant. "You have me."

A tick pulsed along his whisker-rough jaw. His gaze pinched, poignant. He looked like a man waging an inner battle. As if he could not allow himself to believe her.

Trust me, she pleaded. She wanted to be what he needed, his shelter in a storm, a soft place to fall, a love he could always believe in.

"You undo me," he choked, wrapped a hand around her nape and drew her against his chest. There, she breathed in the soap scent of his clean shirt and savored the sweetness of his embrace.

Don't let this end, Lord. She squeezed her eyes shut, holding him tight, holding on with prayer. *Don't let me lose him. Let him love me enough to stay.*

Burke pressed a kiss to her forehead. His reserve evaporated and he held her tight for one revealing moment before he broke away.

"I have a picnic place picked out. Let me show you." He offered her his arm and she accepted it. Hearts beating in synchrony, they headed outside. She locked the door and they drove off in the buggy together.

Winds stirred the grasses in a rustling song as Burke reined Lucky to a stop. The mustang lifted his nose to smell the meadow full of nodding flowers, chirping birds and cool dappled shade from the orchard trees. The fragrance of ripening apples and plums mingled with the summery aromas of sun-warmed grasses and the first blackberries ripening in heaping falls over what used to be a livestock fence.

"The old Holbrook place." On the seat beside him, Lila bounded to her feet. The pale pink calico dress she wore, sprigged with pale blue and yellow flowers and adorned with silk ribbons, dainty lace and pearl buttons made her belong in this meadow dotted with small blue buds, yellow sunflowers and wild roses. "I haven't been here in ages."

"Did you know the family?" He hopped down and reached up to catch her. The sunlight bronzed her as he lifted her, dear in his arms, and set her gently on the ground. Her sweetness filled him and became a part of him.

"No one knows the family." Daisies waved at her ankles as she grabbed the rolled blanket beneath the wagon seat. "There were children about my age, but they never attended school. One day they moved away. Some folks said there was a tragedy. Another said financial hardship. But the property was never sold, no one came to tend it. It's sat here forgotten for as long as I can remember."

"A mystery." It was a mystery how he would ever end things. He hefted the basket and the jug while larks sang and a gopher popped out of his hole to watch them curiously. "You've been here before?"

"As kids, we would come to pick the fruit and eat the berries." She strolled among the wildflowers, her skirts fluttering in the breeze. "Scarlet would climb high into the trees to get the best fruit. She was fearless. Heights didn't scare her. I'm not sure if anything does. We would stand at the fence nibbling on apples or plums and dream about our lives to come."

"What did you dream?" He set down his load and took the blanket from her. Gave it a snap.

"Isn't that a little personal?"

"You're blushing." The edges of the blanket fluttered in the wind.

"I was thirteen." She caught one edge and they both walked backward, drew the blanket tight and lowered it to the ground. "And yes, I'm blushing."

"I'm curious. Now I have to know." The breeze tried stealing the edges of the blanket, but he anchored it with the jug of lemonade and a nearby rock before striding over to help Lila anchor her corners.

"Let's just say it involved a fairy-tale ending and leave it at that." She kept her foot on the blanket corner and stretched, trying to reach a rock.

"I hear those kind of endings are popular with you ladies." He hefted up the rock and set it in the appropriate corner. When he straightened, his shadow fell over her. She gazed up at him with tenderness.

Tenderness.

"Everyone deserves a happy ending." She searched him, as if she could look into his soul. No one had gotten closer in decades. Her caring felt as sustaining and as tangible to him as the sun blazing down.

"Not everyone." The words ripped past his constricted throat. Could she see the scars that had never healed? The wrongs he'd committed?

"Yes, everyone who believes in Him. *And*

we know that all things work together for good to those who love God." Her treasured answer proved she could not see into the darkest reaches, where his secrets lurked. Her love gentled him, shining in her eyes, smiling on her lips, whispering without words from her heart.

He wanted to believe. He wished for nothing more than to be able to slip off his past like a shirt he no longer wanted and simply let go. But the wrongs he'd done were a part of him, something he could not shed.

He wanted to be a part of her world, where goodness reigned and life could be wholesome and safe. Where wildflowers fluttered in a prairie breeze and dreams really could come true.

Not his dreams. He could not be in her life. Before he could gather the words, she spun away, taking his heart with her.

"I kept a close eye on the street," she said as she knelt to pluck a wild rose from its stem. "As close of an eye as I could while I worked. I may have missed a few things, but I still saw enough to make a list. Want to see it?"

"Sure." The word came out rough. The pressure in his throat increased. He tried to swallow but couldn't.

"I had the best time." With the rose in one

hand, she pulled a piece of parchment out of her pocket with the other and handed it to him. "I saw two different men wearing spurs. Spurs aren't common around here. Dobbs wears them, and a few other men in town, but I didn't recognize these men. I wrote down their descriptions as best I could."

"This is great, Lila. The Pinkertons should know about you." The details she'd scribbled down could have described a lot of men, but they also fit exactly two wanted men he knew rode with Slim's gang. One of them could have been Cheever. They must have been dressed to blend in with the ranchers and working folk, doing reconnaissance for a future job.

Not going to happen, he thought, remembering the telegram he'd burned. Tomorrow reinforcements would come, they would arrest Dobbs, round up Slim's gang and stop the violent crime plaguing this little corner of the territory.

"It was like being an adventure-novel heroine." She plucked a sunflower, the stem snapping crisply. "You must feel like this every day."

"Most days the work is mundane, but now and then a mission gives me a few high points." He tucked her note into his pocket.

"Meeting you has been one of them."

"Your eyes are sad."

"I suppose they are." All of him was sad, down to the soul. The flowers in her hand drew his attention. The sunflower's satin yellow petals opened to the light just as his heart was open to her. If she could see his sorrow, then she could see more. "Do you know how I feel about leaving?"

"I do. I'm going to miss you." Her words quivered, as if she were fighting emotion she did not want revealed.

To him, all was revealed. He swallowed hard against the lump rising higher, the tangle of emotions he did not dare feel. He was loved. Lila loved him. Her devotion shone through when she gazed up at him, looking at him as if he were somebody to her, somebody ten feet tall, her beginning and her end. He was her beloved, and she was his.

A dream he could not keep.

He could not dwell on the day to come when he would tie his belongings to the back of his saddle, ride Lucky away from town and never look back. If he stayed in this moment, if he made it last as long as possible then he could hold on to Lila.

"I fear this is our last evening together." She came into his arms just as he reached out to draw her closer. "That's why you seemed remote earlier. You were going to tell me tonight."

"Yes." His arms folded around her. "I just learned the news."

"We always knew you would go." She laid her cheek against his chest. The slight coarseness of his muslin shirt felt comforting. "You don't form any lasting ties."

"I'm not a settling-down kind of man."

"That is too bad." She fought the grief threatening to consume her. If she kept her tone light, he would never know how deeply she'd fallen for him. She'd tumbled so far there was no coming back. "If you were that kind of man, then we could have stayed in touch. Exchanged letters. Formed a long-distance friendship."

"That would have been nice." His muscles tensed. Tendons corded. His voice sounded strained. "It would be better for me if we ended things the way they are. Then what we feel right now can be a memory marred by nothing, the best one I've ever had."

"Or me." She squeezed her eyes shut, not ready to let this end. Tears balled in her throat but she wouldn't let them rise.

Please don't go, she silently pleaded, *don't let this end.* As if he felt the same, he clung to her. She listened to the drum of his heart, thudding in time with hers, and felt the rise and fall of his chest, as they breathed in the same rhythm. They were so similar, and like harmony and melody they were not quite complete unless they were together.

Burke stiffened a second before she heard the crackle of a boot in the grass and the metallic click of a Colt's hammer cocking. She realized the birds had silenced, the gopher had disappeared. The back of her neck tingled and iciness snaked down her spine.

"You are going to have to excuse us for interrupting, missy." Dobbs. His sardonic, mean-edged tone made her knees weaken. "We are in need of your beau."

"Why do you have a gun drawn on me?" Burke's noble baritone held no hint of fear. "What's up, Sheriff? Is there some kind of trouble?"

"It turns out there is."

Dobbs wasn't alone. She recognized the squat little man with the bar mustache she'd described in her paper to Burke. His rifle was aimed directly at her.

She gulped. She'd never looked down the barrel of a Winchester before. Little stars danced before her eyes. A loud drum rushed in her ears like a freight train heading her way and drowned out Burke's words. She felt the vibration in his chest as he spoke, about what she did not know.

Another man stood behind the cover of the buggy, his long-nosed .45 drawn, gleaming in the sun. She didn't recognize him. He was brawny, unshaven, his stubble as black as the unkempt fall of his hair. He wore a red bandana at his throat, a bright splash of color against his black clothes. His cold hard glare made her shiver. The man's gun pointed at Burke's back. Did Burke know? How did she tell him? His grip had tightened on her, so she couldn't move. His every muscle tensed like those of a bear ready to spring.

"It turns out the assistant clerk at the depot is a friend of mine." Dobbs crunched through the grasses, crushing daisies and sunflowers beneath his boots. "Lucky for me, old Harold didn't feel well and went home early or I never would have heard about your telegram."

"Then I guess we have a problem." Burke rolled her out of his grasp and drew with one smooth motion so fast it was a blur. The momentum sent her stumbling onto the ground. The flowers fell from her hand but not her belief in him.

The outlaws circling them responded. Hammers thumbed back, rifles ratcheted, gunmen took deliberate aim as Dobbs swung his arm a few inches in Lila's direction. "It's your call, Marshal. Do we shoot her now or will you put down your weapon?"

"Let her go." He kept his gun trained dead center on Dobbs's chest.

"Sorry, can't do it." The sheriff didn't answer. The voice came behind him, a voice straight out of his nightmares. "If I remember, Burke, you need incentive to make the right shots. Some things never change."

"Olly." He wasn't surprised. Kid Cheever had grown up, wide-shouldered, tall, rangy and he'd finally acquired his father's cold, dead eyes.

"I thought for sure I'd finished you off that day in town." Olly spat out a stream of juice, the plug of tobacco distorting one cheek. "You are a hard man to kill."

"You ought to know. You've tried twice. Twice you have left me to die in the street." He pushed aside the memories of the year spent in the gang, the arguments, his attempts to escape and then the hopelessness when he realized escaping wouldn't matter. He was a criminal, an outlaw, and what was done couldn't be forgotten. "You've been busy robbing trains and banks. What were you doing bothering with a delivery wagon and cattle?"

"Got to eat, and that bank job was a bust. There wasn't much in the tills and the vault was locked. We have to make a living somehow." Cheever cocked his gun and aimed it at Lila, who sat where she had fallen, her big green-blue eyes as round as saucers. Two guns were trained on her now. "It turns out I need a good sniper for my next job. What, didn't you tell the lady what you used to do?"

"Don't, Olly." Burke lowered his gun. He would rather be blasted away than to lose Lila this way. "Just let her go, and I'll do whatever you want."

"You'll do what I want anyhow." Greed and power glittered in soulless eyes. "There's a payroll I want to get my hands on, and tonight is the night."

"You don't want to do this." Burke didn't flinch when Cheever took the gun from his hand. Unarmed and defenseless he tried to think of how to stop the inevitable from happening.

"Sure I do." He laughed at that. "Your little lady doesn't know you were once the most hunted gunman in the Dakotas, does she? Or that last I checked you were still wanted for murder in Wyoming?"

No, please, no. Burke squeezed his eyes

shut for one long moment. He was a courageous man, but he lacked the bravery to face
her. He knew what he would see. Revulsion.
Disgust. Horror.

"Oh, guess I ruined the surprise." Cheever
spat again. "Dobbs, get her up and tie her
good. Burke, don't forget. Her life depends
on you."

He hung his head. She would hate him
for the lies. She would hate him for what
he'd been and because that part of him
would always be inside him. Everything that
mattered to him was lost. Surely this could
not be in God's plan, but he figured God
owed him nothing. God had guided him this
far but maybe no further. Perhaps finally all
accounts would be settled. God might be
through with him, and his impossible quest
for penance would be over.

Olly wasn't going to let him live. It was
Lila he had to save and that was the reason
why he held out his arms for one of Cheever's lackeys to tie his wrists.

CHAPTER SIXTEEN

Night had fallen hours ago, so it had to be near midnight. Lila watched the narrow patch of the sky. From her place on the floor of the buggy and the thick trees blocking the Heavens, she couldn't see much but she knew they were far west of town. The buggy bounced and jostled on sloping roads, unlike the relatively flat lanes on the prairie. The brief glimpse of a mountain peak, close enough to touch, confirmed her suspicions. They were far from Angel Falls, far from anywhere.

The outlaw's words kept spinning through her mind. *Your little lady doesn't know you were once the most hunted gunman in the Dakotas, does she? Or that last I checked you were still wanted for murder in Wyoming?*

Burke hadn't denied it. He'd stood with his powerful shoulders braced, his chin raised radiating integrity like the Range Rider she'd believed him to be. But a gunman? A murderer? No, she couldn't imagine it. Not the man who'd held her with infinite tenderness, who had treated her with immeasurable gentleness. She wouldn't believe it. The outlaw, the one Burke had called Olly, was lying.

"Here we are." Dobbs sawed back on the reins and the buggy rocked to a halt. The mustang's hooves pounded in protest in the dirt.

"Easy on the bit, Dobbs," Burke barked out, harsh and with authority like the tough lawman he was. "Don't hurt the horse."

"A bleeding heart. That's a weakness, boy." Dobbs kicked the brake, tossed down his reins and leather whispered in a strange sliding rasp. Lila couldn't guess the sound until she heard a handgun cock. Dobbs had drawn his weapon. "Even when you had me fooled, you couldn't stop helping folks. You gotta learn the way of the world and I'm about to give you a good lesson. People are only good for one thing, using to get what you want."

"Dobbs, take the gun off her. I've agreed to cooperate." Frustration punched in his words.

"Maybe you've got more lessons to learn. Such as you don't cross me." The threat hung in the sultry air.

What was happening? She couldn't see Burke. She couldn't see Dobbs, only the deep shadows of the dashboard. Bridles jangled, horses sidestepped and boots thudded on hard-packed ground. Before she could protest beefy hands wrapped around her forearms and hauled her out of the buggy. Her elbow rammed into the frame. Her knee struck the step. She fell on her knees to the ground. She couldn't see anything. The forest was too dark. She could not see the men who held her.

"Git up," a disembodied voice spat. "I want ter watch ya walk."

"She's got a real nice walk," another voice, edged with threat, said with a laugh.

Her stomach twisted. What was going to happen to her? The safety of town, of her family and friends was several hours' drive away. No one knew she was here.

"Leave her be." Burke's fury darkened his face and twisted his jaw, apparent even in the shadows. "You hurt her and nothing can make me help you. Nothing."

"There's always something that works." Enough scattered starlight filtered through the old-growth trees to faintly glow on the steel of the sheriff's .45. The muzzle nosed against Burke's temple. "Take him, boys."

Terror for Burke coursed through her.

Vaguely she realized she was being half dragged through the thick shadows of the trees toward an abandoned claim shanty. The moss-covered roof tilted at an angle, as if it were in the process of falling down. A hitching post in the far corner was not. Its thick round logs sank deep in the ground and rose taller than a man's head. The crossbar, waist-high, looked capable of holding the strongest ox.

Without warning, the men holding her let go. She was grateful for the release of their warm, clammy hands, but she hit the ground hard enough to rattle her teeth and knock the wind out of her. Pain slammed through ribs and she rolled to her side, trying to catch her breath. Her lungs gasped, her throat spasmed, tears swam in her eyes. Suddenly her lungs relaxed, she drew in air and swiped the dampness from her cheeks just in time to be dragged along the ground by her wrists and dropped in front of the hitching post.

She wasn't alone. Burke stood, back to the post, ankles apart, a chain gleaming in the darkness. Blood trickled from the corner of his mouth. His hat was gone, his shirt torn. He was hurt.

"Burke." His name escaped her lips, raw with fear for him and herself.

He didn't acknowledge her. Not a muscle flickered as he towered overhead, iron-strong and defiant and invincible. The man he'd called Olly tied his hands behind him and bound him to the pole.

"Your turn next." Olly's silky tenor held a note of darkness. She shivered as his finger-tips trailed the cut of her jaw and lingered on her vulnerable neck. "You are a pretty piece of calico."

"Cheever," Burke growled a warning that didn't sound at all like the tender man she'd fallen in love with. Menace grated in his tone.

As if hit, Olly removed his hand.

Roughly her wrists were bound behind her back and tied to the pole next to Burke's boots. Being tied up wasn't exactly comfort-able. The rope burned the delicate skin of her wrists and dug so tightly it felt as if her bones were about to break. Her shoulders screamed with agony.

Dizzy with discomfort, she drew in fresh air in deep gasps and listened to chains binding her to the post rattle and clink. She recognized the *snick* of a padlock closing. Burke stood above her, as silent at the pine pole they were bound to.

"Hope you're comfortable." Done bind-ing them, the outlaw rose. A sneer that was part amusement and part hatred twisted his shadowed face. He spat a spray of tobacco juice that landed in the darkness. "There was only one chain in the wagon we commandeered, but at least this way you can say your goodbyes to your lady friend. You have time. We ride in an hour."

That sounded terribly final. Lila leaned back, expecting to find the pole and found Burke's calf and knee instead. She looked up at him but saw only his shirt and the underside of his jaw, clenched so tight she could make out the delineation of tensed muscle, even in the near dark.

"I would much rather read about this kind of adventure," she whispered. The wind shifted and her stomach rumbled. "Is that beef I smell?"

"They're cooking supper over a spit. I can see the light," he whispered in return. "I'm guessing one of Lorenzo Davis's cattle."

Her eyes had begun to adjust to the heavy darkness. She saw an old well house not far away, a stable made of rough logs where one of Olly's lackeys was hitching Burke's horse with others, and Pa's unhitched delivery wagon. Faint shadows shifted behind a wooden corral. Probably what remained of Lorenzo's stolen livestock.

In the other direction, the ghostly dance

of firelight waxed and waned. The cookout must be on the other side of the shanty. Men's voices murmured, pots clanged, steel forks scraped on enamel plates. An argument broke out over the best piece of steak.

"I can't get us out of this." Burke's whisper came chocked with emotion. "They took my guns, my knives, even the one I keep in my boot."

"I left my guns and knives at home," she quipped. What was wrong with her? She was on the edge of hysteria. She closed her eyes and tried to stay calm. She had to think. There had to be a way out of this. The books she read always offered a solution.

"When they untie us, I want you to run," Burke's tone dropped below a whisper, barely audible as a cooling wind gusted. "Run and don't look back. No matter what, I will hold them off."

"With what? You are unarmed."

"I intend to improvise. Don't worry. I'm good at it."

"But what about you?"

"Me? I don't matter. Your freedom does." His voice broke, betraying a hint at the depth of his affection for her. An answering tenderness welled within her, sparkling pure.

"Can you reach one of my hairpins?" She

arched her neck toward his bound hands. "How about now?"

"What do you want with a hairpin?" His fingertips brushed the silken crown of her braided topknot.

"Just pull out one and try to drop it into my hands."

"I don't see the reason for it." He twisted as far as the bindings would allow. His spine popped. His ribs protested. His knuckles brushed against her textured braid. "It's not going to cut the rope or break the chain."

"Yes, but I read this in a book once." She tipped her head slightly.

"There." He had to concentrate to work the thin metal clip out of the thick braid. When it came loose, he managed to twist his neck just enough to see the curve of her shoulder and the back of her head. Her hands would be behind her, directly in line with her spine. He released the pin. "Here it goes."

"I didn't get it." She didn't sound perturbed. "So close. It just barely glanced off my fingertips."

"Try it again." While he worked, he kept his senses alert. The clatter at the fire pit grew louder. Everyone must be gathering around to eat, so the guards on them would be at a minimum. He couldn't see anyone watching in the dark, his eyes were still adjusting, but guards had to be somewhere. Neither Olly nor Dobbs would trust him alone, even unarmed and chained to a pole.

"Got it." Lila's whispered triumph was replaced by silence. He felt her inching closer to the post, closer to him. The chain binding the both of them drew tighter as she fought for more give. She went after the padlock.

C'mon, Lila. You can do it. He gritted his teeth as the chain threaded through his bindings shortened and the ropes cut flesh and clamped on bone. The pain was nothing, not when he thought about what would happen if she didn't get away. He'd seen it before. He lived with the Cheever gang for a year. He knew what ruthless men did to a female captive.

Regardless of any deal he struck, any bargain he made, Burke knew Lila would be beaten, raped and shot. He wouldn't be there to save her because they would have already put a bullet through his brain.

"Ooh, almost!" she muttered. The faint click of chain links might have been loud enough to carry, but the wind gusted again, hard enough to rattle the trees and send the boughs of the surrounding forest swishing and creaking. Cold air sang through the limbs, needles rustled and the faint starlight overhead eked out. Huge, scattered drops of rain plopped to the earth like popcorn popping.

Just a little more help, Father. Please. The sky was dark, as if Heaven no longer watched but he did not feel forsaken. A dark silhouette separated from the inky shadows. A guard patrolling the distance from the cluster of horses to the captives was getting closer.

The metallic snick told him she'd done it. She'd picked the lock. Adrenaline spilled into his bloodstream. The gunman was pacing closer, not hurried. He hadn't spotted Lila yet, but he soon would. The chain whispered as she snaked it out of the bindings holding one of his ankles to the post and a foot was free.

The shadow drew closer. He was a tall and skinny scarecrow and it could only be Slim, the head of the gang. Burke's pulse cannoned. Danger closed in only ten yards away. Nine. Eight.

Hurry, Lila. He willed her hands to go faster. He pulled at his wrists, but they were bound. He was helpless to move, helpless to protect her. Six yards. Five.

He felt the slither of the chain against his palm and his wrists came free from the post, but his hands were still bound. Slim carried his rifle, relaxed in the crook of his arm, rain dripping off the wide brim of his hat. Burke tensed, ready to move as the rope tugged and abraded his wrists as Lila worked at the knot. Three yards. Two.

"What the —" The outlaw's gaze dropped to where the woman ought to be. The rope slid free, Burke stepped forward on his free leg, grabbed the nose of the gun while Slim was too startled to move and rammed the flat of his palm directly on Slim's sternum. Without a word, the mighty outlaw crumpled and slid to the puddled ground. The tiniest splash was the only sign he'd been taken down.

"Is he . . . ?" Lila gasped. "Did you —"

"I don't know." He only knew the man was unconscious. Maybe he'd stopped Slim's heart, maybe not, but he'd stopped him. He ripped the chain from his ankle, scanned the perimeter and grasped Lila by the forearm. He pulled her hard against the side of the shanty where the shadows were the deepest.

He had a gun, so he had a fighting chance. He hauled her to the corner of the building, searching the foliage, ears peeled for the slightest footfall or the tiniest splash of a puddle. Nothing. The merriment around the campfire continued, talk turning to how they were going to spend the mill's payroll once they'd stolen it. Whiskey and women seemed the most popular choice.

"Run." He covered her while she dashed across open ground to the shelter of the well house. He followed her, walking backward, gun raised, finger on the trigger. The horses were feet away, tied loosely to a long rope anchored between trees. He chirruped and Lucky answered with a low nicker.

"So far so good." He swiped the rain sluicing down her forehead and into her eyes, just to have one last reason to touch her. He wished for moonlight to see her by. He wished for an eternity to love her through but it was not to be. At least he had the chance to know her and to love her. He was grateful for that. "Untie Lucky as quick and as quiet as you can. Can you ride bareback?"

"I've never ridden," she replied in her low, dulcet alto. "But I've read about characters who did. I can do it."

"Good." He covered her lips with his. One last kiss. Pure love blinded him. Pure devotion filled his soul. He released her, sure it was the last he would see of her. "The second you get on his back, you tell him to fly. You hold on, and you don't look back. No matter what. Do you promise?"

"Will you be right behind me?" Her voice trembled.

"Promise, Lila." He shook her gently. They had no time to waste. He didn't hear danger approaching but that could change in the blink of an eye. "You ride to town and find Jed. Tell him to wait for my boss. Now, go."

"But —"

"Go," he growled. "If you love me, do this."

"I love you. I do." She stumbled back, torn by what he asked, lost in the shadows. "I didn't believe what those men said about you. I know they lied. You are the best man, Burke."

"Go!" He sounded strangled, almost angry. Of course he was. Every moment she delayed put them both in more jeopardy, so she did as she promised.

She raced past the stable, slipped between the horses, untied Lucky and climbed awkwardly, slipping and sliding onto his back. With both hands full of black mane, she leaned against the horse's neck and whispered, "Fly."

The mustang snorted, gathered his muscles and leaped away from the others. She had no bridle to guide him, no saddle horn to grab. She squeezed with her knees just like she'd read about in so many Westerns and clung with all her might. His power glided beneath her and moved through her as he sailed across the yard. Surely Burke would grab one of the horses and follow.

But the rhythmic pounding of Lucky's hooves brought men running. The forest came alive. Gunfire echoed like cannons. Shouts rang and bodies thudded to the ground. The gunfire did not end. That's when she knew Burke wasn't coming. He'd never intended to do anything but defend her so she could escape.

How could he have done such a thing? She broke her promise and glanced over her shoulder. Burke pushed himself out of the mud and onto his knees with rifle raised. He must have been shot. He fired again and again before he tumbled backward, hit a second time.

"Stop!" she screamed but Lucky did not obey. He knew his duty and carried her far away into the night, where black clouds roiled across the endless sky and no outlaw rode out of the dark to chase her.

CHAPTER SEVENTEEN

He had hit the ground hard and feared he couldn't get back up. The first bullet had sliced through his side, grazing neat as a pin between two of his ribs. The second burrowed into his left shoulder. He'd heard bone crack and pain radiated everywhere. Up his neck, across his back and chest, down his arm which hung limp. He couldn't feel it. If he hadn't been able see his arm, he wouldn't know it was still there.

You have to get up, Hannigan. He was still breathing. As long as he lived, no one would charge down this road after Lila. His senses told him someone was untying some horses, a few men remained probably hunkered down behind a rock or a log making sure they were safe before venturing out. He'd lived and worked with criminals enough to know they put themselves first and wouldn't risk an unnecessary bullet wound unless they had to.

That gave him a few seconds to gather his strength and figure out a way to get off the ground. He clenched his jaw and heaved upward.

His body stayed flat in the mud. Wet and cold seeped through his shirt and trousers. Rain pelted his wounds and sluiced down his face. His gun became slick with rain, mud and blood beneath his grip.

He had two more bullets left. He'd taken down four men. That meant five were still alive and gunning for him. He didn't like those odds. It sounded like two were ready to mount up, which meant one thing. He was out of time. He had to stop them right now. *Lord, Lucky has a head start. Now give him wings.*

He exhaled so his shot would be steady, straightened his right arm, drew the rifle an inch to line up a shot with the road and squeezed. The first rider tumbled off his mount and hit the ground. Another shot stopped the second.

"I told you he was still alive, boys," Cheever bellowed. "Now stick your chicken necks out and cover me."

Rain blurred his vision. Weakness made his teeth chatter. He turned his gun toward the squish of boots in the muck, splashing closer in a slow measured step that told him his nemesis knew he was out of bullets.

Defenseless, he stared up at the Heavens, infinitely black and cold. At least Lila had a fighting chance of making it back to town. Even if Cheever's men mounted up, Lucky had too big of a head start. It was a good chance they couldn't catch up with him. That meant Lila was probably safe.

She's worth it, Lord. He gladly gave his life for hers. He coughed and felt a stream of blood rush warmly down his shirt. For the first time since he was fifteen, he was proud of his life and of what he stood for. He would die with love in his heart, not guilt and not emptiness. Love.

"Looks like we have a score to settle, Burke." Olly towered over him, gun in hand.

"Guess we do." He stared at the barrel of the .45 aimed at his heart. "I wouldn't have shot your pa if he hadn't shot me first."

"You got what you deserved then and you'll get it now. Only this time I'll make sure the job is done right. This time you will be good and dead." Olly spat a spray of tobacco juice, thumbed back the hammer and exhaled, ready to take his shot.

That summer so long ago rolled back to him, the scent of growing grass and sun-scented wind and daisies nodding lazily. Before Olly's betrayal, before a life of crime, before his soul had shattered. He could almost feel the boy he'd been, lost and lonely but innocent.

One last try, he pushed with all his strength. Surprised his body responded, he didn't move fast enough. The gun went off, but he grabbed it out of Olly's hands. Before his old friend could draw his holstered second shooter, he fired. He knew it wasn't a fatal wound, he wasn't trying for it. Light bled from his vision, sound from his ears and he hit the ground he could not feel. Darkness claimed him, cold and final. His last thought was of Lila and the first time he'd stumbled into her store and asked to buy a bandage. It was her beautiful face he saw and then there was no more.

He knew nothing for a long while. Pain invaded out of the darkness even when he could not reach consciousness and finally the pain vanished, too. In dream, he heard the rustle of wheat in a mild breeze. Ripening fields rolled around the shanty in every direction. The Dakota sky stretched blue overhead and puffy white clouds sailed through it. The warmth of summer wrapped around him as he pulled a blade of grass from its leafy sheath and popped the raw stem between his teeth. The green taste filled his mouth.

"What are you doing, son?" Pa looked up from hoeing Ma's garden, strong and healthy and whole, his easygoing grin wide.

"I'm lookin' at the cloud pictures." When he tipped his head again and held his hat to keep it from falling, he saw shapes just like his pa had taught him to look for. "It's a wagon!"

"Let me see." Pa came around to look and sidled up close. His big comforting hand settled on Burke's shoulder, engulfing it. "Yep, you're right, son. It's a covered wagon. Looks to me like it is heading west."

"And there's the horse that goes with it." Excited now, he poked his finger toward the sky. "But it's grazing. They must be done travelin' for the day."

"I wonder who they are and where they are goin'?" Pa swept off his hat to rake his hand through his hair.

"Rob, what about my garden?" Ma asked in her gentle, amused way. "Thistles are trying to take over my green beans."

"I see a thistle up in the clouds, too. Want me to weed it?" Pa quipped and everyone laughed.

Ginna came running from helping in the garden. She dusted the dry prairie dirt off her hands and brushed it from the corner of her apron.

"I see a little girl." Her braids bobbed as she tipped her head to study the entire sky. "I see a family stopping to camp for the night. A happy family."

Something warm brushed his jaw and settled on his forehead, a soothing comfort that drew him up out of his dream to surface. Before his eyes opened, pain invaded. He couldn't feel his arm or his shoulder, but everything else hurt. That had to be a good sign. It meant he was alive.

He clenched his jaw, grinding his teeth, to endure it. He did not want to sleep, not even to escape the agony. Gradually he became aware of a rocking movement, the incandescent glow of starlight and the faint flutter and snap of a skirt hem as the winds snatched at it. His eyelids fluttered knowing she was near. His Lila.

"You came." The words croaked out of his dry throat. "You disobeyed me."

"I'm difficult that way, ask Eunice." Humor polished her. She'd never been more beautiful. Gratitude stung his eyes. He'd never thought he would see her again. God had been kind to allow him to gaze upon her one last time.

"The doc says you are hurt pretty bad. You had to go and play the hero, didn't you?" She brushed at his hair, smoothing it out of his eyes, her touch infinitely caring. He heard what she did not say.

"Only a fool lets himself get shot at." Words that were too vulnerable caught in his throat, and he could not say them.

"Exactly. The day I met you, you had two bullet wounds. The day I say goodbye to you, you have three bullet wounds. I'm starting to think you are a dangerous man to be around."

"Finally." The smile cost him, and he couldn't hold it for long. He held up his hand for her to take. Her soft fingers fit between his, a perfect fit. Love brimmed over, leaving him defenseless. "I tried to tell you."

"Everybody did." Her fingers tightened around his in a single affectionate squeeze. "I didn't believe it for a moment."

"You should have." He wished he could sit up. All he could see was the patch of starry sky overhead beginning to gray. Dawn was not far away. "You should have believed it, because it is true."

"Hardly." She looked at him as if he'd hit his head, as if he were talking nonsense. "Just close your eyes. We should be in town before long."

Then he didn't have much time. The wagon bounced and jostled on country roads, making the wagon bed bite into his spine. He lifted his head a scant inch off the blanket he was lying on. It looked like Jed was driving. She must have rounded up half the town when she'd arrived back in Angel Falls. Ardent concern and unspoken affection polished her, made her more lovely than ever. He cleared his throat.

"I was an outlaw. When I was fifteen I rode with Cheever in his father's gang for a year. We robbed stages and banks, innocent folks and not-so-innocent folks. What Olly said was true." He nearly choked on the words. He wished he could erase that time from his memory. He wished he'd never picked up a gun. "I'm wanted for the murder of a deputy in Wyoming. I've committed crimes in the Dakotas, which I've never paid for."

He watched while she shook her head adamantly, fighting disbelief and denial. Her denial wouldn't last. His words would sink in and she would believe him. Her love would die, her regard for him vanish. What would his life be without her love? He was about to find out.

"But you are a Range Rider." Even in the thick dusk, he could see her feelings change. Distance settled between them like the leading edge of a storm. She sat up straighter, away from him, still in denial. "I saw your badge."

"Yes. We had a job go wrong. Olly's pa was furious at me because I refused to gun down anyone else. I'd been pushed too far. I was a kid, but I grew up. I finally learned how to have the courage to stand up to someone that terrifying and tell him I was out. He shot me. So I shot him. The gang left me to die." He could remember the chill of that cold December day when he'd been left for dead in the snow. "A unit of Riders from town got there just before I lost consciousness. I knew they recognized me. I knew I was looking at a hard prison sentence or worse."

"You murdered people?" She shook her head, as if dazed, as if she couldn't make the pieces fit.

"I tried to hurt them instead of kill them, but the one deputy died of his injury anyway." Remorse and guilt of the strongest kind battered him, greater than any physical pain. He would never forget opening his eyes that day and seeing the Rider towering over him, hands on his hips, starkly familiar. "One of the Riders was the first man I'd shot. I thought he'd died, but it turned out the bullet missed his heart and he lived. He remembered me. He saw what Old Man

Cheever did to me. He offered a deal and got the governor to agree. If I worked for them and made up for what I did, I would have the chance to earn clemency for my crimes in Montana."

Here is where she would say she despised him. She would turn away. Perhaps regret ever knowing him. He steeled his heart. He gathered his courage. He was man enough to face her rejection, although it would hurt.

"That explains why you are so good with a gun." The sorrow haunting her belied the attempt at humor. "Jed said it was incredible shooting you did."

"I tried my best." For her. All that mattered was her. That she would have a happy future. She deserved a good man to love her, children and a fairy-tale ending to her life. He would give anything to be that man.

Not in Your plan for me, I know, Lord. He swallowed hard, his confession done and his strength, too. *But I wish.*

"I never wanted you to know." His eyelids drifted shut, he couldn't keep them open. "But you needed the truth. The man you think I am doesn't exist."

"You are wrong, Marshal. In novels, the hero always has a past." Her fingers in his did not move away but remained strongly entwined. "I saw the man you are on the

315

day you stumbled into the mercantile shot and bleeding, on the day you drove the delivery wagon to keep me safe and last night when you took bullets for me."

"All flukes."

"Hardly." She straightened her spine, let the cool early-morning breeze buffet her face and the first rays of dawn brought illumination. "A character's true nature is revealed in the choices he makes through the book. I have seen yours."

"You saw me kill men right in front of your eyes." A muscle ticked along his clenched jaw, as if that tortured him. "You saw me being violent."

"I saw you being protective. We both know what those men would have done to me. You were the only thing stopping them." Her love for him renewed. It felt as fresh as the new day, as hopeful as the pearled light shining over the world.

"You were the one who picked the padlock holding us," he argued as if determined to be humble. "You could have escaped all on your own. I was unnecessary."

"Yes, well, you are a man," she quipped, too choked up to say what she really meant. Although his eyes were closed, he pressed his jaw against the curve of her palm and she knew he heard the symphony of love in her heart.

He did not speak again as unconsciousness claimed him. She sat at his side until the wagon rolled up to the depot. Jed, Dr. Frost, Mr. Winters and Pa carried him to the platform. The whistle could already be heard. She leaned against the edge of the depot building and watched as the train rumbled to a stop, a unit of Riders disembarked and that was the last she saw of the love of her life.

CHAPTER EIGHTEEN

"Whatcha doin', Earlee?"

"Nothing that would interest you." She tapped the excess ink off the pen on the side of the bottle. She'd left the bread dough to rise in two big bowls on the table beside her, covered with light cloths. The yeasty scent already made the kitchen end of the living room smell homey.

"I was hopin' you could come play fort with me." Edward folded his forearms against the table and leaned in. "Everyone's workin'. I'm bored."

"Enjoy it while you can. Next year you will be old enough to help with some of the farmwork." She set the pen on the paper and marked the date, August 30, 1884. "Tell you what. After I walk back from seeing my friends in town, I'll take you down to the creek."

"Honest?" That lit him up. "I sure do like the creek. I wanna watch the crawdads again. Can we have a picnic supper there? Oh, boy. I'm gonna go tell Ma!"

Edward's bare feet slapped across the floorboards. Already he was calling out to their mother, who was resting comfortably in the shady backyard.

She smiled as her brother leaped out the door, all little boy energy. The day ahead held so much promise. An afternoon spent with her best friends, supper by the cool shady creek and while the children played she would start penning her new story. She itched to get her idea down on paper and there was nothing more pleasant than sitting in the whispering grasses with the sounds of her family all around her while she imagined up a fictional adventure.

But first, her letter. With her pen loaded, she set it on the page to write.

Finn,
I know you are concerned for me and feel associating with you might not be in my best interests. I appreciate your concern. It tells me you are still the McKaslin boy I remember, kind to all, liked by everyone before you started spending time with people who weren't good for you. I am certain that part of you is still there, for good is never truly

lost. So you will simply have to endure my friendship, as I like to write letters and you are too far away to stop me.

She drew a smiling face so he knew she was smiling as she wrote. She chronicled the changes on the farm since she'd last written.

The fluffy yellow chicks have tripled in size and are gangling instead of cute, the way they used to be, but always funny. Pa built a summer enclosure for them to scratch in and chase after bugs. They dash around after a prize bug, so focused they run into the screen fencing and each other, bounce off and keep going. The baby calves have grown, too, adorable with their big brown eyes and curiosity. The kittens have taken over the barn, sliding down the remains of last harvest's haystacks like otters at play.

She added a few anecdotes from Edward's latest exploits and the news of the Range Riders in town and the sheriff's arrest. Lila's pa's horses and delivery wagon were returned. Some of Lorenzo's cattle were recovered. Several townspeople who'd been threatened and intimidated by Dobbs had come forward. Good news, all in all.

She signed the letter with a flourish, addressed the envelope and went to dig for her stash of pennies hidden in the room she shared with her sisters. She would stop by the post office on her way to Lila's. That way the letter could go out on the afternoon train.

"The bread is ready." Her sister Beatrice sailed into the shanty. "Don't worry, I'll get the dough kneaded and in the oven. You go have a great time with your friends."

"Thanks." She went in search of her Sunday calico and her shoes. Hopefulness filled her heart. Her and Finn's story wasn't over yet.

Lila waited for the dust from the teamster's wagon to clear before she stepped off the boardwalk and crossed the busy Friday afternoon street. It had been three weeks, almost four, since the sheriff's arrest. Dobbs had been replaced by Clint Kramer, who had been sheriff before he'd lost the rigged election. The Range Riders had hunted down the remnants of Slim and Olly's gang, two of which had fled when Cheevers had been shot and the others had been out setting up to rob the nearby logging company's considerable payroll. Peace and order had returned to Angel Falls. The only thing missing was the gigantic piece of her heart Burke had taken with him.

"Lila, how's the new job?"

She stepped up onto the boardwalk and glanced around. Recognizing the older man seated on a cart pulled by a donkey, she broke into a grin. "Perfectly, Mr. Grummel. How's Mrs. Grummel?"

"Wishing she didn't live next door to that stepmother of yours." He hollered over the clatter of another teamster's loaded wagon rumbling by. "Do you know what business is going in across the street? I heard the storefront was rented but not by who."

"I have no idea." Lila shifted the bakery box she carried to her other hand. "I didn't even know it was rented."

"These days everything changes." Mr. Grummel shook his head. "Nothing stays the same. People come, people go. Oy."

"Have a good afternoon!" She called before the donkey took him out of talking range. Mr. Grummel's hat tipped in answer and his cart rolled away.

She spun on her heels to face the mercantile. The harvest window display Eunice had set up was quite effective. Canning jars and lids, big kettles and drying screens, knives and peelers and a pretty assortment of kitchenware.

Her hand hesitated on the door handle. On the other side of the glass midway through the store she caught sight of her father. Eunice fussed with his hat, tugging as if at a stray thread, perhaps talking about the steps necessary to mend it, a look of adoration plain on her face. A look of contentment on his.

Lila turned the knob, the bell chimed and she crossed the threshold into the store.

"Lila!" Lark bolted out from behind the counter, arms wide and leaped into a quick hug. She rocked back on her heels, bursting with pleasure and flicked a braid behind her shoulders. "Lila, I'm doing real well taking your place. Eunice is letting me post all the sales to the accounts."

"Good job." The store looked the same, but different. Better, brighter and she could still picture her mother at the fabric counter, chatting with customers as she cheerfully measured out bolts of colorful fabrics.

"There's my girl." Pa came over, pride showing. "Cora Sims was just in telling us what fine work you are doing for her."

"Yes," Eunice agreed. "I told her it was the way you were raised. Hard work, lots of discipline. You've made yourself a fine reputation, Lila, but remember, you can come back anytime."

"Thank you." She was content with her decisions. She was her own woman. With a start, she remembered the time. "I'm in a rush. I need to pick up some berries for my sewing circle this afternoon."

"I'll get them." Eunice paraded over to the buckets of fresh blueberries and chose the nicest one.

"I'll put it on your account!" Lark rushed to pick up a pen and ink it.

"I've got deliveries to make," Pa said, giving her nose a tweak. "Don't forget to visit your old man more often."

"How about I come over for Sunday supper?"

"That would be just fine." Pa nodded, cleared his throat and ambled away.

"I'll make pot roast," Eunice decided, "and my sourdough biscuits you like so well."

"I'll forward to it." Lila took the pail of berries, waved goodbye and pushed out onto the street. She was late, late, late. Her friends would be arriving any minute.

As she hurried down the blocks and neared Cora's dress shop, a pretty little buggy pulled to a stop. She recognized the mare, Miss Bradshaw, being tied to the hitching post.

"It's Meredith!" Lila squealed as she spotted her dear friend, lifted her skirts with her free hand and raced in a very unladylike manner, weaving around perfectly innocent pedestrians on the boardwalk. Oh, how she'd missed her friend!

"Surprise!" The willowy blonde in a fashionable cotton print dress pushed away from the post and came running. The jaunty tilt of her hat brim flapped slightly with her gait as she flung her arms wide. "It's so *good* to see you!"

Lila set the box and pail on the bench outside the dress shop so her arms were free. They met in the middle of the boardwalk, hugged and hopped up and down in their excitement. They caught hold of hands, the way they used to do when they were little schoolgirls. "You look wonderful, Meredith. You're positively glowing."

"I'm happy." Joy lit her up, making her lovelier than ever. An engagement ring sparkled on her finger, a beautiful diamond and emerald setting which suited her perfectly. "I blame Shane for it. My happiness is entirely his fault."

"Is he still training your father's horses?"

"Yes. Pa is pleased with his work, and you know my mother. She can't stop fawning over poor Shane. I think he drives out to visit me on the weekends just to escape her flattery." Meredith laughed, her bliss contagious. "I don't see an engagement ring, so Burke hasn't returned to town to propose?"

"Pro-pose?" she sputtered at the notion. Her happiness at seeing her friend evaporated. The misery of losing Burke and the anguish of missing him through the past three, almost four weeks seized her again. In truth, she did not even know if he lived. She tried to smile, tried to keep her heartbreak hidden. "No, Burke was never serious about me. I told you that in my letters."

"Yes, but the heart follows its own path." Meredith gently squeezed Lila's hand, her understanding and support unshakable.

"Meredith! It's Meredith!" Fiona leaped from the wagon seat while it was still creeping up to the boardwalk, leaving her grandmother and her husband behind with a wave. The horses sped along again as she squealed up the step. "You came! You're really here!"

"I couldn't stay away. I missed you all so much!" Meredith laughed, and Lila did, too, as Fiona set down her sewing basket and caught them both. They circled into a three-person hug, skirts swishing together, arms tangling right along with their peals of laughter.

"Let me in!" Kate bounded up, dropped

her sewing basket and joined in the squealing and the hugging. "Meredith, this is the best surprise ever. Are you staying in town over the weekend?"

"Yes. I have to squeeze in all the time I can with my friends while I'm here. Letters are great, but they aren't the same as being here with you. Kate, what is going on with you? You haven't written me hardly at all."

"I have a letter right here. I finally got to town to mail it, but now you're here so you may as well take it with you." Kate pulled an envelope from her skirt pocket and her gaze landed on someone else hurrying up the boardwalk toward them.

Lila glanced over her shoulder. "Scarlet!"

"Ooh! I had hoped you would be here, Meredith!" Her red curls bounced as she set her sewing basket alongside the others. "I loved your last letter about all your little students. They are so funny."

"And fun. I love being a teacher, but I've missed my friends." Meredith reached out to bring Scarlet into the hugging circle. "My next job must not be so far away."

"It's fine to be your own woman," Lila spoke up, "but life is better when you are close to your friends."

"Exactly." They all harmonized, glad to be all together again.

"Hey, is there room for me?" A shy, soft-noted voice asked.

"Ruby." Lila let go of Meredith, breaking apart the circle to make a space. "There's always plenty of room for you."

"Always," everyone chimed.

Ruby flushed prettily, not used to so much attention, and joined them. She was such a pretty person no one noticed the careful patches on the elbows and skirt of her red calico dress. "And to think I almost didn't come. Meredith, I would have been terribly upset to have missed seeing you."

"Is there a problem at home?" Scarlet asked.

"Only of the wild animal kind. I've been run ragged trying to keep the jackrabbits out of the garden," Ruby explained with good humor. "If I don't keep an eye out, they are nibbling on my carrots. Pa took pity on me and agreed to pay the neighbor girl to chase away the bunnies while I'm gone."

Across the street, Lorenzo Davis caught the gentle sound, stopped in his tracks and turned toward them. His gaze landed on Ruby and only on Ruby. His wide shoulders straightened and his chiseled face became dreamy. No one else noticed, just Lila. She wondered if a romance between the two of them was in the future.

"We have rabbit problems, too!" Earlee squeezed into the circle, shaking Lila from her thoughts.

"Hey, you aren't even late," Fiona said in her gentle manner. "For once. I'm shocked."

"No one is more shocked than me." Earlee's gold curls glinted in the sunshine. "Lately I have been so busy with the house and the farm, I don't know if I'm coming or going."

"You should have been named 'Late' instead of 'Earlee,' " Kate quipped and they all laughed together, just like old times, like the schoolgirls they used to be.

So much in life changed. Little girls grew up, they became young ladies who found jobs, married or helped support their families. They were all finding their way in the world, but she knew the best things in life stayed the same. Their friendship was stitched together with the thread of love, a bond too strong to break.

"Come inside," she said. "I don't want to waste a single moment of our time together."

The sun brightened, as if even God agreed. They broke apart and gathered up their sewing baskets. Their merry chatter rose like lark song as Lila retrieved the cookies and blueberries and led the way.

"I don't think the doc was right." Jeremiah Kane pushed his chair away from his desk. The scrape of wooden chair legs against the oak floor echoed in the Helena office that headquartered the territorial Range Riders. Jeremiah rose to his impressive six foot plus height. "You aren't ready to come back, Hannigan. You can't use your arm."

"If I can stand, I can work." Burke leaned back in the corner chair, stretched out his legs and crossed them at the ankles. He wasn't intimidated one bit. "Sure, my arm is in a sling. It's not my shooting arm."

"That's not the point." Jeremiah cornered his desk, came to the front of it and leaned against it. He folded his arms over his chest, a casual stance, but there was nothing casual about his glare. "You push yourself too hard, Burke."

"I have a lot to make up for. What I did was wrong. I was coerced, I was forced, but I still did it." He was a man, unbowed, not that kid who had been frightened into submission. That didn't erase the past. The thing is, the past felt more distant, as if it truly were in the past. "You know it, Jeremiah. You were the first man I shot."

"You shot many, but you did your best to

wound, not kill. Not many outlaws take up that philosophy. That says something, too." He paused a moment. The front door swung open, voices rose and fell near the entrance, and the door closed again. They were alone. "I understand why you are driven, but maybe it's time to ask yourself one question. When is it enough? How do you know when you have paid your debt?"

"Never." The answer nearly choked him. He wanted it to be different, but wanting didn't make it so. Reality was reality and no amount of wishing could change it. How could he let go of what he'd done? "What I took can't be replaced. I caused harm. I took a life."

"That's true. But you've spent almost a decade stopping harm, stopping criminals." Jeremiah, tough as nails, boomed out the words as if with anger, but there was no true anger in them. "Think of all the harm you stopped from happening. The justice you helped to find for honest folks who were victimized. You saved countless lives by getting violent outlaws behind bars before they could hurt anyone else."

"It doesn't feel like enough." But he wanted it to be. He ached with the wish down to the marrow of his bones.

"It is. I've spoken with the governor and

you are officially pardoned. Your debt to this territory is paid in full." Jeremiah softened, a rare show of emotion. "Maybe it's time to forgive yourself. I have, the government has and I'm reckoning even God has."

He thought of Lila kneeling in the wagon at his side, coming back from Slim and Cheever's hideout. She'd hardly blinked an eye when he'd told her his story. He'd been so sure she would hate him, that she would never understand, that she would see what he saw in himself.

"You are no longer that scared kid. You were never like Cheever. You were a good kid in a bad situation, but you grew up and you rectified what you could of your mistakes. You've made a difference. No one could have done more." Jeremiah shoved off the desk. "It's time to let you go. It's been an honor serving with you."

"Go?" They were letting him off the hook, just like that?

"You are free to be whatever you want. A farmer, a shopkeeper, a railroad worker." Jeremiah held out his hand, palm up. "Son, I'm going to need your badge."

His badge. He pulled it off his shirt and ran his thumb over the raised shield. He traced the rifle and horse imbedded in the silver. Those symbols had come to mean protection and commitment and duty. The raised words above proudly proclaimed, Montana Territorial Range Rider.

It was his identity, all he had wanted to be as a boy. He could still remember the feel of the splintered fence against his palms as he stared between the boards in the orphanage yard, watching strong, impressive men ride by on their fine horses. The Range Riders had been briefly in that town, but the impression they'd made remained.

"I want to keep it." He couldn't give up this life he'd earned, the job God had led him to. Besides, he had nowhere to go, nothing else he wanted to be.

"I'm glad you feel that way." Jeremiah almost smiled, a rare show of mirth. "I hear from the boys you found yourself a pretty little calico in Angel Falls."

"I did." Lila's beautiful image washed into his mind like a cool splash of water on a hot July day. Her soft oval face, her cinnamon-brown hair, her green-and-blue eyes shimmering with love for him.

Have You forgiven me, Lord? The prayer rose up straight from his soul. *Are You really giving me a chance?*

"As it turns out, we are making a few changes around here." Jeremiah opened his top desk drawer and pulled out a shining new key. "The governor has decided he wants a branch in Angel Falls. The railroad has brought more population into that area and a lot of crime has followed. We need someone to run that office. Are you interested?"

CHAPTER NINETEEN

A new day's sunshine cheerfully sparkled on the windows of Cora's dress shop. Lila considered the display she'd just arranged, adjusted the angle of the darling straw bonnet and plumped the silk ribbon bow. There. The pretty, summery dress Cora had designed as a sample draped perfectly, surrounded by lovely coordinating accessories. That ought to have passersby stopping in their tracks to take a look.

Monday mornings were slow and Cora had said to take advantage of it. So Lila threaded her way around a table of reticules to the front counter, where a fresh sheet of parchment was waiting. She uncapped the bottle, inked her pen and bent to start her latest letter to Meredith.

I hope you are settled back in your schoolroom teaching your adorable students, all seven of them. We loved hearing about them when you were here. I know we miss you already. Things are good here. It's not exactly an adventure novel these days, but I'm enthusiastic about my life. God may be the One to set my path, but it is up to me to make it all it can be.

The musical chime above the door sang out a melody and let in the sounds of the street and the whistling arrival of the morning train several blocks over. Lila put down her pen and greeted her first customers of the day with a smile. "Good morning, Noelle. Matilda."

"Good morning," the cousins called in unison. Matilda with her dark curls and quiet manner led blind Noelle through the doorway.

"Are you looking for anything in particular?" Lila asked, capping her ink bottle.

"Matilda saw the bonnet in the window display and we were suddenly overcome with the need for new hats," Noelle explained happily. "How is your father, Lila? I meant to catch up with your family at church yesterday and ask about him, but my aunt got a hold of me."

"Pa is fine." Noelle's husband, Thad, had been the rancher who had found Pa after he'd been beaten and rushed him to town and rode for the doctor. "His black eye is gone, his nose is nearly healed. The blow to his head turned out not to be as serious as Dr. Frost first feared."

"Now that the outlaws are rounded up and arrested, he can make his deliveries without fear," Matilda added. "It was frightening for a while. Thank goodness the new deputy turned out to be a great help and we are all safe again."

"Yes," Lila agreed, ignoring the hammering blow of grief that struck hard at the mention of Burke. She didn't know if he'd survived his injuries, or if he was well or if he thought of her at all. He had made a great difference to this town and a lasting difference to her. Pride filled her, chasing away some of the sadness. "We have a new shipment of bonnets from back East. Come with me and I'll show you. I just set them out this morning."

"Perfect," Noelle said happily and with her hand on her cousin's arm wove through the store almost as if she could see.

The front door chimed again and Cora breezed in, looking joyful, as she always did these days. Her wedding was less than two weeks away. She was marrying a very handsome bounty hunter. "Noelle! Matilda! How wonderful to see you. Aren't those bonnets adorable?"

"I have to have one," Noelle answered her dear friend. Cora gave Lila a nod, as if to say she would handle the sale, and hurried over to chat with her friends about hats, the upcoming nuptials and Noelle's baby boy, Graham, who was home with his proud papa.

The door swooshed open with a jingle and a gust of dusty air. Tingles skidded down her nape and trickled along her spine. She turned toward the doorway and stared at the man with shoulders braced, boots planted, one arm in a sling. Dark brown unruly hair framed a face so rugged it could have been carved out of stone. The silver shield pinned to his white muslin shirt glinted in the morning sun.

No, it couldn't be. It was her imagination playing tricks on her. Wishful thinking conjuring up the image she cherished most. Her knees buckled and she grabbed the counter for support. She blinked, but he didn't disappear. The ring of his gait, the power of his stride, the love in his gaze made her see. He was no dream or image but a real, live, flesh-and-blood man striding through the shop toward her.

"Burke." She choked out his name. Tears

bunched in her throat. Joy dawned within her. The deep grief and the pain of missing him vanished. She gathered her skirts, dashing toward him, drinking in the sight of what she'd missed most. His handsome face, his physical strength and his mighty honor. Integrity radiated from him like the goodness of his heart. "You came back."

"To you." His chiseled mouth tugged up in the corners, softening the hard planes of his face. His midnight-blue eyes radiated a depth of caring that betrayed him. He held out his good arm in an invitation. "I came for you. Only for you."

"I lost hope." She stepped into his embrace and laid her cheek against his chest. "I thought I would never see you again."

"For a while there, I did, too. It took a while for me to heal." His jaw settled against the side of her head, a pleasant pressure that made her feel sheltered and safe. He was steely muscle and solid bone against her cheek, and she could feel his heart beating oddly fast and heavily, belying the calm he projected. "I couldn't stay away."

"I thought you were a lone wolf. A man who had no ties and liked it that way." She smiled into his shirt, holding him tight, so very tight.

"I don't want to go through life with nothing to show for it. Loving someone and being loved in return is the only real living there is." His voice smiled, layered with warmth and affection and conviction. His heartbeat slowed, one reliable thump at a time. "I was merely existing until I met you, Lila. Loving you changed me. A lot of things have changed."

"Like what?"

"I'm a free man. I've been granted clemency from the government. So I looked at God and where he seemed to be leading me and then I looked in my heart. Do you know what I found?"

"I'm breathless to know."

"My love for you. There is nothing but my love for you without condition and without end in my heart and in my soul." He breathed in her lilac scent and savored the silk of her hair against his jaw. She felt *right* in his arms, as if this moment was meant to be. Gratitude filled him and he held her tight. So very tight. "There is going to be a new office here in Angel Falls and I'm in charge of it. Since I'll be staying in town, I was wondering if you could do me a favor."

"Oh, I don't know about that. I've done quite a few favors for you. I've read to you, made soup for you and saved your life, twice. You are out of favors with me." Her rosebud mouth curved upward. Her green-blue eyes shone luminous with her love for him.

Her beautiful, precious love. His throat tightened with emotions too great to measure. For so long, he'd believed love happened to other men. That he wasn't good enough to deserve it, that it was something he could lose and vulnerability he couldn't allow. But he'd been wrong. God was giving this one chance, the one he'd prayed for. He would not waste this chance for Lila. He could make his life new and have the happiness he'd once known and lost as a little boy.

"Maybe you can see your way to granting me one more favor anyway. It's a wish, really. The one thing I want or ever will want." He gazed down at her, not used to being vulnerable, but he was tough. He was strong. He could open his heart without condition or end. "You as my wife. Will you marry me?"

"Marry you?" Humor flashed in her smile. Happy tears filled her eyes. Unspoken love glowed there, the greatest gift he could ever receive. A single tear slid down her cheek and she swiped at it. "It would be my honor to take you as my husband. Yes, I will marry you. Absolutely, with all of my heart."

"I love you, Lila." He brushed away another warm, salty tear with the pad of his thumb. "I love you with all I am and all I will be. I will do my best to protect you and cherish you, my best never to let you down."

"I know, because that's you. The best man. My best man." Infinite bliss seemed to lift her from the ground. His lips met hers with the softest kiss that was sweet, pure and true, just like their love. Theirs was a romance story, after all.

EPILOGUE

It was a perfect day for a wedding. Green leaves rustled musically in the warm breeze that blew through the Lawson family's buggy. Cheerful sunshine made the clear blue sky bluer and highlighted the white church where her beloved waited inside. Lila could barely wait for her pa to draw the horses to a halt. Excitement flitted through her like hummingbird's wings. She was getting married! Today she would become Burke's bride.

"Everything is perfect," Eunice declared from the front seat. "I made three trips to the church this morning to make sure everything has been done to my specifications."

Leave it to Eunice to take charge. Lila knew her stepmother meant well. "Thank you for everything you've done, Ma. You, too, Pa."

"Are you nervous?" Lark leaned close to

343

whisper. She looked adorable in her lavender lawn dress, the one they had sewn together just for the wedding.

"No, I'm not nervous at all." It was a big step to marry anyone, but she was certain of her choice. Burke had told her the entire story of his orphanage years, how he had fallen in with the Cheever gang and the near decade of hard service he'd given as a Range Rider. The test of time had proven his character. He was honorable, righteous and brave. "I keep pinching myself, sure that I am dreaming."

"I can't believe it, either," Pa spoke up. While she and Lark had been talking, he had helped Eunice down and now offered his hand to her. "My little Lila is all grown up. It's hard for a father to face."

"I'm grown up but I'm not growing away, Papa." She swooped down from the wagon, landing lightly on the grass. "Burke and I will be just down the street above Cora's shop. It's not far at all."

"I know, but this is a hard day for me. I have to give you away." He cleared his throat, hiding emotion, and helped Lark down next. "At least it's to a good man. I see that now. I wouldn't have gotten back my horses and wagon if it weren't for him."

"Oh, Pa." Lark rolled her eyes. "You might

as well say it. You take him fishing. You said last night at supper Burke was like a son to you. Go ahead and admit it."

"I'll keep my feelings to myself, missy." Pa gently tweaked her nose. "Lila, the door is open. They are waiting for us. Are you ready?"

"Almost." She looked up expectantly. Shadows moved inside the doorway, rushing toward her and took shape. Scarlet with her red curls in a summery dress dashed down the steps. Everyone followed her — Kate, Fiona, Earlee, Meredith and Ruby. Laughter filled the air like a lark song, voices rose and fell with merriment, arms wrapped around her and before she knew it, they were in a circle, arms locked together, her dear friends.

"You look as excited as I felt on my wedding day." Fiona with her dark curls and ready smile looked especially happy this morning. She practically danced in place. "I know you and Burke will be exceptionally happy together."

"If only I had known who he really was, I never would have warned you against him," Scarlet said.

"Or me," Kate agreed. "He's good to you, Lila. He'll make you very happy."

"Yes, he will." She was already transported. Just through that door, her bridegroom was waiting for her. Her engagement ring, a sapphire set between two sparkling diamonds, caught the light at that moment, like a sign from above.

"Is it me, or do you look a little pale, Fiona?" Ruby asked in her gentle, concerned way. "Do you feel all right?"

"Oh, I am probably pale," Fiona said casually. "But I'm not sick."

"Oh!" Meredith was the first to start leaping. "You're expecting!"

"The baby is due around May." Fiona blossomed with happiness. "I have a lot of sewing to do."

"We'll help," Earlee volunteered. Congratulations rose on the wind. So much was changing for them all, such good things. Life, love, families.

"Come, Lila," Pa said. "It's time."

There was a flurry of excitement, her friends gave her more hugs, funny advice and good wishes before they dashed back inside the church. Later there would be a supper party at home for her friends and family with Burke at her side.

Every step she took along the path and up the stairs felt monumental. Sunlight sparkled through stained-glass windows, adding jeweled beauty to the sanctuary. She hardly registered the full pews of well-wishers, or Reverend Hadly at the pulpit or how shy she usually felt in front of so many people.

Her gaze arrowed to Burke waiting for her. How dashing he was in a black suit and white shirt, his thick dark hair tamed for there was no wind inside the church to blow it. He looked vibrant and masculine and invincible, and he was hers. Hers to marry, hers to love, hers to cherish for all eternity. Bliss filled her and her shoes didn't touch the floor as Pa accompanied her down the aisle.

The minister began to speak, but did she notice? Not a chance. All she could see was Burke and the unshakable affection warming his midnight eyes to a gentle blue as he turned toward her.

"Her mother and I do," Pa answered the minister.

In a daze, Lila realized her father released her. Burke gathered her hand in his.

"I'm not nervous one bit," he leaned in to whisper. "Are you?"

"No, only ecstatic. I get to marry you."

"That's my line," he chuckled. "God has blessed me richly today."

"And tomorrow and the rest of our lives." Her confidence touched him down deep.

Once Arthur was settled, the minister continued the ceremony. He could only half listen, he had a hard time focusing on anything other than Lila. She looked beyond beautiful in a white print dress sprigged with tiny yellow flowers — sunflowers, he realized.

Thank You, Lord. He sent a prayer Heavenward. It wasn't easy to forgive himself for that dark time in his life, but he felt that God had. The Lord had looked inside his heart and brought him to Lila. Gratitude left him speechless as he realized the minister was waiting on him.

"I do," he vowed. Never had a man meant those words more. He intended to love, honor and cherish his wife through any hardship and every happiness until he no longer drew breath. She gazed up at him with unfailing love and he had everything he'd ever wanted.

"I do take this man as my husband," Lila breathed, tears glittering in her eyes. "I so do."

Love lit her softly, the same way happy endings came in a fairy tale. With happily-ever-afters and promises that were always kept, never broken.

It was easy to see the future when he looked into her eyes, their loving future. A pretty house for her to make into a home, a close marriage laughing and reading and watching thunderstorms. A baby in a bassinet, maybe another on the way. He saw the years pass, a little boy looking up at the sky to see the pictures in the clouds, a little girl hurrying to join in as Lila tended her flower beds and he hoed up the weeds for her.

A happy family.

Although it was not that time in the ceremony, Burke cupped her chin in his free hand and kissed her sweetly, his wife, his love and the best part of his soul. Understanding laughter rippled through the crowd, the minister cleared his throat and Lila beamed up at him, her infinite love gentle and honest and true.

The sun chose that moment to brighten. Rich light tumbled through the windows and fell like grace on the noble lawman and his calico bride, Heaven's assurance of great happiness to come.

Dear Reader,

Welcome back to Angel Falls. *Calico Bride* is the third book in my BUTTONS & BOBBINS series. I hope when you open these pages, you enjoy revisiting old friends in the BUTTONS & BOBBINS girls and you recognize familiar faces from my previous Love Inspired Historical books. In Lila's story, the BUTTONS & BOBBINS girls have grown up and are starting on their different paths in life. Fiona is happily married. Meredith is engaged and teaching summer school. Lila is working in her parents' mercantile and waiting for her life to begin. When she prays for God to liven up her life, I hope you enjoy the adventure He sets her on with a handsome hero new to town, an undercover mission and forbidden love that cannot end happily . . . or can it?

Calico Bride is a story I dearly loved writing. Perhaps because I was touched by Burke's tragic past and by the dreams he wants and doesn't believe he deserves. I loved Lila's sense of adventure and courage and the lessons she comes to learn about her life and the nature of true love. Most of all, I loved the gentle humor of their romance and the way God leads them softly, surely and inevitably together. I hope you do, too. Ruby's story is next!

Thank you for choosing *Calico Bride*.

Wishing you love and peace,

Jillian Hart

QUESTIONS FOR DISCUSSION

1. Describe Lila's first impression of Burke. How does she react? What conclusions does she draw about him initially? How are they different after he hands her his badge?

2. How would you describe Burke's first impression of Lila? Why is he drawn to her? Why do you think he trusts her with his secret?

3. What do you think about the concern and compassion Lila shows wounded Burke? What do you think of Eunice's lack of compassion? What are the reasons for both?

4. What do you think of Burke's past as revealed initially through his nightmares? How do you think the loss of his family

has affected him? How does this change your perspective on his character?

5. How would you describe Burke? What are the deeper layers to his character? What are his flaws? How would you describe Lila? What are her deeper layers? What are her flaws?

6. What is the story's predominant imagery? How does it contribute to the meaning of the story? Of the romance?

7. Both Burke and Lila look to God to help at turning points and crossroads. When do you see Him in the story? How does He guide Lila? How does He guide Burke?

8. What does Lila learn about compassion through the course of the story? How does the depth of her compassion change for others? For Burke?

9. Burke tells Lila he is a loner, that he likes life better without ties. Why does he tell her this? What deeper feeling is he hiding? What hints does he give through the story to let you know how he truly feels?

10. What roles do Lila's friendships and the

town's characters play in the story and the romance?

11. How did you react when you read about Burke's involvement with a violent outlaw gang? How do you think this has affected him? How does it change your opinion of him?

12. What do you think Lila and Burke have each learned about love and about themselves? How has love changed them?

13. What does Burke learn about forgiveness?

14. What are the ways Lila changes and what does she learn about her life?

15. There are many different kinds of love in this story. What are they? What roles do they play in the meaning of the book? In Lila and Burke's romance?

ABOUT THE AUTHOR

Jillian Hart grew up on her family's homestead, where she helped raise cattle, rode horses and scribbled stories in her spare time. After earning her English degree from Whitman College, she worked in travel and advertising before selling her first novel. When Jillian isn't working on her next story, she can be found puttering in her rose garden, curled up with a good book or spending quiet evenings at home with her family.

The employees of Thorndike Press hope you have enjoyed this Large Print book. All our Thorndike, Wheeler, and Kennebec Large Print titles are designed for easy reading, and all our books are made to last. Other Thorndike Press Large Print books are available at your library, through selected bookstores, or directly from us.

For information about titles, please call:
(800) 223-1244

or visit our Web site at:
http://gale.cengage.com/thorndike

To share your comments, please write:
Publisher
Thorndike Press
10 Water St., Suite 310
Waterville, ME 04901